FAIRY RINGS OF MUCH MEDDLING

Pauline Potterill

Pobo

INTRODUCTION

In this, the sequel to Wishing Wells of Much Meddling, Emily and her family are now living happy, perfectly normal lives. Well, as normal as can be expected in any household with three baby girls. Most days are chaotic, but still normal in the traditional sense. No co-incidences are questioned. No odd occurrences go unexplained.

When the strange white cat appears Emily knows that something is not right. In fact, something is very wrong in Much Meddling. Someone, it seems, is interfering with the very fabric of its existence.

Can the Wells family fulfil thier ancestral role as guardians and save the village? The cats hope so.

Fairy Rings Of Much Meddling

January 22nd

CHAPTER ONE

I t was on the triplets' third birthday that the white cat first appeared, on the wall outside Wishing Well Cottage. Emily became aware of it as she strapped the three children into the back seat of the car. The cat sat, unblinking, scrutinising the activity. Emily busied herself, trying to ignore it. Unusually the children settled quickly, all eyes on the cat. Straps secure, she too felt compelled to look. As her eyes met those of the cat, Emily knew. Things were about to change. There was no going back. The feline stood, its glossy white coat glistening in the early morning light. With a couple of flicks of its white tipped black tail it turned elegantly and slipped off the wall out of sight.

For three years, Emily and Alex Wells, and their three children, Tansy, Lily, and Violet, had led a perfectly normal life. Well, as normal as could be expected in any household with three baby girls. Most days were chaotic, but still normal in the traditional sense. No coincidences were questioned. No odd occurrences went unexplained. Kevin, the cat she had inherited with the house, and his equally unusual female companion, had not been seen since the day Emily and Alex had brought the triplets home from the hospital. The two cats had sat on the wall and watched as all three babies were carried into the house. Then, as Alex had locked the car, the two cats had rubbed heads, made a "Perrrupping" sound, turned and slipped off the wall, apparently content that they were no longer needed. As the months went by, Emily occasionally thought she glimpsed one of them out of the corner of her eye, but in her heart, she knew the cats were gone.

Emily dropped the children at nursery and drove back home. To her relief the wall remained empty but as she opened the front door something soft and warm brushed her ankle. The white cat strolled silently down the hall swishing its black tail: the white tip creating disapproving eddies of disturbed dust, making Emily feel guilty. At the end of the hall the cat turned right and headed through to the outhouse where it did a circuit, apparently searching for something. When it jumped with difficulty, up onto the worktop, Emily was surprised. Then, as the cat climbed into the old laundry basket, that she and Alex used for newspaper recycling, the penny dropped – the cat was female, pregnant, and heavily so! Bowing to the inevitable, Emily lifted cat and basket onto the floor and placed them in the corner of the room. She then went and hunted out Kevin's old bowl and filled it with some cooked chicken from the fridge. With the cat settled she felt the need to tell someone. Alex, she knew, would be busy. As the local blacksmith, he was currently producing railings and a set of gates for a client who was keen to have them fitted by the end of the week. He wouldn't want to be disturbed. Besides, as a Wells, nothing cat related would surprise him.

Instead, she phoned Lou, her friend. Louise and Mike had bought one of the cottages inherited by Alex following the deaths of his Great Great Aunts. These three sisters had each lived to be 100 years old and, like Emily's children, were triplets. Much to Emily's distress, she had been the last person to speak to each of them before they died. The first to die was Angelica, the owner of Wishing Well Cottage. Angelica had given Emily a periapt, a charm pendant, when Emily had been caught in a snowstorm on her way to the airport and had to stay the night. The periapt had drawn her back to Much Meddling and Wishing Well Cottage. It was on that visit that she had met Ruby and learnt that Angelica had died, and had most probably been dead when Emily had slipped out of the house at first light to catch her flight. Emily had helped Ruby to fill out a lottery ticket and Ruby had repaid her kindness by giving her a matching winning ticket, the day before she died. This had given Emily the means to buy Wishing Well Cottage. The third sister, Myrtle, had introduced Emily to their great great nephew Alex, the day before she died, thus completing the triplets' quest to find a bride and secure the Wells' family line into the next century.

"Hi, Em. How's things?" asked Lou. "You sound odd. What's up?"

"There's a cat!"

"Ah." Lou became silent briefly. "Talk to me."

"A white, pregnant cat has marched into the cottage and taken up residence in the outhouse. Despite being white, it has this strange black tail with a white tip, which it waves about like some kind of magic wand!"

"Oooh. So, it is true after all. It isn't just legend. The Furry Cat Mother exists! As your best friend, do I get a wish?"

"Stop it. The last thing I need is a litter of cats with dubious abilities. If there are three of them, I think I might just flip. I was looking forward to a nice, normal life. Everything was going so well", moaned Emily.

"Put the kettle on. I'm on my way over. Let me see this fabulous feline."

* * *

"Wow, what a gorgeous looking cat. Those eyes - like some re-incarnation of Cleopatra," cooed Louise.

"Yes, they are so beautifully outlined. I wish I had eyes like that."

"Careful, one swish of that tail and your baby blues could be yellow. Have you thought of a name yet?"

Emily hadn't. Emily was hoping that the cat would leave, or its owners lay claim. She knew the latter was unlikely. Cats in Much Meddling didn't have owners. They came and went as they pleased. When they went, no-one knew where.

"Anyway, how is Mike? Will he be coming to the party on Saturday? Alex and I are going to need all the help we can get."

"An afternoon spent with a dozen or so 3-year-olds – are you kidding? He's delighted, even skipping a game of squash so he can be there, reckons he'll get more exercise."

"Mmm. Alex can't wait either."

* * *

When she brought the children back from nursery they made a beeline for the outhouse. She had no idea how they knew. They just did. Crouching on their haunches the three children proceeded to stroke the white cat. Despite this rough handling the cat tolerated the attention, rubbing her head against each child's hand in turn.

"That's enough now. Leave the cat alone. You've said hello, now let her have some peace." As Emily shepherded the children out of the room the cat started to knead her bedding looking distinctly uncomfortable. Emily recognised that discomfort. The cat was about to go into labour. She wished Alex was home.

In the kitchen, she gave each child a drink and a couple of biscuits. She looked at pictures they had made and listened attentively as they related their day, all talking at once. The nursery had sung happy birthday to them. There had been three little cakes with their names on and a gift each of a packet of crayons and a colouring book. She helped each one to stick their picture into their scrap book; there wasn't enough fridge or wall space for the triple production lines of artwork. Emily had learnt early on that displaying it all wasn't a viable option. The scrap books, now reinforced with sticky tape, were rather tatty but the contents were intact. As the children busied themselves colouring-in she nipped back to the outhouse to see how her new guest was faring.

The cat was now turning circles and intermittently purring loudly. Every now and then she settled into a curled-up position for a few seconds then stood and continued circling. Emily felt helpless. Should she call a vet? She didn't know. It was a perfectly normal process, but then so was human birth. A scream from the kitchen sent her running down the hall.

Tansy was in tears and a fight had broken

out. Her yellow crayon was missing, and the others wouldn't let her borrow theirs. A quick hunt under the table found the crayon in a gap between the flagstones. The tears dried immediately and Emily breathed a sigh of relief. She knew the peace wouldn't last long but she used the time to start preparing their tea.

When Alex arrived home he was greeted by three excited children all waving sheets of paper in the air and shouting "Snokettee, Snokettee." He looked at Emily for help, but she was as bemused as he was. When she looked at the pictures, which she guessed were of cats, she was none the wiser as to what they were saying.

"Snokettee eer," wailed Lily and started pulling Alex towards the kitchen door. The other children joined in, dragging him down the hall.

"We have a guest," explained Emily. "She turned up this morning and let herself in when I got back from nursery."

As they approached the outhouse the cat could be heard purring loudly, not in a contented way.

"Snokettee," repeated Lily, pointing at the cat in frustration.

"What?"

"Snoketteeee!" added Violet.

"Snow kitty. Is that what you are saying?" asked Alex.

"Yes, Snokettee," replied the children, crouching down in an arc as the cat continued to purr and knead, and drool slightly.

"Is there something wrong with it?" asked Alex. "Its not got rabies, has it?"

"Don't think so, but 'it' is a 'she', and a pregnant she, and, I believe, in labour."

As the cat began to mewl and pant the family watched as the first slippery little bundle appeared. Snokettee shuffled round and began to lick it. Soon a wet little face was visible on a wobbly little head and kitten number one took its first breath. Within the hour two more kittens appeared. As Snokettee cleaned the third one Violet gave an ineffectual clap of her hands, did a delighted skip, and threw her arms around Emily's waist, "We all here now mummy!" There were three, just as Emily had feared.

As the new arrivals suckled, an exhausted Snokettee lay on her side and purred contentedly.

"Right, lets give the new mummy some peace, back to the kitchen," said Emily. "Daddy and I have a birthday surprise for you."

The kitchen was an L-shaped room at the end of the house. It was flagged, as was the whole of the ground floor. The back wall had two long low mullioned windows with leaded panes which looked out onto the garden and the well. The left-hand wall had a door in its centre leading through to a utility room and pantry. Beyond the door, the room widened left and had another mullioned window with lead panes looking out, this time to the front of the house. The far wall had floor to ceiling cupboards flanking a cooking range and an open fire. Hanging from a beam over the fire was a large cauldron. This large vessel was used every year, during the Well Blessing Ceremony, to feed the village. At the left side of the range sat two old leather wing-back chairs. It was in these two chairs that Emily had sat with Angelica and poured out her heart to the old lady. It was here that she had been given the periapt, a beautifully carved interlocking pair of tiny limestone rings. This charm was now lying back at the base of the stalactite, from which it had been cut, in the cave end of the cellar beneath the house. The centre of the kitchen contained a well-worn and well-loved pine table, with a selection of wooden chairs. A big rug at the door end gave the children a play area, and a floral sofa under the window gave visitors somewhere to sit.

Emily made the children sit at the kitchen table and close their eyes. "Anyone cheats and they don't get their surprise. Eyes shut tight."

Taking three extra large buns from the cupboard she and Alex quickly lit the three sets of candles. They then placed the buns silently on the table in front of their brood.

"Okay. Eyes open." As the children stared at the candles Emily and Alex burst into 'Happy Birthday' and then explained about making a wish and blowing out the candles. Lots of 'phewphing' and coughing later all nine candles were extinguished.

"Again, again," cried the children.

"No, not today. On Saturday, at your party, there will be proper birthday cakes with more candles to blow out. Daddy has something else for you now." With that, Alex went into the back porch and wheeled out the first of three red tricycles. She and Alex had discussed getting different coloured ones but decided in the end to get identical ones. A selection of different coloured handlebar tassels meant that each child could choose their own. It wasn't long before the children were crashing madly round the kitchen as they learnt to control their new vehicles. Finally, around 7pm, fed and exhausted and having said goodnight to Snokettee and the kittens, Emily and Alex managed to get all three into bed. After a quick gathering up of scattered clothing, which she threw onto the laundry floor, she emptied the drier, transferred the contents of the washing machine into it and set it going. Then she filled the washing machine and set that going too. Carrying the laundry basket full of clean clothes, she went back to the kitchen and put the kettle on, folding and sorting clothes as she waited for it to boil.

CHAPTER TWO

O n Saturday the children were awake early and Emily, for once, didn't mind. She needed to get up as she had lots to do. She decided to let them stay in their pyjamas until it was time for them to get washed and dressed for the party. When Alex came down, she left him with the girls whilst she went to check on Snokettee and the kittens. All seemed well. The three tiny bundles were snuggled into their mother who was purring contentedly. Emily washed and filled Snokettee's bowl and then went back into the main house, locking the door behind her to keep the cats safe from exuberant children.

The morning passed quickly and soon it was time to get the girls into their party frocks. After a row as to which dress belonged to which child, despite them being identical, all three were eventually dressed. She combed the last head of hair and sent the girls into the kitchen to play. Just as she reached the bottom of the stairs the front door opened, and Lou and Mike came in dragging a Nathan who didn't seem too pleased at having to go to a birthday party for 3-year-olds. "I'm 4 and nearly a half", he announced holding out three parcels. "These are for the 3-year-olds! I have to say, 'Happy Birthday like you mean it'. Where are they?"

"Nathan, what did I tell you!" snapped Louise.

"Thank you, Nathan. They are in the kitchen," said Emily hiding a smirk.

Nathan ran down the hall and into the kitchen with his father close on his heels.

"If I said he was hard work I don't suppose you'd have much sympathy."

"Nope, I've got treble trouble. Generally, they are quite sweet, but when they aren't..." said Emily. "Best go and supervise the unwrapping."

They reached the kitchen in time to see Alex handing Mike a can from the fridge and cracking open one of his own.

"Don't start that yet. I need you two to re-arrange the furniture in the living room."

"It's just one. Don't worry. It's a kids' party. We don't want to greet the other parents smelling of alcohol," said Alex.

Nathan plonked the three parcels on the rug in front of the girls who took one each. As Lily started to examine hers, and her little fingers tried to find an edge to tear, he huffed and grabbed it from her ripping the paper off. Lily started to howl, and Mike grabbed Nathan.

"Nathan! That is her present! Let her unwrap it. Half the fun of getting a present is unwrapping it."

"She wasn't doing it right."

"That doesn't matter. "

"Nathan," said Alex. "Why don't you help us men get the front room ready for the party. We're going to make a pirate ship. Come on." With that Nathan happily followed the two men out of the kitchen.

"Pirate ship?" queried Louise.

"Yes, Alex's idea. I think it might work quite well. He plans on pushing his beloved Chesterfields together to make a boat and getting the kids to 'sail' the seven seas in it. His idea of a padded cell, I think. If it works, it will keep them all in one place for a bit. James is coming too –never misses an opportunity to entertain, especially if there is any potential to increase his flock." James, their neighbour, and Much Meddling's vicar, had become a major part of their lives and a terrific help over the years. He, and his housekeeper Anna, had helped Emily when she first moved to the village. Together they had helped Emily host her first Well Blessing Ceremony. This, an annual event, involved providing food for the entire village after all three Much Meddling wells were blessed. This ceremony could be traced back over 400 years and was said to protect the village from drought and ensure its prosperity.

Lou and Emily supervised as the girls opened their presents: three beautiful little summer dresses.

"Oh, Lou," they are so pretty," said Emily. "These must have cost you a fortune. You shouldn't have."

"Probably not, but I couldn't resist. I never get to buy anything pretty. There are lots of fun boy outfits and I do enjoy dressing Nathan, but… you know."

For the next hour Louise helped Emily get ready for the party whilst keeping an eye on the triplets. They made lots of bite-sized sandwiches and cooked some sausage rolls. They put crackers, cheese straws and crisps into bowls and cut sticks of carrot and pieces of cucumber. They drained mandarin orange pieces and mixed them with slices of melon. The food, covered in cling-film, was laid out on the kitchen worktop ready to be uncovered and moved onto the kitchen table. A selection of drinking vessels sat alongside various juices and squashes. Finally, there were three birthday cakes. Each one had three candles and a child's name spelt out in tiny pink and blue flowers.

At 3pm the guests started to arrive. Despite all the planning it was chaos for the first 20 minutes. Emily tried her best to intercept all the presents. The children would get to open them later when she could record who had given what. Once the final guest had arrived and all the children had been press-ganged onto the SS Chesterfield Alex and Mike, both dressed as pirates, did a great job of keeping the children entertained, even Nathan. Nathan was a crocodile. They had given him a small green sleeping bag to wear. This very effectively prevented him from running around and being too rough with the younger children. It had green scaly spines down the back and shoulder straps to keep it in place. His arms were green, and he had a large crocodile head made from a bicycle helmet and green felt, with a red tongue and big white teeth. He writhed around in the 'sea' snapping at the boat, whilst the little pirates shouted, 'Shiver me timbers' and 'Yo, ho, ho' and tried to hit him with ping pong balls.

Halfway through the party a large green and red parrot arrived, cawing 'Pieces of Eight, Pieces of Eight". It was James, very apologetic. One of his parishioners was ill and he had had to visit her. He had come as soon as he could. He immediately entered into the spirit of the party, leaping about and making the children laugh by running away from the crocodile. He then told them that they needed to watch out for a seagull which was known to poop on passing ships. Did they know what a seagull looked like?

"Yes", they all shouted.

"How many legs does it have? James lifted one of his big, clawed feet in the air and then the other.

"Two." They chorused

"Does it have a mouth, a beak or a snout?" James made elaborate gestures to indicate the choice.

"A beak."

"Does it have arms or wings?" James flapped his arms about.

"Wings!" All but one yelled. The one, an angelic looking little girl with a very serous expression, said," Haven't you ever seen a bloody seagull, Vicar?"

The adults in the room did their best to contain themselves and James was very glad that his face was hidden by the parrot head.

"Hannah, yes I have seen a seagull but, you know, you shouldn't…"

At this point Emily leapt in quickly. She knew full well that if James made a big thing of Hannah's swearing then all the children would pick up on it and she didn't want the triplets' birthday to be forever more known as 'That Bloody Party!

"Okay everyone! Time for some food. Who's hungry?" Right, then! Hand-wash first." The adults on toilet duty made sure all the children arrived in the kitchen suitably ready and got them seated round the big kitchen table, napkins round their necks to protect their party clothes. There was the odd fight over who got what but generally it all went well, with just the odd spillage. The party was now coming to an end. Those parents who hadn't stayed started to arrive to collect their off-spring. The children were now getting restless and wanting to get down from the table. It was time to wrap things up. Emily produced the birthday cakes and told them all to shut their eyes. With the help of Louise, she quickly lit the candles whilst Alex drew the curtains, it being light outside. The room was now lit only by the candles. She told them to open their eyes. As she and the other adults started to sing 'Happy Birthday' the children did their best to join in. As the triplets blew out their candles to great cheers and the room went dark a couple of the children burst into tears. Apparently, the brief darkness was a bit much. The curtains were quickly opened, and the crying stopped abruptly as goodie bags were handed out, along with a slice of cake each wrapped in a party napkin.

As the crowd started to thin out, a stocky, well-dressed gentleman walked in, asking for Trevor. Trevor, a skinny introverted child, was sitting on the rug, busily colouring a picture book. The little boy quickly gathered his belongings, eager to show his father what he had received in his goody bag. The man thanked Emily. He placed an arm, revealing an expensive watch and cuff link, round Trevor's shoulders and shepherded him towards the hall. Standing in the doorway blocking their exit was Lily, glowering. Slowly raising an arm and pointing an accusing finger she said in a forceful voice, "Bad man."

Alex grabbed her and scooped her out of the way, "I'm sorry," he laughed, apologetically. "I don't know what that was about. Lily, say thank you to Trevor's daddy for your present."

"No. Bad man!"

"Lily," snapped Emily.

"Children! No accounting for them," laughed the man. "Come on Trevor, lets get you home." He steered his son out of the kitchen and down the hall. Emily and Alex exchanged glances. As Emily closed the front door, she tried to dismiss Lily's outburst as a childish eccentricity but, try as she might, her heart couldn't. Trevor, an only child, seemed happy and relaxed enough. There was no sense that anything was wrong there. She had never met the man before. Trevor's mother, Suzanne, usually picked him up from nursery. She was pleasant enough but wasn't known to socialise at all with the other mothers. She just collected Trevor and left. She was quite a bit younger than most of them and she must have been very young when she had Trevor. Just how young, had been a hot topic of speculation until it was noted that a new addition to the nursery, Michael, had an exceedingly good-looking father – one of two, it seemed, and gossip moved on. Suzanne and Trevor were left to get on with their lives. Although quieter than the other children Trevor was a normal little boy. Why on earth Lily should have taken a dislike to his father, Emily had no idea.

Back in the kitchen, guests gone, the triplets were tearing round on their tricycles, doing circuits of the kitchen table, rubber tyres squeaking on the flags. Emily had fully expected them to be tired after the excitement of the party, but apparently not. Louise had the kettle on and was sorting out cups so that they could all have a drink. So, Emily went to see what state the living room was in and investigate the noise which was increasing as she approached.

Opening the door, she found herself in the middle of a sea battle. Two pirates, Alex and Mike, were valiantly defending the SS Chesterfield from a large green parrot and a crocodile. Ping pong balls filled the air, batted aside by wooden cutlasses. She said nothing, just draped the handful of bin bags she had been carrying over the door handle, and left them to it. Hopefully they would bag the bodies when they were done.

With all the 'children' occupied she and Lou enjoyed a moment of relative peace. The tea was very welcome, and the two women concluded that the party had been a success. Emily was a little disappointed that she hadn't had the opportunity to use her cartoon plasters but relieved that she had been able to hand back all the children intact. Not a single head injury despite all the running around. No-one had been sick and only a single puddle had needed mopping up. As they finished their drinks the children were starting to get fractious so she announced 'quiet time' and took their tricycles off them. She gave them all a drink whilst they did a bit more crayoning and then ushered them all upstairs to get ready for bed. She would save the present opening for the following day when the children were fresh, and Alex could help her to keep things under control.

CHAPTER THREE

O n Sunday the children were up early, as usual. Emily got them settled at the kitchen table; bibs tucked round their necks. Alex fished three boiled eggs out of a pan, deftly tapped and rolled them on the kitchen worktop and then peeled off the shells. Next, he popped each one into a mug, squirted in some tomato ketchup and then mashed each egg in turn, stirring in the ketchup. 'Egg-mashed-up-in-a-cup' was a treat the triplets loved. For this, they each had an 'eggstra' special spoon and 'eggseptional' toast. Emily grabbed two slices of toast from the toaster then buttered and sliced them into strips, discarding the crusts. She gave each child a couple of strips each and a spoon with a pixie shaped handle. As the girls tucked in Emily suggested to Alex that the girls should open the rest of their birthday presents, once they had eaten.

Gathering the girls on the kitchen floor rug Emily placed all the gifts in the middle, sharing them out as per the name tags. As one or two tags had come adrift she had to guess who these gifts were from, which wasn't too difficult as she just had to gather three gifts with matching wrapping, at least one of which had a label. Once done, she found she had one parcel that didn't fit with the rest. Assuming that she would be able to work out who it was from, by a process of elimination, she picked up pen and paper and took note of who had given what, whilst Alex supervised the unwrapping. Assuming most people had given three matching gifts, they had the girls open these at the same time.

Amidst a mound of crumpled paper, the children amassed their own little piles of matching hats and gloves, soft toys, colouring books, T-shirts, and, to the thrill of their parents, some noisy electronic books, and other noisy devices to torment the already stressed.

Finally, there was the mystery parcel. All it said on the label was 'to the girls, on their 3rd birthday'.

Emily took off the outer wrapper, to reveal three matching white boxes. The girls, who had been watching closely, held out their hands. She gave a box to each. As little hands struggled to remove the lids, against the vacuum inside each box, Emily and Alex, itching to help, sat on their own hands. Intent on the boxes, no one noticed the white figure which slid silently into the kitchen.

Tansy was the first to open her box. Inside was a wad of tissue paper and in its midst a chain. Tansy delicately picked it up. As the chain slid and unravelled, an enamel fairy-shaped pendant appeared, dangling from its shiny links. Soon, there were three pendants, each with a fairy, each one with a different coloured dress. The girls were delighted. Emily was none the wiser as to who had sent them. Unseen, Snokettee headed back to her litter.

* * *

The day was bright and fresh and predicted to be dry all day. The present opening complete, the Wells family trooped next door to the church. James asked the congregation to pray for a number of residents in the village who weren't well, naming them as he did so. Albert Dewhurst, the retired blacksmith, was the only name Emily knew and automatically looked at Alex with concern. Alex shook his head dismissively, and pointed at his hip, whilst mouthing 'He's okay'. She remembered Alex had mentioned that Albert was waiting for a hip replacement and had just been provided with a walking frame, not that he was using it, it seemed.

After the service they collected Violet, Lily and Tansy from Sunday school and chatted to a few of the people they knew. Leaving the church, they crossed the road to the pond on the village green. Alex produced a packet of bread crusts so that the children could feed the ducks. This was something that they now did every Sunday unless it was raining. As a family, it was something that they all enjoyed, and it kept the children occupied for a while whilst either Emily or Alex went home and got lunch ready. Alex handed out a couple of slices to each child. Tansy always managed to throw the bread farthest onto the water. She intuitively made use of the breeze and she had a natural throwing technique older than her years. The ducks, which had arrived at their feet as soon as they reached the pond, quacked cheerily and gobbled up their treats. Emily watched for a while and then left them to it.

Back in the cottage she went to check on the cats. The three little kittens were now 5 days old and still snuggling into their mother for warmth. Looking closely, Emily could just see that at least one of the kittens was showing signs of its eyes opening at the inner corners. All three were now quite a bit bigger than when they were born. It was difficult to tell what their colourings were. Nestled into Snokettee's white fur and black tail was a muddle of black, white and grey furry limbs. It was impossible to tell if each kitten was one colour of if they were all mixed. She restrained herself from picking any of them up but gave Snokettee a stroke.

"I hope you can control your offspring, Snokettee. It is going to be chaos when they start running around. We shall have to find names for them all soon." Emily watched for a while before going to get lunch ready.

* * *

In the afternoon they bundled the children into the car and drove out of the village and up into the hills. The air was clear and fresh and there wasn't much sun to warm it, but they knew that it was fairly sheltered in the valley where they were going. Parking the car on the verge next to a stile they made sure that all the children had their waterproofs zipped and their jeans tucked inside their red Wellington boots. Climbing over the stile they headed across a field, steering the triplets round the sheep droppings, to the base of a bracken-covered hill. Here a small stream trickled down the hill side from a spring up on the moors. Falling over a small limestone outcrop the water formed a shallow pool. Over the years parts of the limestone had fallen off and the pool was lined with a mixture of crumbled rock and well-worn pebbles. Spilling over the shallow depression, that held the pool, the water continued on its way along the edge of the field following the slope of the hill. Emily sat on a rock and watched as the children splashed about in their Wellingtons. Overhead peewits circled and cried.

"Build a dam, Daddy, build a dam," yelled an excited Tansy. This was something they had done on a previous visit which had kept Alex and the girls occupied for ages. The children collected stones and moss and Alex constructed a dam. They let the water rise until it reached the top of their Wellingtons. Alex produced a makeshift boat, fashioned out of bark with a twig mast and a plastic sail cut from a milk bottle, and floated it on the water. Then, using a branch as a lever, Alex destroyed the dam. They all laughed gleefully as the water rushed away carrying the boat with it. Laughing, they ran alongside as the boat negotiated rocks and branches. Once or twice it got caught up in eddies, circling briefly before moving on. In her haste to keep up Violet fell full length but got back up and carried on running without complaint. As the water level returned to normal, the boat got wedged under a branch at the side of the stream. Alex retrieved it and carried it back to the pool. The children paddled and splashed and threw stones at the boat until a surprisingly accurate shot from Tansy destroyed the mast, and Emily and Alex decided it was time to go home. Emily watched as Alex swung Tansy up onto his shoulders and then scooped up the other two, sitting one on each hip. She still marvelled at how lucky she was to be married to this marvellous man. His physique still took her breath away. Seeing other women's response to him gave her secret satisfaction. Their blatant attempts to steal him away should have worried rather than amused her, but she trusted him implicitly. Although she wouldn't admit it, even to herself, her heart believed in the periapt sitting in the cellar beneath their home. Besides, she knew he loved her. She felt it, every time he looked at her, and he adored his three girls: three girls who used him as a human climbing frame and placed their entire trust in his ability to keep them safe and to right every wrong. She followed, as he trudged along talking animatedly, telling them some story he was making up, adding ridiculous facts that the children were challenging. She smiled to herself. She was so, so lucky. The thought scared her a little. What had she done to deserve all this? Then she remembered the cats. Things weren't perfect. Things were about to get complicated.

Together, she and Alex strapped the girls into the back seat of the car. Damp and muddy, they fell asleep on the drive home.

CHAPTER FOUR

D espite the bright sunshine, a fresh breeze whipped Emily's hair into her eyes as she crossed the green to the village store. She was glad to step into the warmth of its interior as the door closed behind her, its bell tinkling rudely. She took her time wandering up and down the two aisles, filling her basket and perusing the magazines. Alex was picking the girls up from nursery, so she had a few precious hours to herself. At the till she chatted happily with Jake, the young man who was currently managing the store. Since Carla, the previous owner, had left, there had been a series of people working there. Jake, a graduate, was currently running the place whilst looking for permanent employment that would make use of his degree in earth sciences. He was charming and enthusiastic and did an efficient job of ensuring that the shelves were always stocked and the produce in date. Emily really hoped he would stay, unlikely as that was.

"So, how are the girls?" he asked, running his hand over his artistically shaven head. "I heard the party went well."

"Yes, I think it was a success – no casualties! How are you? What have you been up to?"

"Not much, still no interviews. I am getting really sick of filling out applications and doing on-line tests and the rest of the crap they make you do before telling you they don't want you, or don't tell, just leave you waiting. If I had the money, I'd go off travelling. Still, at least I have a job, and some money, which is better than most of my mates."

"Ah, you'll find something. In the meantime, we are all very glad to have you here."

She stopped by the bakery to get herself a pasty for lunch and a couple of loaves for the girls' sandwiches. There was a queue, as per usual, at the counter. Diets weren't that popular in Much Meddling. Diets weren't a consideration, for 'normal' people. Diets, along with gyms, were obsessions of city people who spent too much time looking in mirrors and at each other and not enough time looking at what God had provided for them. Or so Emily had been told, when, on a previous occasion she'd regrettably teased someone about the amount of cream cakes they were buying. When she had thought about it though, she realised, that even on the coldest days you could always find locals valiantly trekking up through the woods to the crag that overlooked the village, or strolling across the fields to one of the streams that cascaded down from the surrounding limestone hills. The majority of villagers did get a reasonable amount of exercise. She, like them, liked nothing better than to wander through the woods looking and listening to the sights and sounds that surrounded her. The scenery was always changing: a new bud, a fallen log sprouting toadstools, the fleeting glimpse of a deer, the knocking of a woodpecker. Then, out of the wood and up through the bracken to the crag, the sense of achievement at having made the climb and the satisfaction of looking down on the village and out across the surrounding hills to the Yorkshire moors beyond: the elevation helping to put the world and its problems in perspective, the ancient solidity of the crag reducing the significance of one's own worries.

Lost in her thoughts, she jumped when a hand was placed on her shoulder.

"Sorry, didn't mean to startle you, but talking to you wasn't working." Behind her in the queue was Mags, one of the members of the book club that Emily attended. "Are you coming this week? I am afraid that I am only half way through the book. Have you read it? I don't suppose you get much time."

"Actually, I've nearly finished it. I read in the car whilst waiting to pick the kids up from nursery. I like to make sure I am on time so usually get there early. I wouldn't miss the Book

Club meetings. They are my 'Me Time'. I don't get much of that. How's Dave?"

"Oh, he's fine. He's working for Cartwright's now, the haulage company. Lots of long-distance stuff. So, he is away a lot. Can't say I like that, and he isn't too keen, but the pay is better. He should be back for Thursday though."

Reaching the front of the queue Emily chose and paid for her items, which now also included 5 custard tarts. She said goodbye to Mags and headed home.

The afternoon passed all too quickly and just as Emily was beginning to wonder where Alex was with the girls, the phone rang. It was Alex, sounding a little odd, which alarmed her. He assured her that they were all okay, but he was having to get the Range Rover's windscreen replaced and didn't know how long it was going to take. He'd explain when they got home.

She went to check on Snokettee and the kittens. Snokettee was looking tired but content, her pride suckling enthusiastically. The kittens were still a furry mass of little legs but it was clear that despite having Snokettee's white tipped tail, they were all distinctly different. One was sleek and black, one was white like Snokettee, and one was a fluffy grey with a possible hint of ginger. They were just adorable. Emily sat quietly and watched them for a while, and Snokettee watched her. Staring into the cat's eyes she felt a connection, a shared knowledge and understanding, a shared bond between mothers, two mothers of triplets. She told herself that she was being silly, but the cat continued to stare into her eyes, and she found that she couldn't turn away. When finally Snokettee blinked, she looked back at the kittens. Suddenly she was overwhelmed with the same feeling of love she always had when she looked at her own children. Aghast, she looked back at Snokettee. The cat was now purring contentedly and looking knowingly at Emily. Emily would look after these kittens as she would her own children, and Snokettee, equally, would look out for Tansy, Violet and Lily.

* * *

When Alex and the girls got home, Emily was disturbed by his behaviour. He explained that a cat's eye had been kicked up by a passing car and broken the windscreen. She understood why he would be annoyed and hassled by it all, but he appeared to be being evasive. He obviously wasn't telling her everything. When pushed, he got angry and said he'd explain later. This was completely unlike him. The girls however, seemed happy enough. Whilst getting the girls' tea she tried to make light conversation with him, but he was distracted and irritable and she gave up.

When the girls were finally in bed and settled, she went to look for him. She found him sitting in the front room with a can of lager in his hand and another two empty ones on the coffee table in front of him. She sat down on the edge of the sofa, a suitable gap between them. He didn't look at her. He took a large swig, emptying the can. He crushed it noisily and threw it into the unlit fireplace. It ricocheted off the side and back, bounced off the hearth and came to land on the rug, dribbling lager and leaving sooty marks. Emily didn't say anything. She waited. Eventually, he turned towards her.

"I could have killed her. I didn't listen. I should have known. I should have realised."

"What are you talking about? You said it was just the windscreen. I don't understand."

"Lily didn't want to sit in the middle seat. None of them did, but I made Lily. What option did I have? She fought me Emily, but I thought I knew best and I am bigger and stronger than her. I thought she was just being stupid. I thought she was just having a temper tantrum, but she knew – she knew, and I didn't listen. I'm her father and I am supposed to look after her, but in the end, she had to look after herself!" He was in tears now. This big man was sobbing, and Emily still didn't understand.

"Alex, what are you talking about? What happened?"

"I was driving along. It was bedlam. All the kids were making a noise, but Lily was screaming and trying to wriggle out of her harness. Then this car overtook us. The cat's eye came through the windscreen and embedded itself in the back of Lily's car seat. If she hadn't managed to undo her harness and slide into the floorwell, she'd be dead. It would have gone straight through her little chest."

"Oh, Alex," gasped Emily.

"She knew, and she told me, but I didn't listen!"

"Alex, you couldn't have known. I would have done exactly the same. You can't blame yourself. The girls do play up. They are kids and they don't always comply when we need them to."

"But I'm her Daddy, Emily! She should be able to trust me."

The pair fell silent, lost in their own thoughts. Emily wondered how Lily had managed to undo her harness. They weren't designed for little fingers to undo. It shouldn't have been possible. At times, Emily struggled to undo it. She snuggled up to Alex, relieved that he didn't resist her, and wrapped her arms around him.

"Well, I guess one good thing to take away from this is that the girls, despite their young age, can take care of themselves."

"Huh!"

"Would you like another can? I could do with one," said Emily.

"Yes, please. You know, when the

windscreen was fixed, all three climbed back into their seats as if nothing had happened. We need a new car seat by the way - the garage loaned us one. Lily didn't complain when she was strapped in and even spent the journey home playing with the cat's eye. It's on the table in the hall. She insisted on keeping it."

* * *

The following morning Emily wondered how the girls would be when she took them to nursery, but they all happily piled into the Range Rover and quickly settled as she strapped them in, yesterday's drama a distant memory. She dropped them at nursery. Then she drove to Mothercare and picked up a new car seat. As she put the box in the boot of the Range Rover she was shocked to see the old car seat. She hadn't expected that, but then what else would Alex have done with it. She sat it upright and turned it to face her. Emily went cold. There was a deep slash in the fabric and padding and a huge dent in the back support which was split. Lily couldn't have survived that impact. When she examined the harness, she was stunned. The metal locking device in the centre of the buckle had disintegrated. It looked like it had melted. Emily found she was shaking. Lily was three years old. She couldn't have done that. She, Emily couldn't have done that, not even Alex! Was the buckle worn? Could it have given way just at the right moment to save Lily? Could it be that simple? How long had they had it? It got used practically every day. Frantically she checked the other car seats. No, they were fine. She tried to dismiss it. She didn't want to think of her daughter like that, but images of Myrtle, standing by the Wishing Well Cottage hearth holding a cast iron cauldron with a broken handle, wouldn't go away. Emily and her friend Louise had returned from a walk to find Myrtle, the third of the Wells triplets, standing by her hearth holding the cauldron which had been sitting by the fire. Myrtle had calmly told Emily that she needed to get the cauldron handle fixed as she would need it for the annual Well Blessing Ceremony. The cauldron was the only vessel big enough to feed the whole village. Its handle, which was wrought iron and curved to support the cauldron, had no longer been doing its job. Myrtle had told her to take it to the blacksmith to get it fixed. This was how she had met Alex.

She closed the boot and drove home. Just as she was getting out of the Range Rover, she was startled by the roar of a black Mercedes, scattering gravel as it set off round the green. As it drove away, she caught a brief glimpse of the driver who looked very much like Mr Earnshaw, Trevor's father. She could only assume that he had been at the vicarage. It was the only logical explanation. But why? He didn't live in the village, and she didn't think James knew him.

Inside she went to check on Snokettee and the kittens. They were doing fine. The little furry muddle of limbs was constantly moving. Occasionally, one would separate and climb on top of the others to slide back down as Snokettee licked it. Emily smiled, she couldn't help herself.

"We shall have to find names for them all," she said to Snokettee. "Do you think we should ask the girls? How about a naming ceremony this weekend? You think so? Good."

She then went and made the beds and set the washing machine going before tidying up the breakfast things. She then had a spot of lunch and a quick glance at the local paper before going to pick up the triplets.

CHAPTER FIVE

On Thursday evening Emily made her way to a two-storey apartment above the bakery, for the book club meeting. When she arrived she found everyone deep in discussion about St Peter's, the Young Disabled Unit. Situated on the outskirts of the village, just past Fare Well Cottage, St. Peter's was a large granite building set in its own grounds. Emily and Alex had donated Fare Well Cottage, Myrtle's old house, for the use of relatives of the YDU's residents. It seemed that the owner of St. Peter's, who hadn't been well for some time, had deteriorated. Everyone was concerned as to what might happen, should she die. Cheryl, a nurse at the YDU, was being grilled as to the current situation and likely outcomes. It was known that the owner and her 2 sons had been at logger-heads for years, the sons trying to persuade their mother to either sell the place or turn it into an hotel and conference centre.

"We have no idea," said Cheryl, "it has been going downhill for years. The management committee have been doing their best but there is no money. The old lady has been gradually handing over responsibility to them but without her input the home is struggling to survive. It needs investment, and there isn't any money."

"I thought those places made a fortune. My father-in-law is in Long Acres and you wouldn't believe the money my wife's family are paying out every month – it's scandalous," muttered Tony, one of the newer members of the group, whose pessimistic attitude was getting him a bad reputation. The more charitable members of the group felt that his bitterness towards life probably wasn't surprising, as he had recently been made redundant. The less charitable members thought the latter wasn't surprising.

"Really?" said Cheryl. "Just think what you would pay to stay in a motel for a week, and all you get there is your bed made and a help-yourself breakfast. Care costs. Even minimum wage adds up when it is 24/7."

"Yeah, but, how many inmates have you got?" It was obvious that Tony wasn't convinced of the expense and was doing some maths of his own.

"At the moment 12, *clients*", she said pointedly, "but we need at least 15 just to keep our heads above water and 20 before we can afford to update the place."

"Does it need updating?" asked Emily, and wished she'd kept her mouth shut as all eyes now turned to her, the millionaire in the room.

"Yes, but there is a lot of maintenance needed before that. The roof leaks, meaning that we can't use some of the rooms on the upper floor any more, and the boiler isn't adequate to heat the whole place anyway now that we can't augment it with the open fires due to health and safety. Social Services have stopped sending us clients because we no longer meet their regulations and their payments made up nearly a third of our income. A lot of money needs putting into that place, and soon. It would be a real shame if it closed."

There were a lot of agreed mutterings and surreptitious glances at Emily. To divert attention from herself she asked, "So, Cheryl, what would you do with the place to make it profitable?"

"Well, if it was down to me, I'd fix the roof, replace the boiler and ensure that it met the regulations for Social Services to refer clients to us again. That way we could fill enough beds to start making a profit with which to update the place. It is a fabulous building and could be really spectacular – a wonderful place for people to live and rehabilitate but I guess we will have to wait and see what her sons do with it. Actually, I don't even know if Lady Agnes plans to leave it to her sons, and I don't think the management committee does either."

That silenced everyone. After a pause the

host, Sonia, suggested they discuss the book they had read.

A little later, as Sonia refilled Emily's wine glass and asked her if she would like some cake, Emily realised that she hadn't heard a word of the last 10 -15 minutes. She had been deep in thought about the Young Disabled Unit. Despite it being so near to Fare Well Cottage she had never been there. As Fare Well had been inherited by Alex, before they were married, she had had very little to do with the arrangements. Alex had dealt with that. She had just helped with the setting up of the cottage ready for use. Now she wished she had taken more of an interest, but at the time she had had enough to do looking after Wishing Well Cottage.

She sipped her wine and forced herself to concentrate on what was being said. It seemed that the book discussion had concluded and everyone was now catching up on local gossip, chatting in small groups, and she wasn't in one. The people either side of her were turned away talking to their neighbours. She tried to catch the thread of what was being said, but struggled to find anything to say to join in with either conversation. Instead, she stood and crossed the room to Mags, "So, Dave didn't make it back in time?"

"No, he had the opportunity to pick up an extra load. It meant a detour, but he will be back tomorrow."

"So, got any plans for the weekend?" asked Emily.

"No, not really. How about you?"

"Oh, we will probably take the girls out for a walk somewhere. We all enjoy it and it wears them out nicely," she said with a grin.

"Have you taken them to the donkey sanctuary? I bet they would like that. My little ones used to love it."

"That sounds like a brilliant idea. I'd love that, never mind the children."

* * *

When she got home, Alex was engrossed in a film. She gave him a quick kiss and left him to it. Violent science fiction didn't appeal to her. Heading down to the outhouse she switched on the corridor light and opened the door. Snokettee and the kittens were all snuggled up together, Snokettee purring and the kittens making squeaky little sucking noises. Snokettee briefly opened her eyes, shuffled a little and settled again, content that there was no threat. Emily shut the door and went to the kitchen. On the table she had a quick sift through the mess of crayons and drawings left by the children and was amused to realise that she could tell which child had created which picture. When she picked up Lily's she was shocked by what appeared to be a large house with a very heavily crayoned black cloud over the top. In the foreground was a man. He was holding and swinging what looked like a spade. The picture was definitely Lily's but it wasn't her usual style. This was darker and quite menacing. The crayon strokes were viciously applied and had a certain maturity about them. Had Alex seen it?

She went back to the living room but it was obvious that the film was nowhere near ending, so she headed upstairs. A quick peek into the children's room and, happy that all was well, she went to bed.

She slid between the sheets and, knowing that she was unlikely to get to sleep before Alex joined her, she switched on her laptop and searched on St. Peter's, Much Meddling.

There were a number of articles written by local historians and, although St Peter's YDU did have a website, it was very basic and looked like it hadn't been updated for ages. She quickly exhausted the website, which consisted of an external photograph of the building, a couple of the grounds and some internal shots of the sitting room, dining room and a bedroom. It all looked very pleasant, but out-dated. She turned to an article by local historian, Arthur Bramble.

The article had a wonderful ink sketch of the front of St Peter's when it was first built in 1823. Built by the Victorians in the style of an Elizabethan manor house, with castellated turrets at the corners, it was 3 storeys high with the turrets making a 4th storey. It was built in granite with mullioned windows and two flights of stone steps leading upwards to meet at a grand entrance with portico and balustrade. An archway under the steps gave entrance to the basement of the building. The property was square and imposing and spectacularly beautiful. Emily was fascinated.

Skim reading the article she discovered that the building was originally called Sycamore Park Hall and had been built by Lord Archibald Noblet Earnshaw. The family had made their money during the Industrial Revolution processing cotton, and had lost a significant amount of their fortune as a result of the American Civil War of 1861. Emily was fascinated to read about the Lancashire Cotton Famine. When the Northern United States had blockaded the Southern United States' ports, preventing the export of cotton, the Lancashire workers had no work, causing great hardship and starvation. However, when imports had resumed, Lancashire mill workers had refused to process slave-picked cotton from the Southern United States and at great suffering to themselves and their families. This lasted nearly four years. As a result of their support and in acknowledgment of their suffering the Federal American government had sent a gift of food, and Abraham Lincoln had sent an address, commending the people of Lancashire. Wow, she had no idea. How did those people survive with no income for that long? She just couldn't imagine that. Would people do that today? Today there would be pictures all over the news and the internet, but back then, when most people couldn't read, or, if they could, couldn't afford newspapers, how did people get to know and understand what was happening on the other side of the world. Their compassion was astonishing. Would so many people here be prepared to starve, to effect change for people that they didn't know, and at the other side of the world?

CHAPTER SIX

In the morning Emily woke as Alex slipped out of bed.

"What time is it?" she asked, noting that it was still completely dark outside.

"Five fifteen. Sorry, but I need to get the furnace going, I have an early 'shoeing'. One of the Bradley's dray horses threw a shoe yesterday and it is needed for an appearance at a market tomorrow. It is the only time I can fit the horse in. I'll check on the girls on my way out." With that, he kissed her and left.

When she woke again, it was to Violet bouncing on the end of her bed, shortly followed by Tansy and Lily.

"What do you think about naming the kittens this weekend?" she asked. "I want you all to think of a name each. It won't be long before they are running about." This wasn't met with the enthusiasm she was expecting. If anything, they seemed puzzled by the suggestion.

Herding her troop downstairs she sorted out breakfast for them. Once they were eating, she remembered Lily's drawing. She waited until Lily had eaten most of her food and was using her spoon to play with the rest of it. She placed the picture in front of Lily. "What is this about?" she asked.

Lily looked at the picture and flung her spoon at it, splattering her work with cereal, "Bad man." She slipped down from her chair and ran over to where the other two were now playing on the rug at the other end of the kitchen. Picking up a doll, she cuddled it and kissed it gently on the forehead.

Emily stared at her child, then at the picture. Who was the 'bad man'? Was it Trevor's dad? If so, why, and how was Lily to know?

* * *

On her way back from dropping the children at nursery she was still mulling over Lily's drawing. As she approached the village and Fare Well Cottage, a large ginger cat ran across the road, pausing mid-way, just long enough to force Emily to stand on the brake. The cat headed into the driveway next to Fare Well. Just before Emily set off again, the cat jumped up onto the wall and sat silhouetted against a pale blue sign with faded gold lettering. Emily tried to read it but had to drive a bit closer, into the entrance.

St. Peter's Young Disabled Unit
Rehabilitation and Independent Living

At the bottom of the sign were contact details. On impulse she drove through the large wrought iron gates, which looked like they hadn't been closed for a very long time. The drive was lined with sycamore trees which had self-seeded in recent years as the lawns had obviously not been cut as needed. The road curved gently round to the right and then the tunnel of trees ended to reveal a gravelled parking area, on which sat several cars. To the left was St Peter's, situated in the building that was Sycamore Park Hall. It sat square and magnificent, looking out across a manicured lawn and the valley below. At the bottom of the lawn was a scattering of hawthorn bushes and a huge wood. Beyond that, she knew, was one of the roads leading away from Much Meddling. No wonder she had never seen the place before. On closer inspection of the building, Emily was dismayed to see peeling paint and what looked like sagging curtains at the upper windows, a couple of which were boarded up.

* * *

At a second-floor window, unseen by Emily, two pairs of amber eyes watched with satisfaction. Settling down, and tucking their paws underneath their pristine furry bodies, they leant against one another and purred quietly.

* * *

As Emily sat and admired the building,

a door, in the arch under the double flight of steps that led to the main doors, opened, and out marched what looked like Mr Earnshaw, Trevor's father. He was heading straight for her. Alarmed, she froze and watched as the lights on the black Mercedes, parked in the row ahead of hers, flashed. Oblivious to Emily he opened the door, climbed in, and slammed it. Then he drove off scattering gravel again.

* * *

Having observed this departure, the two cats jumped off the windowsill and hopped nimbly onto the bed in the room. Seeking a hand each, of the bed's occupant, they snuggled into her side in an effort to provide comfort. The elderly lady fondled her companions, and drew strength.

* * *

Emily headed off down the drive and into Much Meddling. Instead of driving home she drove down the back street, behind the shops, to Alex's forge.

"Hello, love. What you doing here?" asked Alex.

"Have you got a few minutes? I'd like to talk."

"Ooh," said Alex, laughing, "sounds ominous."

Emily smiled. "I wanted to talk to you last night but there wasn't time and I'd like to talk to you when the girls aren't around". Seeing the look on his face she added, "Have you seen Lily's drawing?"

"Drawing, what drawing? How about, if I come home for lunch, about 2 o'clock? When I have finished these two pieces, I can let the furnace go out and I'll be done for the weekend. I don't suppose you could get me a pasty from the bakery?"

With that, she left him to it. She walked through the yard to the large wooden doors that separated the forge out-buildings from the high street. She unbolted and stepped through the smaller person sized door set into the larger ones, and made her way to the bakery. She bought a couple of beef pasties and returned to the car.

* * *

Back at the cottage she collected up the breakfast things, cleared the floor of toys and went to check on Snokettee. She worked it out. The kittens were now 10 days old. They were so tiny, with their little ears flat to their heads still, but their fur was longer now and they looked more like proper cats. Emily crouched and held her hand out to Snokettee to sniff. The cat leant forward and rubbed the side of her face against Emily's hand. Emily was pleased. It felt good to have a cat, cats, about the place again. Since bringing the triplets home she hadn't had time to miss, or even think about, the absence of Kevin and his companion. She still couldn't bring herself to refer to the other cat as Angelica. Everyone else did. Her friend Lou loved to torment her and would pointedly mention Angelica at any opportunity. The thought that the cat was the re-incarnation of the former owner of Wishing Well Cottage amused her. She had also named her own cat, Ruby, after the previous owner of Bode Well Cottage, where she and Mike lived. However, Lou hadn't met either of the old ladies, and Emily had.

* * *

Alex arrived shortly after two as he had said. She pulled the two pasties out of the oven and put them on plates. She plonked a pot of tea on the kitchen table and they both sat down and took it in turn to ladle chutney onto their plates. As they tucked in, both of them found their eyes straying to the picture at the other end of the table, where Emily had deliberately placed it. Alex reached over and dragged it to him. Emily waited. When the suspense got too much she said, "Well, say something. What do you think it means?"

Alex carefully laid the picture on the table. "I think it means that they are taking after their great great great aunts."

Emily held her breath.

"Myrtle in particular was a good artist. Have you seen the landscape of the Great Storm, she did? It is in Fare Well Cottage; very dramatic and atmospheric."

"I meant, why do you think Lily drew it? What do you think it is showing?"

"Well, it is obviously a house and a man gardening, just before it rains."

"Don't be obtuse," snapped Emily. "That is St Peter's, with Trevor's dad waving a spade about and something bad is happening. Lily has drawn the 'bad man'. I have just been to St Peter's and it looks just like that," she said, stabbing at the picture, "AND, whilst I was there, Trevor's dad came storming out, slammed his car door and drove off in a rage."

"Did he have a spade?"

"No! This isn't funny," snapped Emily.

"He had probably been to see his mother."

"What? You know him?" screeched Emily, in a pitch higher than she had intended.

"Yes, Simon's brother and I were at school together, not the same year, but I knew them. Until the party, I hadn't seen Simon for years, didn't recognise him immediately. He is a lot younger than his brother, Thomas. Don't know where either of them lives now."

"And, you didn't think to mention this on Saturday?"

"Why? I know most of the people round here."

Emily fell silent and continued eating her pasty. So, what was his mother doing at a Young Disabled Unit, surely she'd be too old. Then, she might only be in her fifties, early sixties. Then it dawned on her. "Is his mother Lady Agnes Earnshaw?"

"Yes, she owns St Peter's. It was her that set it up as a Young Disabled Unit back in the 80's. Her family were really unhappy about it, but it was what she wanted to do, and when her husband died, she went ahead and did it. Sycamore Park Hall has been in the Earnshaw family for generations; well, they were the ones who built it, back in the 1800's. It was really successful. The grounds made it a lovely place for people to recuperate."

"Well, it isn't that way now. According to the book club…"

"Oh, I should have known. What have you been gossiping about now?"

"Apparently Lady Agnes has deteriorated and it is possible she may die. Everyone is concerned what will happen then. Her sons have been trying to get her to sell it for years. Cheryl, she's a nurse at St Peter's, said that it needs a lot of investment, the roof, the heating…"

"Whoa, whoa, whoa," said Alex, "I can see where this is going and No, we are not putting any money into that place."

"That isn't what I was suggesting, but, it wouldn't do any harm to talk about it."

"I don't think you have any idea what it would cost to do up that place. It is enormous. The problem belongs to the Earnshaws. As for Lily's drawing, I don't know. I really don't know."

CHAPTER SEVEN

Saturday was dry and clear, but there was a definite chill in the air. Alex was busy outside chopping logs, when the phone rang. It was Anna, Emily's first friend in Much Meddling and the lady who had helped her when she first moved in to Wishing Well Cottage. She had introduced Emily to a number of the villagers. Anna was also James, the vicar's, housekeeper.

"Hi, you back already?" asked Emily, looking at her watch, puzzled.

"No, still at Geneva airport. Our flight has been delayed. So, I thought I would give you a call and see if you are up for a 'girl's night out' sometime next week, say Tuesday?"

"Yeah, sure. I'll check its okay with Alex and have a word with Lou. How was your holiday?"

"Absolutely brilliant! It was lovely to get away and I have had such a great time. The snow was perfect. It was snowing when I arrived and then it was sunny for most of the week. I have some terrific photos to show you. How are you two, and the girls?"

"Great. The girls had their 3rd birthday, and Alex and I survived the party. James was hilarious, dressed as a parrot."

"I'll bet. He does love an audience. Oh, flight's just been called. Better go. Speak to you later. Can't wait to see you. I have some *news*! Bye," and she was gone.

"Bye," said Emily, to no-one.

Emily tapped a few buttons and waited for Lou to answer her phone. "Hi, Lou, it's me. I've just had Anna on the phone. Are you up for a 'girl's night out' on Tuesday?"

"Sure, I don't think Mike is doing anything then. So, anything new happened since the kids' party?" asked Louise.

"Well, the kittens have grown. Their little ears are starting to stand up and they are moving around more now their eyes are open. I so want to pick them up and cuddle them. They are absolutely gorgeous."

"Have they got names yet?"

"No, we are doing that this weekend. I have asked the girls to each think of a name."

"Can't wait to see what they come up with. Nathan is pestering for a dog, which would be lovely, but I am not sure I want the responsibility. They are a bit more tying than a cat. I still miss Ruby. It doesn't happen as often now but I keep thinking I have seen her out of the corner of my eye, you know, amongst the bushes or up a tree. Anyway, better get on. So, Tuesday 8pm at The Three Wells as usual?"

"Yes, okay, see you then," said Emily. Then, after checking Tuesday was okay with Alex, she texted Anna to confirm.

* * *

After lunch, which was delayed by the arrival of their on-line groceries delivery, the family set off, at Emily's suggestion, to the donkey sanctuary that Mags had mentioned. They drove through Much Meddling and out onto the fells, climbing up into the hills to High Dudgeon, a small village about 15 miles away. The donkey sanctuary was set in its own little valley, on the edge of the village. There were a few other cars in the car park. Two had their doors and boots open whilst adults stuffed tiny feet into multi-coloured Wellingtons, zipped up little jackets and issued exasperated instructions to "Wait!"

Soon Emily and Alex and the girls set off towards the pay booth where they were met with the usual exclamations and compliments for having three identical little girls. Wherever they went, outside Much Meddling, they caused a stir. Emily wished people wouldn't pay them so much attention. The girls were beginning to take on the airs of royalty. Alex shepherded them through the gate and they followed the signs to the donkeys. Some of the animals were in stables and others out in a 'viewing field'. This had a raised platform next to the fence to allow smaller visitors a clear view. There must have been about 20 donkeys there, some looking fit and healthy, other ones not so. Reading the information plaques attached to the fence Alex and Emily were dismayed to read some of the harrowing stories of the donkeys, now at the sanctuary. How people could be so uncaring and cruel was beyond their comprehension. They were glad the children couldn't read yet. They also, thankfully, weren't interested in looking at the plaques, which had some awful pictures of the donkeys at the time of rescue.

Strolling round the stable yard, Alex lifted the girls, one at a time, so that they could see into the stables. They moved along the row, following the sanctuary's tour route, looking at donkey after donkey and were just about to follow the last arrow, directing them to the tearoom and shop, when they realised that Tansy was missing. Alex jogged back along the route they had come, but there was no sign of her.

Turning to the remaining two triplets he said, "Lily, Violet, do you know where Tansy went?"

They both pointed to a small hole in the fence at the side of the stables. It was too small for either Alex or Emily to get through and they couldn't see Tansy. Alex stopped a passing sanctuary employee and explained.

After a key had been obtained Alex was led round the back of the stables to an enclosure which wasn't on show to the public. Here were the sickest animals. Tansy had climbed into a stall and was standing in front of a donkey, resting her forehead against that of the animal. Her hands were gently caressing the sides of its neck. The donkey was standing unsteadily. It was thin and weak and its coat was dull and matted. Looking at its feet, Alex was horrified to see that its hooves were long and curved upwards. The animal looked like it was on little rockers.

"Tansy, come here," called Alex.

"Daddy, help the donkey."

"Tansy, come here."

"No. Help the donkey. Daddy, please help the donkey," and she turned back and put her forehead against the donkeys face again.

Alex looked at the attendant, who explained that the donkey had only arrived that morning and that the vet was due on Monday.

"Daddy!"

To the attendant's horror Alex opened the stable door and inspected the donkey's hooves. He then explained that he was a farrier and, if he had the right tools in the Range Rover, would attend to the donkey's hooves. He looked at Tansy and realised that there was no moving her, so he left her with the donkey and the attendant.

"What, you left her with a wild, sick

donkey. She is three years old, she could get trampled, or bitten!" snapped Emily.

"I doubt it. One of the staff is with her. She'll be fine. Why don't you take these two and get a coffee or something. It is going to take me a while to cut and trim those hooves."

It was well over an hour before Alex and Tansy found them. Having had their fill of orange juice and cake, Emily had taken the girls into the sanctuary shop. She now had her arms full of cuddly donkeys, donkey colouring books and a copy of 'A Donkey's Life' for herself.

"I am going to have to come back tomorrow," said Alex. "I have done what I can for today. The donkey has had enough for now."

"What, we were going for a walk tomorrow."

"Blame your daughter. I'll come in the morning. We can still go for a walk in the afternoon."

Tansy led the way back to the car, seemingly content that the world was a little better.

CHAPTER EIGHT

On Sunday morning Alex and Tansy left the house early, to go to the donkey sanctuary. Tansy had insisted on going with him and he was happy to take her, both because it was good to spend time with his daughter and because she had actually been a great help, keeping the donkey calm. It wasn't often that he was able to have time with just one of the triplets and it was really enjoyable to get to know them as individuals. They were all so different, which came as a constant surprise. Why this should be, he didn't know. Tansy was the most boisterous of the three and the most physically capable. She was a bit of a Tom-boy, which he liked. Despite her small size she appeared to have no fear, beyond basic self-preservation. When, yesterday, they had discovered that she was missing, he had been concerned, naturally. However, he realised that he would have been more concerned had it been one of the other two. Tansy, he had been sure, was off on some adventure of her own making, and he had been right. He was proud of the way she had sought out the sick donkey and how she had asserted herself to help it.

At the sanctuary, they were treated like honoured guests. The staff were again apologetic for the hole in the fence which had allowed Tansy through, and were quick to assure Alex that the hole had been fixed. They were also most grateful for what he was doing for the donkey. Alex suspected that this wasn't the last time he would be helping out here, and he honestly didn't mind. In his line of work he dealt with horses all the time, but this was different, not just because this was a donkey, but because it felt good to help the animal. He was supplied with tea and a large slice of chocolate cake, and a steady stream of staff, mainly female, came and peered into the stall whilst he worked. There was also a degree of fascination with the role Tansy was playing. It was obvious that the donkey trusted this tiny little girl. Again, she stood at its head, resting against it, stroking its neck and muttering soothing noises.

When Alex had finished, the animal swayed slightly, still weak and unsteady but anatomically sound, getting used to relying on different sets of muscles to stand. They left the donkey to feed and rest. After much thanks from the staff and encouragement to visit, any time, they headed home, Tansy humming happily. Clipped to her jacket pocket was a badge with

'Tansy, donkey sanctuary helper – free pass', printed on it.

* * *

Not long after Emily, Violet and Lily got back from church, Alex and Tansy returned, chatting happily like old friends, pleased with their days work. Alex related how remarkable Tansy had been and how good it had felt to him to be able to help the animal. It was visibly less stressed, once it was able to stand properly.

After lunch, Emily led the family through to the outhouse and Snokettee.

"Right, did you think of a name each?" she asked the girls.

They all looked at her. None of the children said anything. So, Emily picked on Lily, the most precocious of the three.

"Lily, do you have a name?"

Lily, appearing vaguely exasperated, crouched down and pointed at the black kitten, "That's Marigold, and that's…"

"Lily," Emily interjected, "let the others choose. Tansy, do you have a name?"

Tansy pointed at the grey kitten, "That's Spider."

Violet quickly pointed at the white kitten, "That's 'Whoops-a-Daisy."

Then all three children turned and ran off into the kitchen, leaving a bemused Emily and Alex to stare at one another, dumbfounded.

* * *

Later that afternoon, trudging along the top of the crag, on the hill that overlooked Much Meddling, Alex put his arm round Emily. She leant into him and they stopped to admire the view. It was always different, always spectacular. The trees changed with the seasons and the light changed with the time of day and the weather. The lack of leaves on the trees allowed the buildings of the village to show through the branches: the rooftops of the high street, dark and shiny wet. Although it wasn't raining the tiles retained the dampness from the early morning mist. Nothing really dried out at this time of year. On the grass below the crag the girls were running about with their arms wide, banking into the breeze and laughing. Alex gave Emily a squeeze and a peck on the cheek, then ran off flapping his arms and 'cawing', towards his little girls. He grabbed Violet, the nearest, and swung her up and round, rotating twice before plonking her back on the ground, giggling delightedly. Both Tansy and Lily ran at him, swinging on his arms, "Me, Me." He wrapped an arm round each child, lifted them off the ground and bounded down the hill. Sliding to a halt, he twirled on the spot, before putting them down and faking exhaustion.

"Again, again," they pleaded.

He was just about to give in when he spotted a lone figure jogging along the top of the ridge. "Look, Uncle James. Bet I can get there first," and he set off running up the hill, rapidly followed by the girls.

James was out training for his next marathon, which he used to raise money for St Peter's, the Young Disabled Unit. Tansy reached him first and virtually flew into his arms. Pummelled rapidly in succession by Lily and Violet, also arriving at speed, he stopped. Tousling three dark curly heads in turn, he grinned, "You lot look like you are having fun, I could see you all running about from back there," and he indicated back, the way he had come. "Lovely to see you all, but I'd better not stop. You soon get cold this weather." Freeing himself from the triplets, he set off again, waving goodbye.

As they set off back down through the woods Emily said, "I must ask James about St Peter's. He probably knows what is going on. Lady Agnes was one of the people he listed for us to pray for this morning, and I am sure that it was Mr Earnshaw I saw leaving the vicarage the other day."

"James probably does know, but he has confidentiality to think of so may not be willing to tell you."

Emily sighed, "But it won't hurt to ask. Anyway, Anna is back now. I bet she can find out."

"You know, you are turning into a right gossiping busybody," he said laughing.

"Aren't you curious? Don't you want to

know why Lily thinks he is a 'bad man'? I don't like unsolved mysteries. Talking of which, we still don't know who gave the girls those necklaces. I have accounted for everyone at the party."

"Does it matter?"

"Of course it does. I need to thank them."

Dropping off the crag and heading downhill, the path disappeared into the wood that covered the lower slope of the hill, and could be quite dense when the foliage was at its fullest. At present, only the few conifers were green. Entering the wood, Emily and Alex noticed that the children had disappeared. This was something that often happened, at some point, on their trip to the crag. It usually didn't take Emily and Alex long to find them, but it was taking increasingly longer as the girls learned and grew more inventive with their hiding places. So far, however, they hadn't learnt to be quiet as well. Little giggles usually gave them away, especially if Alex did his usual of pretending to have difficulty finding them. Once he had found them all it was discovered that mummy was missing, and the girls ran about until they found her. Suitably exhausted, the family headed back home.

Back home, Emily checked on Snokettee and was surprised to find the kittens all on their own. Snokettee had obviously slipped out the cat-flap. The kittens were all huddled together in their basket, forming one furry ball. So, Whoops-a-daisy, Marigold and Spider, what do you think of your names? I guess it won't be long before you are all scampering about, climbing here, there and everywhere."

Just then the cat-flat opened and in strolled Snokettee, dead mouse in mouth. Emily decided it was time to leave. Whatever happened next, she didn't want to witness.

CHAPTER NINE

Tuesday's 'girl's night out' couldn't come soon enough for Emily. Once she had dropped the children at nursery, shopped, cleaned up the breakfast things and put on a load of washing, she got herself a cup of tea and sat down at her laptop. She did a property search covering a wide search area and with 'unlimited' price range, and filtered on 'most expensive' first. There was nothing the size of St Peters. The nearest was £4.85million. She couldn't imagine what St Peter's would be worth despite it needing some work. St Peter's problems weren't something that she and Alex could fix with a donation, even if Alex was willing. She brought up a number of Sycamore Park Hall articles and read more about its history.

It seemed that the Earnshaws had been quite influential, a number of Manchester's municipal buildings being provided by them. Housing for their workers had been built close to their mills, with fresh-water taps in each street. They were also early adopters of gas street-lighting, which was very popular as it made the streets safer, reducing crime. During the cotton famine they set up soup kitchens although not all the Earnshaw family approved of the strike, causing family rifts. During the Crimean war two of the Earnshaw's sons were killed in action. During the First World War another generation of Earnshaws lost three sons, and a daughter who had gone to France as a nurse. Sycamore Park Hall grounds had been used as a training camp for newly recruited soldiers. During the Second World War the Hall had been used as a hospital for injured airmen. In the 1970s ghost tours of the Hall had been popular and a TV documentary made. This article was accompanied by two grainy black and white photos showing 'the ghosts'. Even for the 1970s they were of poor quality, obviously a publicity stunt to raise money.

* * *

Having fed Alex and the girls, and then tucked the children into bed, she went and got changed. She did her hair and put on a bit of make-up, grabbed her coat and bag, kissed Alex, and headed out the door. Outside it was bitter and the wind had picked up. Wrapping her coat around her she trotted down the drive, along the street past the vicarage and Anna's row of cottages, crossed the street and entered the welcome warmth of The Three Wells pub. Richard, the owner, greeted her and automatically grabbed a glass and filled it with red wine for her.   Richard was one of the people who helped her with the village's annual well blessing by supplying drink, cutlery and crockery. They had become good friends. After a brief chat he gestured over to the window where Anna was already sitting, and returned to his other customers. Emily trotted over and hugged Anna gleefully.

"So, tell me all about it," said Emily, doing a little dance, "and, this *news* you mentioned, then left me hanging."

"Nope, I want to wait for Lou to arrive first. You tell me what you have been up to. This party sounded fun. Wish I had been here for that."

So, Emily told her all about the party and the pirate ship. Finally, she told her about Lily calling Mr Earnshaw a 'Bad man'. Anna listened attentively and raised her eyebrows at this latter. She was about to say something when Lou slipped into the chair beside her, and another round of greetings ensued.

* * *

Alex waited until he was sure Emily was settled in the Three Wells then went up to their bedroom. After a brief search he found the brown wrapped parcel containing the three little white boxes, which Emily had put safely out of the way of the children. The fairy necklaces were to be kept for special occasions only, she had told them. He took the boxes and sat on the edge of the bed. Opening the first he studied the pendant carefully. The chain appeared to be gold, and the fairy also gold but with enamel paint. An expensive gift for a three-year-old especially compared to the other gifts given by parents of the party guests. Alex fingered the pendant and then turned it over to inspect its back for hallmarks. What he saw, sent an icy chill up his spine.

* * *

The women were now on their second glass of wine. Anna worked her way through the photos on her phone. There were beautiful snaps of snowy mountains with glistening glasses of various amber coloured beverages held aloft in the foreground. Happy smiling faces grinned in panoramic shots from mountain restaurants. Then she stopped the photo show, mid-week, looking coy. The other two looked at her expectantly. After a pause, either for effect or from embarrassment, she swiped to the next photo and said," This is Sasha, we met at the hotel bar the third night and, well…"

Both Emily and Lou cut her short with excited congratulations. Louise ran to the bar and came back with a bottle of Prosecco and some tall glasses. As the bubbles settled and the girls pumped her for information, Anna positively glowed. She and Sasha had spent the rest of the holiday, when not skiing, together.

Despite being French, he lived in Halifax, was an architect and was coming to visit the following weekend. Emily and Lou were ecstatic.

"So, we get to meet him?" said Louise. "I can't wait. Let me see that photo again." Anna handed over her mobile. "Yes, I think you have done well there. Nice and rugged, very good for curling up with on a cold night. Er, how old is he? He looks a wee bit younger than you." Anna obviously wasn't going to answer that one, so Lou continued, "What are his eyes like?" she asked, swiping madly, "Have you got a photo without his sunglasses? Ah ha, here we go. Oooh, beautiful deep-set eyes, all crinkly round the edges when he smiles, and all loved up, staring deep into the camera at you. Our Anna's in lurve," teased Lou.

"Will you stop it. I am not a teenager. Yes, I know I have been on my own for quite a while now. It is hard starting all over again, getting to know someone new. Anyway, tell me about you two. What has been happening in Much Meddling in my absence?"

* * *

Back at the Cottage Alex was still reeling from the possible implications of what he had found. On the back of each fairy pendant was a thin sliver of calcite. The periapt that Emily had been given by his great great aunt was made from the same material, hers cut from the stalactite which had formed over millennia in the cave beneath the cottage. Putting the pendants back in the cupboard where he had found them he went back downstairs, and down into the cellar.

* * *

Lou was keen to know how the kittens were doing. She hadn't seen them since the party. She was also eager to know their names.

"Yes, we have names. Are you ready for this?" Emily asked, keeping the others in suspense. "It was really weird. The girls were so matter of fact about it, as if it was obvious what their names were. So, why was I asking! They rhymed off the names and then just turned and went back to playing in the kitchen." She took another swig of her wine and continued, "So, ladies, our kittens are 'Marigold', Whoops-a-Daisy' and, wait for it, 'Spider'."

Lou and Anna grinned. Emily shrugged her shoulders, "Just out of curiosity I looked up ''Marigold'. It stands for eternal love. As for the other names...? One of the staff at the nursery is always saying 'Whoops-a-Daisy' when any of the children fall. But, 'Spider', where did they get that from? Anyway, talking of mysteries..." and Emily went on to explain about St Peter's and Mr Earnshaw. She also related a bit of the history she had read about the building.

"So, "said Lou, conspiratorially, "let's see. We have a failing Young Disabled Unit with a sick owner. We have a money grabbing son (probably expecting to inherit and having previously stated that the place should be sold). We have said son, publicly shamed as a 'bad man', seen angrily leaving said establishment and also a mystery trip to the local vicarage from which he was also seen leaving, angry. Hmmm! We know that he isn't always angry – we both saw him at the party. So we can deduce from this that something at each of the visits made him angry. We need more information. Anna, you find out why he was at the vicarage? Em, you visit St Peter's charity shop and pump them for information, and call Cheryl. Find out what happened when he visited the YDU. What she doesn't know she can surely find out. Me, I have my own sources".

* * *

Down in the cave end of the cellar, where the dim glow from a bare bulb cast shadows and the only sound was his own breathing, Alex stood and stared. Deep in thought he watched as a globule of liquid slowly formed and eventually dripped from the tip of the stalactite in the ceiling onto the stalagmite at its base, on which sat Emily's periapt: the resultant sediment, slowly and imperceptibly beginning to re-join the two into a column and assimilate the calcite periapt once more. Alex continued to stare, deep in thought. Who had given his children periapts? Why would anyone do that? He found he was equally livid and scared. He, Alex, didn't believe in such stuff, but others did. He tried to think back to the party. It could have been any of the parents. Just because Emily had accounted for all the other presents didn't mean that one of them hadn't also given the box with the periapts. Any one of them could have slipped the box in with the other presents. Was it accidental that it didn't have a label, or deliberate? He had to find out who had given it. As another drop of liquid fell, he blinked, and an image of Lily's outstretched arm and accusatory finger filled his vision, and the words 'Bad man' rang in his ears.

CHAPTER TEN

Emily had drunk way too much. As Alex opened the bedroom curtains and let in some light, weary as it was on that January morning, Emily groaned. He took one look at her and laughed. "Don't worry, I'll take the girls to nursery. You go hurl, or whatever you need to do."

"I am not that bad, give me some credit," protested Emily, "but coffee wouldn't be a bad idea." Slowly she roused herself and crawled out of bed. She put on her dressing gown, wrapping it tightly against the chill air. When she got downstairs she was pleased to see that Alex had got the girls' breakfast well under way, and there was a mug of coffee for her. After that, and some toast, she felt a bit better. She felt even better when the front door closed as Alex, and the noise that was the girls, left for the day. She carefully gathered the crockery and put it on the drainer, put cereal boxes back in cupboards, crawled under the table for the odd spoon, and put the margarine back in the fridge. Then she wet some paper towel, wiped the back of a chair clean and crawled back under the table to wipe up jam, some milk splashes and something else that she couldn't identify, even after sniffing at it.

The cats were alright and still looking cute. She watched them for a while then went into the living room, drew back the curtains and plumped the odd cushion. Next, she gathered up the plate, mug and packet of biscuits left by Alex the evening before. At this point she decided that she needed another coffee.

* * *

Louise was having a similar morning, but also had Nathan to contend with. He only attended nursery three days a week and Wednesday wasn't one of those days. He was currently smashing cars into the skirting board. When Lou told him to stop, he proceeded to smash them into each other. To distract him, she switched the TV on, and the Disney channel. This rarely had an immediate effect but normally worked. Today took a little longer than usual, or perhaps it just seemed that way to Lou. Once the crashing stopped, she sipped her coffee and picked up her phone.

"Hi, how are you?" asked Emily, "and please whisper your answer."

"Getting by, getting by. Were we singing 'Auld Lang Syne' last night at some point?"

"My throat feels like that's possible. Did you buy a bottle of Prosecco? Let me know how much and I'll go halves."

"Not necessary, my love, I got Richard to put it on your tab," grinned Lou.

They chatted for a while sharing their misery, until a crash and howl at Lou's end sent Lou running into the living room to Nathan. Some angry words ensued and then she came back on the phone, "That was Nathan. He's okay. The pile of books he had built collapsed when he stood on it. Mike is going to be livid when he sees the state of his atlas. Look, I'd better go. Speak to you later."

* * *

As the morning wore on Emily felt better. She made herself some lunch and then decided that some fresh air would do her good. The ground around the shady side of the village pond glistened and the leaves were crisp under foot. On the water two mallards and a moorhen motored about, navigating the remains of that night's ice. She trod carefully until she passed the trees. She decided to walk to the end of the High Street on the sunny side, and back on the shady side when she had hopefully warmed up. She strolled past the dentist and then hurried past the estate agents' window; she still avoided Gerald, the estate agent who had sold her Wishing Wells Cottage and who still tried to 'chat her up' at any opportunity. She glanced into The Little Teacups Café and nodded at the new owner, Lesley. Lesley had taken over from

Jessica, the young woman who had gone off with Emily's ex-boyfriend Grant. Over the past few years Jessica had sent postcards to Emily to let her know that she and Grant were now living together in Naples. Despite their history, Emily liked Jessica and was glad that she had thought to keep in touch. Jessica and Grant appeared happy together, and although Emily would never have seen Jessica and Grant as a couple, their relationship seemed to be working.

Emily continued, crossing a couple of side streets, each one lined with terraced houses that stopped at a stone wall separating the village from the wood on the slopes of the crag. A well-worn stone stile at the end of each street gave access to the woods. She passed the GP surgery next and then Bode Well Cottage, where Lou and Mike lived. The street continued, the properties here thinning out and set further back from the road in large gardens with substantial ancient trees. It was a pretty walk in sunshine but not in the cold. Emily had no intention of walking as far as Fare Well Cottage today. After watching and listening to a robin for a while, its cheery tuneful notes making her smile, she crossed the road and turned back towards the green.

She walked past the hairdresser's and a couple of other shops and came to a halt outside St Peter's Charity Shop. She hadn't intended to come here when she left the house. Now that she was here, should she go in and 'pump' the staff for information? What was she going to say? She was no good at interrogating people. She had enough trouble making small talk. She thought of Lou. Lou would have been straight in there, chatting merrily and asking question after question. If Lou found out that she had been here and not gone in and asked, she would nag her mercilessly. She rehearsed a few lines in her head. 'Hello. How's business? Are you planning a closing down sale? Tell me, is it true that Lady Agnes' son is planning on selling St Peter's? How bad a man is her son? So, what is going on up at St Peter's, the book club... demands... to know?'

She continued to study the stock in the window. There was a ladder-back chair draped with an embroidered tablecloth, an elegant occasional table that had a pretty blue bone china tea service laid out on it with a Tiffany style lamp, and a matching jug and ewer stood on the floor surrounded by a selection of glass vases. A small bookcase held a number of ornaments and old books, some nicely bound in leather and others with printed coloured pictures depicting exciting adventures. Finally, she decided that it wouldn't do any harm to just go in and look. She needn't say anything.

She pushed the door, setting its little bell tinkling. Inside was a bit warmer than the street, but not much. Emily muttered hello to the lady behind the counter, who looked up from the crossword she was doing, smiled, and said, "Hi."

On the chair next to her a large tabby cat stood, stretched its back up into an arch, rotated on the chair's cushion and settled back down, one eye on Emily. Emily strolled slowly round the shop, aware that she was being watched and feeling awkward. There didn't seem to be anything she wanted to buy but she grew more and more uncomfortable, feeling that she ought to buy something. Having done a circuit of the shop, which wasn't large, Emily stopped and let her eyes travel round the upper shelves. There she spotted a large catering sized metal teapot. She asked to have a look at it. Whilst the lady got some steps to bring it down Emily inspected some of the books on the shelf nearest to her. The collection was of local history, and she was fascinated to find that two of them dated back to the early 1800s, and were illustrated. She put them to one side and had a look through the rest of the books and found one from the 1900s, 'A History of Much Meddling - 1400 to the present day'. This had a publishing date of 1969.

Having retrieved the teapot, the lady handed it to Emily who gave it a quick inspection. This would be just the thing for serving tea at the Well Blessings; it would probably hold about 20 cups worth of tea. As she paid for her purchases the lady said, "You interested in the history of this place then?"

"Yes, I have lived here 4 years now and it was only recently that I went to St Peter's. I had no idea how big it is. You can't see it from the road."

The cat, now sitting on the counter, purred gently.

"No, when I was little, we used to play in the woods, but you had to be careful not to be seen from the house. That was back before it was a Young Disabled Unit. The family didn't like us kids playing there. Don't blame them. If it was my place I wouldn't have wanted kids building dens in the trees either." "It is a fabulous building but it looks like it needs a lot of work," said Emily, hopefully.

"Yes, it has been losing money for years, ever since Lady Agnes became ill. She was the driving force, had loads of ideas to make money and it was really successful. Don't know what is going to happen now."

"What do you mean?" said Emily, "Sorry, it is probably none of my business," and then mentally kicked herself, not wanting to silence the woman.

"No, that's alright, it's no secret that St Peter's needs a lot of investment if it is to keep going. There is a management committee but they don't have the authority to make major decisions."

"I believe that Lady Agnes has two sons. Are they no help?"

"You're joking. They are useless. The one son that visits is always rowing with his mother and has no positive suggestions to make. It sounds like she gets more depressed every time he turns up. Her other son lives abroad somewhere, I think. The pair of them would sell the place if they could and probably will when the old lady dies unless it can turn a profit in the meantime."

"Doesn't this place help?" asked Emily, indicating the shop.

"It barely covers the shops bills. We volunteers freeze to death most days. We wouldn't mind so much, saving money on heating, if it didn't affect sales. Customers, generally, do not stay long." The tabby rubbed its head against the woman's hand and then strolled over to Emily who automatically reached out and offered hers. The cat sniffed it and then leant on Emily. The woman smiled, as if encouraged by the cat's behaviour, "I hope you don't mind me saying, but aren't you the lady who owns Fare Well Cottage, the accommodation for St Peter's relatives?"

"Er, well, my husband, but yes, I suppose I am," said Emily.

"I thought so. I probably shouldn't be saying this but, as it's you, I don't suppose it can do any harm…"

Emily waited, trying not to show disapproval of any breach of confidentiality, which might put the woman off.

"Well, he, the son, turned up with a

friend. Together they walked round the whole of the building and the grounds. There was no explanation given to the staff but one of the cleaners recognised the friend. Guess what? He is an estate agent. What do you make of that?"

"Really," said Emily, shocked. "No, they can't sell the place; that would be dreadful. Where would the residents go?"

* * *

Back home, armed with this piece of information and flush with her current detective success, she phoned Cheryl. There was no answer. Disappointed, Emily left a message, suggesting that they get together at some point that fitted in with Cheryl's shift pattern at St Peter's; perhaps Friday when Lou could join them, and hopefully Anna.

* * *

Alex had been struggling to concentrate all day. That was the second shoe he had over flattened. He threw it into his water bucket and picked up another length of metal. He thrust this into the furnace and watched as it started to glow. Still, the necklaces given to his children played on his mind. He was certain that whoever had given them, deliberately anonymously, had known exactly what they were doing. He didn't believe that the necklaces had any power, what-so-ever, but there was motive behind this 'gift'. Just sending them was a message. Someone had a reason for targeting the triplets. Who and why? Simon Earnshaw made no sense. The more he thought about it the more he dismissed him, despite Lily's 'Bad Man'. What possible reason could he have? Alex needed to talk to someone. He didn't want to worry Emily; there was no logical reason to worry, but he couldn't help it. The calcite on the necklaces served no structural purpose and had, he was certain, been put there deliberately to create periapts. Talking to James was the next obvious choice but, as the vicar, it didn't seem appropriate. Briefly he considered getting them exorcised, but that was giving credence to any power they may have. He dismissed that as stupid. Mike maybe.

* * *

That evening, after the children had been put to bed, Emily and Alex sat down together to watch a bit of TV. When the adverts came on she told him of her visit to the charity shop and the news that Simon Earnshaw had had St Peter's valued. Alex automatically bristled at the mention of Simon, despite the lack of any tangible link, his mind immediately going to the three little boxes in their bedroom and his daughter's drawing. He longed to share his fears with Emily but resisted the temptation. She didn't need to know. There was a lot she didn't need to know. Knowledge, that he thought had died; knowledge that he thought had been buried, with his great great aunts.

"Are you listening to me? I said that Simon

Earnshaw has had St Peter's valued, AND, whilst his mother is still alive. It isn't even *his* yet. Can you believe that?"

Yes, he had to admit that that was definitely out of order. Everyone knew how much that YDU meant to her. "Sorry, yes, but there is nothing we can do about it."

"If it had a new roof and boiler then maybe they could get more residents..." said Emily biting her lip.

"No, no, no, no, No!" said Alex. "Absolutely not! It would cost a hundred grand or more to re-roof that place." He looked at Emily, who looked crest-fallen. "Okay, suppose we did. That bastard Simon will just sell it anyway, and all we will have done is to increase its value for him." As the adverts finished Alex settled back into the sofa, muttering expletives.

CHAPTER ELEVEN

After a number of texts between Emily, Anna and Cheryl, arranging to meet at Emily's for lunch on Friday, Lou decided that she needed to follow up on her part of the challenge to investigate the goings on at St. Peter's. With Mike at work and Nathan at Nursery she had a few hours to herself. Having heard from Emily about the YDU valuation she decided to see if she could wheedle anything out of Gerald, the local estate agent.

When she walked through the door Gerald was delighted, presumably relishing the possibility of selling Bode Well Cottage. He offered her a seat, and after initial pleasantries said, "So, what can I do for you?"

"Well, Mike and I have been wondering about putting a conservatory onto the cottage and wondered what that would do to the value of the place?"

"I see," he said, straightening his tie and slicking down his hair, "I would need to visit and know what sort of conservatory you were going to add, to give you a proper valuation." As Lou smiled at him sweetly, he continued, "I'd need to know what sort of conservatory you have in mind and how big? It would need to be in keeping with the style of the property. In the case of Bode Well Cottage I would advise using an architect to ensure that whatever you choose enhances the look of the place. I can recommend an architect if you like."

"I was more hoping for just a 'ball-park' figure at this stage. Do you do many valuations round here?"

"Well, most of them. The only other estate agents operating round here are based in the local towns."

"Just out of interest, if we were to put ours on the market what do you think it would be worth?"

"Without seeing inside, I would put it in the region of £650,000."

"Oh, that much," cooed Louise, "and where would you advertise it? Do you do those county magazine ads? You know, the glossies?"

"Well, we aren't that big but, in that case, we would probably hand the sale over to our sister office who could put it in Lancashire Life for you and probably the Yorkshire one, too. See, here," and he reached behind him to a shelf where he picked up a copy of Lancashire Life, flicked through the pages and then pointed out a 4-page spread of properties, "it would appear in here," he said proudly.

Louise studied the pages. "Do any of these other agencies cover Much Meddling?"

"Well they might but it would be unusual, we are a bit too far out."

Louise thanked him, said she and Mike needed to think about the conservatory, made her excuses and left. Crossing the street she headed into the store and bought herself a copy of Lancashire Life.

* * *

As Emily sorted and folded a stack of washing, the doorbell rang. It was Mr Swire, come to collect his ointment. Emily had first met the old gentleman not long after she had moved into Wishing Well Cottage. It was through him that she had learned about her expected responsibility as the herbalist for the village. The fact that Angelica, the cottage's previous owner, had died, had made no difference to the villagers, they still expected their medicines. Emily had consulted the doctors at the local surgery who had eagerly paid her a visit, keen to satisfy their curiosity as to what Angelica had been doing all those years. Collectively they inspected the jars and numerous herbs etc. that filled the front room of Wishing Well Cottage. They had scrutinised Angelica's 'patients notes' and decided that they couldn't fault her 'prescribing'. Her herbal remedies wouldn't do any harm and were obviously, in most cases, doing some good. Together they helped Emily concoct more ointment for Mr Swire, and told her that provided she didn't take on any more 'patients', she was okay to follow Angelica's notes. So, she had learnt to make most of the remedies which, at the time, she was glad to do. She didn't want to alienate any more of the villagers. Bidding Mr Swire welcome she led him into the front room and noted that he was limping slightly.

"You know I would have brought it to you," she said.

"I know luv, but I need to keep movin'. It don't do to sit too long. When ya get to my age there's them what get keen to lock you up. When I go, it'll be in me own bed, and I ain't goin' yet. So, you'd better get busy on another batch o' that ointment." Sucking on his dentures he ferreted in his pocket, pulling out a selection of items in turn: a rather grey and crumpled handkerchief, a set of large keys, a ball of rubber bands, some Victory 'V' lozenges and finally, with a struggle to free it, a jar of honey which he plonked on the table. The jar of ointment he rammed in his pocket, taking up the space left by the honey. Then he slowly crammed in all the other items. "Thanks, luv." Just as he reached the front door he turned and took Emily's hands in his. Looking her in the eye, he said, "You tek care now. You do what you 'ave to do!" With that he left, leaving Emily wondering what on earth he was talking about.

* * *

The kittens were now 16 days old and Snokettee was spending more time out hunting, despite Emily feeding her. With Snokettee absent Emily took the opportunity to take a few photos on her phone. The kittens being so small, she could fit all three into close-up shots. They were adorable. She tried out their names, calling them in turn, "Marigold", "Whoops-a-Daisy", "Spider." They may have turned their heads at the noise, but that was all. Not that she was expecting anything more. Just then the cat flap went, and in slid Snokettee with another mouse. Emily left.

* * *

When Alex got home he went up to the bedroom to shower and change. Whilst there, he took the opportunity to slip a note into each of the boxes. The notes read, 'please talk to me before letting the girls wear these. Alex'. He would have liked to remove the boxes altogether but he hoped their presence, as opposed to their absence, would delay him having to talk to Emily for as long as possible. The only 'special occasion' that he could think of was the Well Blessing in March, and that was a few weeks away yet.

The girls, he was pleased to see were lively and happy, playing noisily together. When they saw him they ran at him, and dragged him over to their play mat, all talking at once. He sat cross-legged and joined in their play, up-righting a carriage and putting it back on the wooden train track. It was good to spend time with them. It was good to know that they were all safe and well.

CHAPTER TWELVE

Anna arrived first, shortly followed by Cheryl and, about 10 minutes later, Louise. Emily quickly cooked some prawn pasta which she served with a mixed salad of greenery, tomatoes and olives, and some garlic bread. She poured each of the ladies a glass of Sauvignon Blanc and told them all to tuck in. With the meal under way she decided it was time to get to the purpose of the meeting. For the benefit of Cheryl she explained about the girls' night out and how they had discussed what Cheryl had said at the book club, about the future of St Peter's being under threat. She also explained that, if possible, they would like to do something to help. Therefore, they would like Cheryl to tell them what she knew about The Earnshaws. Emily added that she had seen Simon Earnshaw leaving St Peter's looking angry. Seeing that Cheryl appeared reluctant to talk she added that she knew about the valuation.

"Well, said Cheryl, "I don't suppose it is a secret. He has been arguing, noisily, with his mother about it for a long time now. Everyone at St Peter's knows and probably half the village. He was livid the other day, probably the one you are talking about, because we had admitted another resident. He had specifically stated that we weren't to admit anyone else. Sister told him that she took her instructions from Lady Agnes, not him. He then hissed something in Sister's ear, don't know what, she wouldn't say, but we reckon it was along the lines of 'I'll remember that once I am running the place.'"

"How is Lady Agnes?" asked Anna.

"Not good. She had another stroke recently and although she is making progress, she needs a lot of help. She gets very frustrated because she can't speak clearly and struggles to find the right words. Her son, Simon, isn't very patient with her. It is very sad."

"So, what can we do to help?" asked Louise.

"With Lady Agnes?"

"No, I meant with St Peter's. I would have thought that Lady Agnes has appropriate help."

"Sorry, yes. I really don't know. Without more residents and more money coming in the place will close," said Cheryl, "even if Lady Agnes survives for a few more years and her son doesn't get his hands on the place."

"Right," said Lou, "we need to know how much money we would need to raise," deliberately not looking at Emily, "to attract more residents."

At this point, Anna, who hadn't said much so far said, "We should ask James. He does a lot of money-raising for St Peter's. He may have some idea of what is needed. He also knows people on the management team, and Lady Agnes."

"Talking to James was your mission," said Lou, seriously, "have you not completed it yet?"

"I haven't had a chance. Have you completed yours, whatever it was? You mysteriously kept that to yourself, agent Parker."

At that Lou gleefully produced her copy of Lancashire Life and opened it at the pages shown her by Gerald and explained that if St Peter's were to be sold it would probably be through these agents. Further detective work by her had found on-line pictures of the individual estate agents. If one of them could be identified as being the gentleman that accompanied Simon Earnshaw round St Peter's, then it added weight to the theory that Simon had had St Peter's valued. They may also be able to get some information out of the agent. The others looked sceptical, but Lou was adamant that the more they knew the more the agent might let slip. Cheryl said she couldn't help with the identification as she hadn't been there when the 'valuation' took place, but she could show the pictures to others on her next shift, if she could have some copies. Lou reached in her bag and with a flourish, waved a wad of papers in the air, before setting them down on the table in front of Cheryl. They were copies of screen shots.

Emily produced the books she had bought at the Charity Shop and gave the ladies a bit of the history she had read online. The others were fascinated by the old photos and the earlier pen sketches of the 1800's, so elegant and beautiful. Knowing the different uses to which Sycamore Park Hall had been put, stately home, army camp, rehabilitation centre, private home and then a Young Disabled Unit, made the women more determined than ever to at least find out how they could help to keep it going.

Suddenly, Emily was startled to feel something brush against her leg. She looked down and there was Snokettee. Emily pushed her chair back and picked up the cat. The others were delighted and even more so when Snokettee did a lap of the table and nudged each of the women with her white furry head before slipping back to the floor and heading for the hall. Emily followed her, puzzled as to how Snokettee had gained entry to the house. Only the external cat-flap was open as far as she knew. Snokettee, however, proved her wrong by disappearing through the internal flap to the outhouse. Alex must have opened it.

Emily turned to find her guests behind her in the hall. "Can we see the kittens?" Anna asked.

So, Emily unlocked the door and the

women squeezed up together in the doorway squeaking little noises of delight. One by one Emily pointed out first Whoops-a-Daisy, then Marigold, and finally Spider who might, and Emily couldn't be certain without closer inspection, have had some cobweb hanging off one ear. When Snokettee sat in front of her litter Emily decided it was time to leave the cats alone. She shepherded the women back to the kitchen still cooing and expressing their delight.

When Alex got back with the kids, the women were surprised how quickly the afternoon had passed and quickly made their excuses and left.

Alex announced that he hoped it was alright but he had arranged to go for a drink with Mike that evening. Emily was disappointed as she wanted to talk to him. However, having had two social events of her own recently, neither of which had included Alex, she felt she couldn't object.

* * *

Alex pushed his way through the doors of The Three Wells, scraped a stool away from the bar and hitched himself up onto it. As he waited to be served, he mulled over how he was going to explain his crazy story, and it *was* crazy, to Mike. Although Mike had lived in Much Meddling for nearly 4 years now, Alex didn't know how much he knew about the folk lore and traditions of the place, or the ancient feuds. Mike had been fully aware of Alex's Great Great Aunt Angelica's gift of a pendant to Emily, but what, if anything, did he know of it as a 'periapt'? Had Emily confided in Lou and had she discussed it with Mike?

Soon one of the staff, Ash, took Alex's order and quickly presented him with a couple of pints and two packets of crisps. After the odd pleasantry and commenting on it being a busy night Alex found himself a table in a quiet corner and sipped thoughtfully, watching the door. When Mike arrived, he waved and called him over, holding a pint in the air.

Mike sat and gratefully took a sip. "Cheers, mate." Ripping open a bag of cheese and onion crisps he said, "So, what's up?"

"Something, and maybe absolutely nothing," began Alex. "At the girls party, do you by any chance remember noticing someone add a parcel, about this big," and he spread his fingertips to indicate a cube approximately 10cm square, "to the kids pile of presents? It was plain brown paper with a luggage tag, so would have stuck out from all the other gifts."

Mike shrugged his shoulders. "No. Why?"

"Well, we don't know who it's from. Apart from saying 'Happy 3rd Birthday to the triplets', there was no other message."

Mike studied his friend. There was obviously much more to this than just a badly labelled children's gift. Filling his mouth with crisps, he crunched for a while, waiting. He could see that Alex was struggling to continue, weighing up what to say. As encouragement he offered, "So!"

Alex took a deep breath and to Mike's consternation changed the subject, "Do you remember how Emily first came to be here, in Much Meddling?"

"Uhuh! She came back to thank your relative for putting her up for the night and apologise for leaving, in the middle of the night, without saying goodbye. AND, for the necklace she gave her. Then she won the lottery and was able to buy Wishing Well Cottage, met you and got married. So?"

"Don't you think that that was all just a little too neat?" asked Alex. "Didn't the fact that Emily was the last to speak to each of my Great Great Aunts before they died was odd? As co-incidences go, don't you think that it was all just a little too convenient?"

"What, you reckon Emily 'did 'em in'?" sniggered Mike.

"No. I don't". Alex tried another tack, "Okay, what stories have you heard about my Great Great Aunts?"

"What, the rumours that they were 'witches'?"

"No! Okay, yes, but they weren't true. They had a lot of knowledge, about herbs and their uses and possessed great empathy and intuition but there was no casting of spells as some people seemed to think. The Wells family had enemies, going back generations, and my aunts did tend to play on those rumours. Having people think that you had 'powers' was, I imagine, very useful."

"So, what has all this to do with an anonymous gift?" asked Mike.

So Alex explained about Emily's necklace being a periapt and the giver of the children's fairy necklaces having added calcite to turn those pendants into periapts. Mike was puzzled as to why Alex was so apparently worried. Surely he didn't believe that they had any power. Then he realised, that they didn't need to, they were working perfectly well as inanimate objects. The mere fact of their existence had created an irrational fear in Alex. Logic was telling him one thing but his primal instinct as a father, something completely different.

"Look, mate. They are just stones."

"Yes, I know, but who ever did this, do *they* believe *that*? They knew what they were doing. There is motive behind this. Whoever did this is sending a message."

"Who's sending a message?" It was Richard, the publican, "sorry I couldn't get to you earlier – very busy tonight. I thought whilst there is a lull I'd say hello. I haven't seen you for a bit."

"Hi, Richard, pull up a chair. I really thought that the old ways had died with my aunts. After all, there is no-one of that generation left now," said Alex.

Mike explained what they were talking about and asked Richard if he was aware of any ill-will towards the Wells family. As the pub landlord Richard tended to hear all the local gossip. He wasn't aware, and also had no idea who might have left the gift. The story of the periapts didn't surprise him. He had lived in Much Meddling most of his life and was aware of the local rumours and the folk lore that had been handed down through the generations, that was scoffed at by most. He knew though that there were those that still believed in it all, fewer now, but they still existed.

"Have you asked James?" said Richard. "He was at your party and he gets to hear all sorts of stuff."

CHAPTER THIRTEEN

On Saturday morning, when Emily announced that she was taking the girls shoe shopping, Alex sent out a few texts. As soon as Emily and the girls left the house, he sent more to say that the coast was clear. Before long Mike turned up, shortly followed by Richard. Alex laid the three necklaces out on the kitchen table for the others to examine.

"How old do you think these are?" asked Mike, "they don't look new to me." He picked them up one by one. They were all different. Although a matching set, each fairy's pose was individual: one faced left, another right and the third was facing forward. Their wings were delicately crafted with such a thin layer of enamel that they looked almost translucent as light reflected back from the gold beneath. Their beautiful flowing dresses were richly coloured but their limbs and faces were a light peach. Each face was subtly different with a kind and serene expression. Mike found that he felt a little uncomfortable at how captivating they were.

"I agree. I have been wondering about that; the gold is kind of a different colour of yellow than you get nowadays. I plan on taking them to the forge to see if I can remove the calcite and check if there is a hallmark underneath. That should give us a date and the goldsmith. I am going to track down who gave these things if it is the last thing I do. No-one," and he thumped his fist on the table, "messes, with my little girls…"

"Woah, calm down," said Richard.

"I mean it. When I get my hands on whoever did this."

"Did what?" It was James. He had let himself in and just entered the kitchen.

Alex turned to him, "You don't know do you, who gave these," pointing at the necklaces, "You didn't see someone put this box," indicating the brown packaging and label, "amongst the other presents?"

James stared at the packaging, then at Alex. His mouth worked, bewilderment written across his face. Then he said, "It was me."

There was a collective gasp, followed by silence, whilst everyone attempted to process this new information, all the time staring at James. Fingering his dog collar whilst gathering his thoughts and trying to extricate himself, from whatever 'bother' he had got himself into, he added, "When I got here you were all busy. Emily was making coffees and you were in the living room playing pirates. I just put it with the rest of the presents. Then, I didn't think any more about it. It had a label on it. What's wrong?"

Mike was the first to compose himself, "the label only said who it was *to*, not who it was *from*."

"Oh, Lady Agnes," said James. "That's why I was late turning up for the party. I knew she wasn't well, so when she asked to see me, I went."

"What, Lady Agnes Earnshaw, at St Peter's?" said Mike, "Louise has been going on and on about her lately."

"Well, yes," said James.

"Earnshaw!" snorted Alex, his eyes popping out of his head. "An Earnshaw sent these," and he scooped up the necklaces, his fist closing round them. Turning, he grabbed his car keys and stormed out of the house. By the time the others made it to the front door Alex was driving off through the gates and away down the high street. Mike ran back inside and got his jacket. He found his car keys and he, James and Richard piled inside his car. Together they set off after Alex.

* * *

It hadn't taken Emily long to find shoes for the girls. Finding three pairs in the same size usually limited the choice on offer. Helpfully the children liked the same style, or were indifferent. Emily knew that wouldn't last but for the time being it made life a whole lot easier. On one occasion she had made the mistake of taking just one of them, on the basis that they all had the same sized feet, but the girls complained so much about the choice that she didn't try that again. As they drove back through the outskirts of the village Emily thought she glimpsed Alex's car heading into St Peter's gateway and would have dismissed it if the girls hadn't pointed and said, "Daddy, Daddy." She was puzzled, but quietly pleased that this might mean he was coming round to the idea of helping to raise money to keep St Peter's going. Sometimes he could be funny like that. Sometimes he just needed a little time to consider. Then, as she approached the one-way section round the village green, she spotted Mike, travelling at increasing speed in the opposite direction. And, it looked like he had James and Richard with him. One glance at Wishing Well Cottage drive told her that Alex's car was gone. Intrigued, and a little concerned now, she did a loop of the green and followed them.

In the far distance she just caught sight of brake lights indicating that Mike had probably, also, turned into St Peter's. She followed up the driveway and was just in time to see James, Richard and Mike disappear through the front door. Alex's car was abandoned at an angle directly outside the front door. It took her a while to get the girls out of the Range Rover. So, when she and the children walked through

St Peter's entrance none of the three men were to be seen. Ahead was a flight of stairs and three lifts. To the right was a reception desk, but no receptionist. Emily looked around briefly and then headed up the stairs with the triplets in tow. She now found herself in a much grander space with a marble floor and columns. This was obviously the original main entrance; the lower level having been for servants. Looking to the front of the property she had a magnificent view out towards the lawn and the far hills. To her right was what appeared to be a dining room and to the left a recreation room where a number of residents were amusing themselves watching TV or playing ping pong.

"Hi," a young woman propelled herself towards Emily, "can I help you; the staff are a bit busy at the moment."

Emily looked down and smiled, "I think my husband is here and three other people, er, James, the vicar, is one of them. I don't know if you know him." The woman grinned, spun her chair and pointed towards the stairs and upwards. Emily thanked her and shepherded the triplets, who were staring in awe at the woman's wheelchair, away up the stairs.

As Emily neared the top of the stairs she could hear raised voices. It sounded like Alex was arguing with a nurse and James was trying to calm everyone down. She followed her ears and entered the room. It was large and light, with windows on two walls, and it was expensively furnished. Several large oil paintings and a collection of framed prints of, presumably, family members adorned the walls. In the corner between the windows a turret room was visible. It was a lovely apartment, beautifully and expensively decorated at some point in the past. Now, though elegant, it was shabby. The carpet was threadbare and the drapes faded. In a wingback chair with its back to the window sat an elderly lady with a blanket over her lap. She looked weary. Spotting Emily and the girls the lady turned her attention from Alex and the nurse. The argument stopped as everyone turned to follow her gaze which had settled on Emily.

"Alex," said Emily, "*What* are you *doing*?"

Alex looked stunned. When he saw the look of disappointed bewilderment on her face, he felt ashamed. Not able to meet her gaze he sought out his little girls, worried how they were reacting to his behaviour. The girls had dispersed themselves about the room. Tansy was stroking two cats which were sitting on one of the large window seats. Violet had gone to stand by James, and Lily, head tilted slightly, was standing a couple of feet in front of the old lady, apparently studying her.

Alex whispered to Emily, "*She*," pointing at Lady Agnes, "gave the girls periapts." Seeing Emily's puzzled look, he added, "the mystery necklaces. They are periapts! And, *she* sent them!"

"What? When did you find that out? Why didn't you tell me?"

"I didn't want to worry you. I have only just found out who sent them. Her!"

As they looked at Lady Agnes, Lily stepped forward and took the lady's hand. Gently she turned it over and straightened out the fingers which were curled. Then she turned it again and laid it flat so that she could stroke the back of it. Gradually the tension in the lady's face and shoulders visibly eased, and along with it, the tension in the room.

As Lily stared into the lady's eyes she stared gratefully back. Working her mouth, she slowly formed the words, "'ank... you. I... knew... you... come." After squeezing Lily's hand with her good one the lady turned her attention to the keyboard on her lap and slowly but purposefully rolled the mouse and clicked it. From the corner of the room came a whirring as a printer sprang into life.

The nurse went and gathered up the paper and held it out for Alex, "I believe that Lady Agnes wants you to read this."

"'ank you, Si...ster. I'm ...oh...kay ...now. You...may...go."

Alex took the paper. With the wind taken out of his sails he went and sat on a window seat and read. When he had finished he handed it to Emily. When she had finished she asked

Lady Agnes if it was okay to tell the other three, James, Richard and Mike, as she was sure that they would also want to help. At Lady Agnes's nodded approval, Emily paraphrased the letter. For many years there had been a feud between the Earnshaw and the Wells' families. Lady Agnes knew that asking for help as an Earnshaw would be unlikely to work, especially when she had two adult sons to turn to. St Peter's was her life's work and she couldn't bear the thought of it being sold and the residents evicted. However, she knew that when she died, her sons, unless she disinherited them, would sell the place. The only chance was if St Peter's could be shown to be a viable business. Unfortunately, she no longer had the strength or mental ability to make that a reality. As a last resort she had turned to the only people who might be able to help her. Using 'the old ways', in the hope that they worked as her ancestors believed, she had sent the periapts. Whether or not they possessed any actual power didn't really matter, as she expected a Wells to be curious enough to come ask, WHY?

Alex had been thinking whilst Emily was talking. Now he addressed Lady Agnes, "But I still don't see what this has to do with us, apart from the mere matter of us being *millionaires*, why would we help? This place needs thousands, probably hundreds of thousands, spending on it. Why should we care who owns it. If your sons don't care, why should we?"

"You ...good... pee... pul. This...good... home...to...many."

The printer whirred again. James picked it up and handed it to Alex. Emily leaned in to look. On the paper was a family tree. It took the pair of them a little while to understand what they were looking at. In 1981 Agnes Worsley had married Lord Earnshaw, becoming Lady Agnes, and subsequently had two sons, Thomas and Simon. However, working back through Agnes's family line it could be seen that Agnes's mother was one Millicent Wells, daughter of Edward Wells and sister to John Wells, Alex's grandfather.

Emily turned to Agnes, "You and Alex are both descendants of Angelica, Ruby and Myrtle Wells' brother, Edward Wells."

Lady Agnes nodded.

"Really!" scoffed, Alex. "So, how come I have never heard of you? I have lived in this village all my life and not once have you been mentioned. According to this tree you are Great Aunt Millicent's daughter. She never had a daughter!"

Here James intervened, "Look, we can easily find out. I only need to look in the church records. If, that is alright with you, Lady Agnes?"

Lady Agnes nodded and pressed a little buzzer by the side of her chair. Shortly after this, the door opened and one of the nurses came in. "Show...them...round...please. 'ank...you."

Lily gave the lady a brief hug and then

went and grabbed Alex hand. Violet grabbed the other. Together they dragged him towards the door. "Tansy, come on," he said. "Put that cat down, we're leaving."

Emily could see that Alex wasn't convinced and she had to admit that it was puzzling as to why he didn't know of Lady Agnes' existence. In a village this size it seemed ridiculous. At least he had calmed down. Whatever part the periapts played in this, real or imagined, it seemed that the most intuitive of her daughters, Lily, was content to be friends with this mystery relative. Also, from Emily's on-line reading she really couldn't see Lady Agnes as any kind of villain. After all, the lady had set up the Young Disabled Unit. Bad people just didn't do that kind of thing. Emily believed that the periapts were harmless, but their gift had been a really clever way of getting the Wells family to visit.

Before following the nurse Emily smiled and winked at the frail figure that was Lady Agnes. As the others disappeared through the door she went back, took Lady Agnes' hand, "Don't worry, he'll come around. I want to help and I have friends who will. You aren't on your own."

"ank...you. Please...bring...girls...again."

"Yes, I think they'd like that. Take care."

* * *

St Peter's was a large building and the tour

took quite a while. As Sycamore Park Hall it must have been very impressive. The commanding views from most of the rooms gave it an elegance and grandeur that would have been breathtaking in its heyday. Emily and Alex's wealth was substantial, but it wouldn't have built one wing of this place. How rich did you have to be to build a stately home like this? Sadly, it was now a shell of its former glory. Paint was pealing, ceiling roses were crumbling and the window frames, which appeared to have been replaced piecemeal over the last couple of decades, were in need of replacing again. The large upper rooms had been divided to create more bedrooms, but half of those on the top floor were unusable due to damp. Outside, there was a large stable block and sundry outbuildings, again in various states of disrepair. Emily's initial enthusiasm was taking more and more of a beating the more she saw. Did Lady Agnes have any idea what it would take to rescue this place?

Before saying goodbye the nurse took them back inside saying that she had something that she wanted to give them. From behind the reception desk she produced a manila folder containing several sheets of paper stapled together in batches. She explained that the sheets were minutes of St Peter's Management Committee meetings for the last year. Then she handed over a card with an invitation to attend the next meeting, to take place at 10am the following Thursday, saying that Lady Agnes would be pleased if they would attend. Alex just glowered at it. So, Emily took it and thanked the nurse.

* * *

Late afternoon Emily noticed that she had a voice mail from Lou suggesting that they pay Anna a visit, no reason. Emily immediately texted Lou to say 'No' she was not going to visit Anna and that Lou should leave Anna and Sasha alone, to enjoy their weekend in peace. She was sure that Anna would introduce him in her own good time. It turned out, from subsequent texts, that Lou had already been for a stroll past Anna's cottage and was able to report that Sasha had a rather nice 2.0 litre MX-5 convertible in a very tasteful blue with, what she was fairly certain were, leather seats. Had the top been down she would have given them a prod and a squeeze.

CHAPTER FOURTEEN

At church there was no mention of praying for Lady Agnes this week. Emily wasn't sure if this was tact on the part of James, or just the fact that Lady Agnes was actually better than previously. Either way Emily was glad. She knew that any mention would only re-ignite Alex's smouldering irritation. Since they left St Peter's, Alex had refused to talk about what had happened. Until the girls went to bed he used them as a verbal shield, engaging them in play and excluding Emily, deliberately choosing activities that Emily didn't usually join in with. After that he engrossed himself in an audio-book, whilst doing a jigsaw: something she had never known him to do before. His mood was a little better when he woke up and he did initiate conversation with Emily but she was well aware that one reference to Lady Agnes or St Peter's would ruin things. So, she decided to bide her time.

* * *

Anna was having a lovely weekend. She

and Sasha were getting on well. She had been nervous that what had been natural and enjoyable, in the sociable holiday surroundings, would feel awkward and unnatural in the small confines of her own home. In the resort they had been on neutral ground, with hotel and restaurant staff to deal with the mundane. Here, in Much Meddling, she had the responsibility of hosting and catering. Their relationship was very new and having him in her home, after living alone for so long, was all just a bit too domestic and too soon. She had regretted inviting him, feeling that she wanted to get to know him better before spending the weekend together. However, when his car pulled up outside earlier than she had expected, her heart skipped a beat, but with joy, not alarm. She had let him in, they had kissed. She had taken his coat and led him into the living room, offered him a drink and they had started chatting, catching up on their journeys home and the past week. It all seemed just easy and natural.

She was fully aware that both Louise and Emily wanted to see Sasha. So, she deliberately took him on a walk round the village and up to the crag whilst she knew that Emily and family would be in church and whilst Lou, if Nathan permitted, would be having a lie-in. If she was up, it was unlikely that she would be out and about in the village on a Sunday morning.

Together Anna and Sasha strolled round

the village green, past the shops and up the first side street of terraced houses. At the end she led him over a high stone stile, its slabs worn smooth and concave by generations of feet. Together they strolled through the trees on the lower slope of the hill, as it gently wound its way upwards. They stopped for a while trying to spot a cuckoo that they could hear somewhere high in the treetops. Sasha spotted it, silhouetted against the sky, hanging on the vertical trunk, hammer-drilling itself a hole. After watching for a while they set off again, disturbing squirrels and the odd rabbit as they went. Ahead they could see that the trees thinned out revealing a steeper slope: they were approaching the end of the wood. Sasha stopped and turned Anna to face him. Taking her face in his warm hands he gently tilted her head back and looked deep into her eyes. Tucking a stray strand of her hair behind her left ear, he kissed her. Eagerly, she kissed him back and snuggled herself inside the folds of his open jacket as he wrapped his arms around her, pulling her close. When she broke away, surprised at the intensity of her body's response, she found he was smiling at her. In fact, he was grinning from ear to ear. "Come on. Let's get this walk over with."

* * *

Louise cleared away the breakfast things, reaching under the newspaper that Mike held spread open in front of him. He lifted it slightly, just enough for her to retrieve his plate. Taking a stack of plates over to the dish-washer, a mug dangling from each of three fingers, she opened the door and placed the items inside. Looking inside the adjacent cupboard she snapped, "You used the last of the dishwasher tablets, didn't you. Why didn't you put them on the list? I could have got some yesterday."

"Sorry, I forgot. I was in a rush to get to Alex's. I'll get some later."

As Lou started noisily emptying the dishwasher and piling the contents next to the sink, he said, "I'll wash them okay. Just leave them. Actually, I could do with some fresh air. I'll go now."

"What? Mike!"

"Sorry, I'm just a bit ratty. I didn't sleep last night, not sure why. Nathan didn't help, of course. Do you want to come?"

"No, but you can take Nathan. Maybe it will wear him out a bit. I've got plenty to do here, and a bit of peace would be lovely."

* * *

Anna and Sasha quickly made it back to the stile and were just approaching the high street when Anna spotted Mike and Nathan, crossing the road ahead of them. She broke step but Mike had seen her so she kept going. At least Louise wasn't with them.

"Hi, Mike, Nathan, I'd like you to meet Sasha."

Sasha held out his hand and Mike shook it. "Pleased to meet you," they both managed to say, in unison. Then Sasha looked down, "Hi, Nathan."

Nathan looked at Sasha. Then he looked at his father and back at Sasha. Then he looked at his father again, and said, with apparent surprise and even greater disappointment, "He's a real man, not a toy boy!"

Mike spluttered and laughed nervously. Anna bit her tongue. After a brief pause, Sasha howled with laughter. Anna, who had turned rather pink, started to giggle and said to Mike "Tell Lou I'd like a word with her at some point!"

Nathan stared around him, not sure what he had done but liking the effect. He started to laugh too. As Anna joined in, Mike muttered his apologies, and something about dishwasher tablets. He then said, "Nice to meet you," and quickly ushered Nathan away.

* * *

After saying goodbye to his congregation James headed back into the church. Inside the vestry he placed a large key into the lock of a thick wooden wall-mounted door. Behind the door sat a deep cupboard lined with shelves. On the shelves sat a collection of large leather-bound tomes. Selecting a couple he slid them out and placed them on the vestry table. Dusting them off, he opened the one entitled Saint Peter's Church, Births 1922-1962. Searching through the pages he eventually came to an entry for 2nd May 1955 - Christening of Agnes Susan Worsley, daughter of Clive Worsley and Millicent Worsley. The second tome was entitled Saint Peter's Church, Marriages 1932-1961. James searched backwards through the pages from 9months prior to Agnes's christening date, on the assumption that she wasn't illegitimate. After 8 pages of marriage entries he found what

he was looking for, an entry stating - 12th June 1953 marriage of Clive Archibald Worsley and Millicent Ann Wells. He made notes of the names and the dates and put paper slips in the pages so that he could find them easily again. He was sure he would need to actually show Alex, rather than just tell him, if he was to convince him that Lady Agnes really was a Wells' descendant. Further searching confirmed that Millicent Ann Wells was sister of Alex's grandfather John Wells. Next James did a search for the marriage of Agnes Worsley to Lord Earnshaw. After an hour's search, he gave up. Christenings of the Earnshaw sons, Thomas and Simon were found but no marriage of Agnes Worsley and Richard Earnshaw. Of course, they could have got married elsewhere but it was odd that, with both families being local, they hadn't been married in Much Meddling. He would need to ask Lady Agnes.

* * *

After lunch the Wells family drove out of the village and up into the hills. Alex parked the four-by-four in a windswept gravel car-park on the edge of the road. Together Emily and Alex un-strapped the children and zipped up their jackets. Then they all set off uphill through the bracken which spread out, brown, russet and flat, in all directions. Further on their goal came into view. A scattering of white across the top of an open stretch of moor could be seen, where the bracken and heather gave way to limestone. Large weathered sheets of it lay, like cracked icing which had melted slightly, the edges smooth and round. In the deep cracks moss and lichen were colonising their own micro-habitats, laying the foundations for larger plants. Here and there the odd small sapling of heather could be seen, sticking its head tentatively above the rim of rock. Emily loved this place, and so did the children. They happily investigated for hours, peering into the crevices, seeing what treasures they could find: tiny fantastically shaped limestone rocks, a fossilised shell, insects and the odd broken egg shell. Some crevices had water in them and some disappeared to unknown depths. Alex, familiar with the area steered the children to the safer parts. When they were older, he would show them the caves.

* * *

When Mike got home, and Nathan was suitably engrossed in a world of his own, he told

Louise about meeting Anna and Sasha, and at how Nathan had embarrassed him.

"No! Really! I told you," she said laughing. "You really have to watch what you say in front of him. Coz he'll only repeat it. So, tell me about Sasha, what is he like?"

"He seemed okay. We didn't talk for long."

"Really! That's it. That is all you can tell me."

Mike thought a bit. "He has a sense of humour, and Anna looked better than I have seen her look for a long time."

"Oh, I see, so you noticed Anna! But, not her young man," she teased. "Typical".

CHAPTER FIFTEEN

W ith Alex at work and the kids at nursery Emily spread the papers from the manila folder, given to her by the nurse at St Peter's, on the kitchen table. She folded over the top flap of a ring pad and placed a biro and a yellow highlighter pen next to it. Then she got herself a cup of tea and set about making notes of what might be needed to make St. Peter's profitable again. What this might be she didn't know, but she at least wanted to familiarise herself with the documents before the meeting on Thursday.

There was a pile of meeting minutes going back over the last year and some other documents which turned out to be running costs and annual maintenance + the odd quote for work which needed doing. The amounts were staggering. The utility bills alone came to nearly double her old salary as an IT trainer. On top of that were the home running costs, which were twice that again. The income from the current number of residents would barely make a dent in the annual outgoings. The home must be in debt. No wonder Simon wanted to sell the place. Maybe it would be better for it to be taken over by one of the large care home businesses that could afford to invest in the place. Maybe, patching the place up wasn't the best outcome for the residents. The more she looked at the paperwork the more she was disheartened and the more she realised that, just raising a few thousand, and she had no idea how they would do that, wasn't going to solve St Peter's problems. She was also a little alarmed that St Peter's had trusted the Wells family with all this private information. How much faith was being placed in them when there really was, as Alex had said, no real reason why they should help? She was pondering on this when a movement of something white, over by the door, caught her eye.

Snokettee strolled into view with a small grey bundle in her mouth. Emily automatically pushed her chair back from the table, in an effort to increase the distance between the two of them. However, Snokettee quickly closed it, hopped onto a free chair and up onto the table. Emily shrank back, not wanting to look but unable to take her eyes away. To her delight she found herself looking, not at a dead rodent but, at Spider. Emily moved her chair back up to the table. Snokettee approached, and pushed her soft white head against Emily's hand and allowed herself to be stroked. When Snokettee moved away Emily reached out tentatively towards

Spider and presented her finger tips. Spider, sniffing Snokettee's scent pushed her head into Emily's hand. Soon, Snokettee had deposited all three kittens on the table. Wobbly and not yet fully able to stand, the three vied for Emily's attention. She joyfully complied. When mother carried the first kitten away Emily picked up the other two and followed. She watched for a while as the family settled back into the outhouse and then left them to it.

Happier and far more positive than before, she returned to studying the paperwork, which was now in disarray. Several tiny puncture marks peppered the documents and one sheet in particular was gummed and somewhat soggy at the edge. Tearing off the wet bit she laid the paper on the table and smoothed it out. She was about to put it to one side when something familiar caught her eye. At first she didn't know why, but then realised that it was the business logo of the solicitor she had dealt with when buying Wishing Well cottage. However, they were local solicitors so there really was nothing unusual about finding one of their documents here. She glanced at the content and was about to put it on the pile for donations when the name M. Wells leapt out at her. It appeared that St Peter's had been paid £72,000 by Godling and Little solicitors from the estate of Ms M Wells. Could this have been Myrtle? She looked at the date and worked out that this would have been 3 months after Myrtle had died. Emily sifted through the papers until she found the family tree given them by Lady Agnes. She then saw that Lady Agnes mother, Millicent Wells would have been 80 in 2015. Had she died then? If so, the money was probably from her.

* * *

Alex had spent his lunch time hunkered over a tiny piece of metal, his large fingers struggling to delicately manipulate tools that were too big for the task. Despite his deep mistrust of the little fairy pendant he was reluctant to damage the metal work. As a smith he fully appreciated the craftsmanship that had gone into making the figure and, deep down he felt that it was wrong to damage it. Instinctively he felt that it deserved respect. Adjusting the lamp so that it shone at an angle, to better illuminate the metal's edge, he succeeded in raising the gold lip. With a little more work he was able to free the sliver of calcite. Re-angling the lamp he held the little fairy, face down, and studied her back. In the centre he was surprised to see a flattened lump of gold which was partially obscuring the remains of a hallmark. Using his phone he brought up a list of hallmarks and studied them. The gold was clearly 22 carat, but the date letter was almost obliterated. However, he could clearly see Queen Victoria's head. If the date letter was a 'C' then the pendant had been made in 1851 or, if it was a 'G', 1855. Alex was engrossed in removing a second sliver of calcite when a noise by the door alerted him to the fact that he had a customer. A teenager, in high-vis. jacket, jodhpurs, boots and helmet was standing holding the reins of a pony, rhythmically slapping a crop against the side of her left riding boot.

* * *

Lady Agnes concentrated, one finger laboriously tapping away at her laptop, trying to anticipate any questions that might arise at the meeting on Thursday. On a windowsill, at the other end of the room, the two cats stared at the world outside, patiently awaiting developments.

* * *

That evening, Emily and Alex only spoke to each other in the course of dealing with the children. They had just got the three of them washed and into bed when the doorbell rang. Alex went and answered it. Once Emily had got the girls settled she went downstairs and followed her ears to the sitting room. It was James. He had some news. Wanting to leave James and Alex alone for a while, in the hope that Alex would open up to James, she offered to make some drinks. In the kitchen she put the kettle on and took mugs out of the cupboard and dropped a teabag into each. Then she grabbed a pile of plates and some biscuits and put them on a tray. When the kettle eventually boiled she filled the mugs with water, then gave the bags a stir and a good mashing, before throwing them into the sink. Then she topped up all three mugs with milk. She did a bit of biscuit arranging to take up a little more time and then carried the tray out of the kitchen. As she approached the sitting room she was relieved to hear Alex laughing. She busied herself with the tray, giving each of them a plate so they could help themselves to biscuits. James was apologising for causing so much upset by bringing the periapts into the house but was pointing out how ironical it was that he, the vicar, had brought them. Of course he had had no idea what they were and was a little annoyed that Lady Agnes had used him as the vehicle for their transport. Why she had not just asked him to invite the Wells family, he didn't know. Alex frowned and then raised a knowing eyebrow. "So, what is this news?" he asked.

"Okay. So, with Lady Agnes' permission, as you witnessed, I did some research." James then produced some printed photos of sections of the church records. "I am happy to show you the originals if you like but these prove that the family tree she gave you is correct. Your father, Alex, as you are aware had a sister called Millicent who married one Clive Worsley. According to the church records they had a daughter called Agnes. Her christening took place on 2nd May 1955."

Alex begrudgingly picked up the papers,

and let out a deep sigh.

"What we don't have, is a record of the marriage of Agnes to Richard Earnshaw, assuming of course that they were. We would need to know where, to be able to check. Next time I see Lady Agnes I will ask her." Then, turning to Emily, "are you coming to St Peter's management meeting on Thursday?"

She glanced at Alex to gauge his reaction. He just looked resigned. So, she nodded. "I have been looking through the folder they gave us, trying to work out how much it would take to get the place into a position to make a profit. Have you any idea?" looking at James, "You have been raising money for the place for years."

"It probably needs a few hundred thousand pounds; the roof leaks, as do some of the windows and I believe that the boiler needs replacing. It is getting harder to raise money as most of the people in the village are a little fed up of giving. It really needs outside money, outside the village I mean. I raise 2-5 grand a year by running and through the Comedy Caravan, but that is nowhere near enough." The Comedy Caravan Club was a local show that appeared in different clubs around the area. James took part in it with his stand-up comedy act. The money he raised went towards his 'Believe in Change, Pennies for Heaven' charity that supported St Peter's.

"So," said Emily, "how on earth does Lady

Agnes think that we can help? Is she expecting money from us?"

"No way," said Alex. "No matter what we do, her sons will just sell it anyway, and as I said before, all we will have done is to raise its value for them."

"Let me just go to the meeting on Thursday and see what is said," said Emily. "I'd like to help if we can. Raising money could be fun."

CHAPTER SIXTEEN

Emily drove Anna and James, picking up Louise on the way, to St Peter's. Once again, Emily was impressed with the grandeur of the building. She would have loved to sweep up the steps to the original front door. Louise had no inhibitions and strolled up the left-hand flight to admire the view. Then her ladyship, having waved majestically to her public below, continued her parade down the right-hand steps. Rejoining her companions, she took James by the arms and waltzed him through the ground floor front door into the reception area.

Louise came to a halt, looking at all the pink hearts, "Oh, crap! It's Valentine's Day."

"Language your ladyship," said James.

"My apologies, your vicar-ship! Em, remind me to go to the store on the way home."

James greeted the receptionist, who obviously knew him. The lady led the group upstairs to a landing at the rear of the building and asked them to please wait, whilst she went inside. A few moments later she returned to say that the staff had nearly finished the progress reports on the residents and would be ready for them soon. A few minutes later the door opened and they were invited in. The room was another large one, with windows that looked out onto the woodland behind.

At a long oak table sat a number of people, Lady Agnes seated at its head. They were told to help themselves to drinks from a side table and offered seats at the table.

When everyone was settled Lady Agnes began, "Well...come. 'ank ...you...for...cum... ing. Sis...ter...will...take...the...mee...tin...g."

A middle-aged lady in a crisp blue uniform popped her glasses on and smiled round at the assembled group. "As Lady Agnes said, thank you all for coming. I am Sister Colette Jones, I have been the nurse manager here at St Peter's for the past 11 years and I am hoping that this meeting will generate some positive outcomes for the future of this wonderful home. Perhaps we could start by everyone introducing themselves."

Emily inwardly groaned. She hated this. It was like being back at work again. One by one the party introduced themselves. Emily didn't remember any of their names. There was the St Peter's administrator who was taking notes, 2 nurses and a therapist. Just as they had finished there was a knock at the door. The nurse nearest the door got up and opened it. In wheeled the young lady that Emily had met briefly on her previous visit, followed by the cook and the maintenance man who had all been asked to join the meeting. The introductions continued. Everyone was enthusiastic in their praise of the work being done and of the home in general. Anna briefly said that she lived in the village but had never visited St Peter's and that she would really love to help. James, who everyone already knew, said that it was very important that the work at St Peter's was allowed to continue. Now it was Emily's turn.

She said that she was new to the village but she would really like to help. Phew! Her turn had passed. She breathed a sigh of relief.

Louise now had the floor. She said that she hadn't lived in Much Meddling for very long either but thought that it was a marvellous place, with wonderful people and once they knew that St Peter's needed help they would rise to the occasion.

Then the young woman in the wheelchair introduced herself, "I am Sophie Hargreaves. I have been a resident here for just a couple of weeks now. I broke my spine when I came off my horse and have spent the last 9 months in hospital. I am unable to return to my flat as it isn't wheelchair accessible. So, I am here until I can sell, and buy somewhere new to live. The reason I have been invited to join this meeting is because I wanted to represent the residents. They are a mixed bunch with physical and mental conditions. In the short time I have been here I have learnt what a wonderful job the staff are doing, not only to provide a home, but to help us to come to terms with our limitations and to provide us with the means to live with them, and to surmount them. This place has so much potential. It is in a fabulous setting and it would be a real tragedy if it closed. I want to help"

There was a round of applause and heartfelt thanks. When everyone settled down the cook and gardener basically said who they were and agreed that St Peter's needed to survive.

Colette, the nurse manager, then set about detailing all the problems that the home was facing, both physically and financially. As well as the roof, some windows, and the boiler there were bathrooms that needed repairing and modernising, wiring that needed replacing and a whole list of minor repairs. There was no money to do any of it. Essentially, they didn't currently have enough income from residents to cover the running costs. They anticipated that they had 3months and then there would be no option but to close. It was a stark message. Emily looked around the room. Everyone it seemed was waiting for someone else to say something.

Then Louise spoke, "So, how much money is needed to make up the difference between the income you are getting and that which would be enough to break even? In the short term, how much do we need to raise to keep the place going?"

Colette looked at Lady Agnes, who nodded. "We need another £2,750+ a month to cover staff pay and running costs."

"Okay, so that is a start. That's do-able," said Lou confidently, ignoring the surprised looks of the others. "After that, how much is needed to start making some repairs so that the upper rooms can be occupied to bring in more income?"

"From the quotes we have had, and bear in mind some of them are up to 3 years old, we would need at least £450,000 just to do the basics. By that, I mean make the building sound and bring it up to code to meet local health authority standards."

There was silence. They all looked at Lou. "That would be a bit more difficult. Hmmm. Three months you say."

When it looked like no-one was going to speak, Lady Agnes said, "Mo...tea, an'...thin...king...caps!" Everyone laughed. There was a brief interlude whilst people helped themselves to drinks and biscuits. Having broken up the formality of sitting round the large table people now started to chat, bouncing ideas off each other.

"Suppose we aim for £4,000 a month and split the amount between us?"

"What if we put on some charity events?"

"Could we do tours of St Peter's?"

"Could we do weddings?"

"I am not cooking for weddings," said the cook, "and I think you'd need to wait for better weather for that."

"Are there any assets that can be used or sold, land for instance?"

"Are there any tradesmen who would be willing to work at cost?"

After about an hour Colette said that she needed to excuse herself, along with the rest of the staff, as there was work to do in the home. With the staff gone, it was just Lady Agnes, the administrator, Emily, James, Louise, Anna and Sophie left.

James took up the reins, "As the chief fund raiser for this place for the last few years, I have to say, that this isn't going to be easy. Does anyone have any immediate idea of what we can do now to cover the first month's shortfall?"

"Well," said Emily, "I do have one idea but I need to talk to Alex first."

"Good," replied James, "I will see if I can make some more bookings for the Comedy Caravan, and I will make an announcement in church on Sunday and on our website asking for donations."

"How about a 'bring and buy' sale and a craft fare?" suggested Anna.

"Yes, that's a good idea," said James.

"I will talk to the other residents and

pester their relatives," said Sophie, "I realise that it would be unethical for the staff to do so but there is nothing to stop me," she grinned.

"Lou, any ideas?" asked Emily.

"I can't help thinking that we need something a bit bigger and bolder if we are going to make enough difference. It will also need to be something sustainable. Let me think."

James then took it upon himself to wrap up the meeting and suggested that they meet Lady Agnes again on Tuesday with an update.

* * *

When they stopped outside the store to let Lou out to get a Valentine's card James remembered that he had forgotten to ask Lady Agnes about her wedding. "Ah, well, it can wait until Friday, and there won't be as many people there. I'll feel better asking her about it in private."

Lou said goodbye and disappeared off into the store muttering about commercialism and day-light robbery. "Ah, married bliss," said James. "Talking of which, how are things with Alex? Has he calmed down yet?"

"Oh, he's still touchy. Better, but still touchy. Conversation is generally fine so long as I don't refer to St Peter's or Lady Agnes etc. It has been quite a strain all week. I am so glad you came round on Monday, otherwise I don't know what things would have been like."

"Well, you know where I am," he said as he

got out of the car, "I'll drive on Friday. See you. Take care."

* * *

Back in the cottage she dumped her bag and jacket in the hall and walked into the kitchen. On the table was a huge, expensive bunch of flowers and an equally impressive large red envelope. She took a generous sniff at the bouquet and then picked up the envelope. Pulling out a chair and sitting down she peeled back the flap and pulled out the card. 'To the most wonderful wife in the world', it read. Inside, Alex had written, 'You really do mean the world to me. I know I have been an idiot and I mean to make it up to you.' The card and message were cheesy but the emotional relief meant the world to her.

Putting the kettle on, she grabbed a mug and a tea bag and opened the fridge for some milk. She groaned slightly and then laughed. In the door, slightly warping the plastic frame, was a bottle of pink fizz. Squashed between the shelves was a Valentine's meal deal. Pulling it out to inspect it she decided that actually it all looked quite good. She decided to make a positive effort to accept the meal in the spirit that it was intended and not be mean about it. After all, it was Alex' Valentine's Day too; no need for him to spend most of it cooking.

She went up to their bedroom to change her shoes. Laid out on the bed was her black dress, pearl necklace and matching earrings. Laid on the dress was a small white envelope with her name on it. She carefully prised it open and pulled out a gilt-edged card which said, 'Mr Alex Wells requests the company of Mrs Emily Wells for dinner at 8pm on this Valentine's Day. P.T.O.' on the back he had written 'I will get the kids to bed, please make yourself scarce, (i.e., stay upstairs from 6.30pm), until I come to escort you to dinner at 8pm.'

* * *

As soon as Alex arrived home she ran into his arms. He was obviously delighted by her response and held her close, laughing, as the pair of them were buffeted by the arrival of the triplets joining in the group hug. Seeing him happy was such a relief to her. Having her family around her, was the icing on the cake. As their eyes met and locked, she grinned at him, and when he grinned back she knew she had her old Alex back.

* * *

That evening as she 'made herself scarce' she headed into their en-suite to discover that Alex had arranged candles round the edge of the bath, complete with a strategically placed box of matches. There was a stack of clean towels and a dish with a selection of bath bombs placed on a stool. It was so thoughtful of him. Sadly, her planning hadn't included luxuriating in a bath. Now she didn't have time. Still, she appreciated the thought that had gone into the evening, and she could enjoy her bath another night. As she stepped out of the shower and wrapped herself in a towel, she discovered that the wall mirror had steamed up revealing a heart and arrow and the message 'I love you'.

At 8pm there was a knock on the bedroom door. She opened it, and there was Alex, looking magnificent, in a suit and tie and freshly shaved. He must have put his clothes somewhere else in the house and got dressed there. He looked her up and down approvingly and then presented her with a small corsage of pink flowers. She waited whilst he pinned it to her dress. He then bowed slightly, said, "Shall we," and held out his arm for her to take. Together they walked along the landing. The stairs proved to be too narrow, so Alex took her arm again at the bottom. To Emily's surprise, instead of heading for the kitchen they turned right. To her greater surprise there was a smartly dressed young man standing to attention outside their sitting room. "Table for two, sir? This way, please."

Inside, the sitting room had been transformed. The two chesterfield sofas had been pushed to one side, and in the middle of the room was a large table set for two. In its centre was a magnificent candelabrum. Other candles adorned various surfaces, the entire room lit only by candles and the glow of the fire. The effect was magical.

The young man pulled out a chair for Emily and expertly moved it forward as she sat. He then, almost silently, uncorked and poured her a glass of Champagne. It was only as the man was filling Alex' glass that she realised that it wasn't the pink stuff from the fridge. She looked at Alex, who winked and raised his glass to her. He knew exactly what she was thinking. As they took their first sip the waiter brought two starters. Removing silver covers he served first Emily and then Alex. This was no meal deal. This had been freshly prepared, and by a professional. Briefly she mentally ran round their kitchen. If she had known someone else would be using it, she would have cleaned. What horrors lurked? She emptied her glass and decided not to think about it. The waiter refilled it. She thanked him and took another sip, and felt better. Yes, she thought, the champagne was perfectly chilled, just like her.

The food was wonderful. All her favourite dishes were served, scallops, steak with seasonal vegetables, and Crème Caramel. There were extra little surprises between courses and a different wine to complement each dish. Finally they were served cheese and biscuits, and coffee with a liqueur. As he left the room the waiter said goodnight and turned up the music which had been playing quietly in the background. After they had had their fill of food and drink, Alex got up and took Emily by the hand, pulling her to her feet. "Remember this song? It is the first one we danced to together."

"Yes, and I nearly did the splits in those stupid shoes I was wearing, but you caught me."

They danced and chatted for a while, remembering old times. Then Alex pulled her to him and pressed his lips against hers. Without separating he swept her up into his arms and carried her to the sofas which were neatly pushed together. "I thought about this at the kids' party," he said, as he lowered her onto the SS Chesterfield. Kicking off his shoes he climbed on-board beside her, deftly unzipping the back of her dress as he did so.

At some point, in the wee small hours of the morning, Alex extinguished the last of the candles and led Emily upstairs to their room.

CHAPTER SEVENTEEN

When Emily woke it was to Alex gently touching her shoulder. "Oh, what time is it? I've got to get the kids to nursery."

"No you don't. I just wanted to let you know that I am taking them. Go back to sleep," said Alex. "I doubt you are fit to drive."

"What about you? And, what about work?"

"I didn't drink nearly as much. I knew one of us was going to have to take them. As for work, I got Albert to stand in for me." Albert was the retired blacksmith that helped out now and again. Though retired, he didn't want to lose his skills and was usually happy to help.

"Is Albert fit to work? What about his hip?" asked Emily.

"I can't keep him away. He doesn't want to sit still. Besides, I haven't any bookings this morning. He won't need to do anything unless someone just turns up. When I get back I want to talk to you about St Peter's." Emily blinked and raised her eyebrows. "I know. You don't need to say anything. I have been beating myself-up enough over it. Anyway – gotta go." With that he kissed her and left.

When she went downstairs she was pleased to see that the kitchen was immaculate, just the kids' breakfast things in the sink and a half finished mug of coffee on the table. In the sitting room everything had been returned to normal. It was as if last nights meal had been a dream; a wonderful dream.

Then she remembered that she hadn't given Alex the Valentine's card and box of chocolates that she had got for him. She pulled them out of a cupboard and sat them on the kitchen table with the card propped up against the chocolate box. She thought a while and then opened the envelope and added an extra message. 'Sorry. I forgot to give you these. I plan to make it up to you.'

Next she went upstairs, found a sheet of paper and an envelope, and wrote a note. 'Mrs Emily Wells requests the company of Mr Alex Wells, for dinner at 8pm on this post-Valentine's Day. P.T.O.' on the back she wrote. 'You get the kids to bed for 8pm then we can eat in peace.' Then she got out a clean pair of his jeans and a T-shirt and laid them on the bed with her message placed on top.

She got herself a bowl of cereal and a coffee and pondered on how to approach telling Alex her idea to help St Peter's. It wasn't long before he arrived. When he saw the card and chocolates he laughed. "I wondered if I'd given you long enough." As Emily frowned he added, "to nip out and get me something."

"Hey, they were in the cupboard, over there. I planned on giving you them at dinner but we didn't come in here. Then we were, kinda busy after that."

Alex opened his card and read. Looking up and smiling affectionately at her he said, "I love you too. Thank you. So, St Peter's! I am really sorry that I was such a fool over the children's necklaces. I can't believe that they got to me so. I was actually scared, Emily. I thought someone was targeting our kids. I didn't know that it was possible to feel like that. I am a big strong man and I just felt helpless. It made me so angry."

"Why didn't you tell me?"

"I didn't want to scare you, and worry you. I also, didn't think you would understand."

"What! Why?"

"You never believed that the periapt, which was given to you, had any power."

"I didn't think you did either," blurted Emily.

"I don't, but I am a Wells and I can't escape the fact, that during my life all sorts of things have happened: things which could be explained as co-incidence until you add them all up, and then it seems very unlikely. Logically the periapts don't work; it is ridiculous to think so.

But, just the thought that someone else might think they do and would use them against our children..."

"Oh, Alex, I wish you'd told me."

"Anyway, whether they work or not I have 'de-activated' them! I have removed the calcite and feel much happier about them. The calcite is staying at the forge until I find out where it came from and can return it."

"Lady Agnes," said Emily puzzled.

"No, that isn't what I mean. The calcite needs to be returned to the stalactites from which they were cut."

"You're kidding!"

They talked for a while, Emily incredulous, that he was serious. Despite him professing that it was superstitious nonsense she knew that he would only be content when he knew that he had done all that was possible, to keep his girls safe.

To change tack slightly she asked him what it was he wanted to say about St Peter's. Essentially, he did want to help because he thought it important that the home should keep running. He was happy to help fund-raise as well as provide physical help if he could. Emily was delighted and told him that she had an idea to help but didn't know what he would think about it. She reminded him that although St Peter's Charity Shop was making a profit, just, most of the money they made went on rent and utility bills. The shop, generally speaking, was pointless. She didn't know what the running costs were, but if those costs could be eliminated, it would be profitable. What she had in mind was re-housing the shop. At the forge there were a number of outbuildings and Alex's old flat. As these could be accessed via the wooden door to the high street it wouldn't be far for customers to go. She didn't know what state the buildings were in but, what did he think?

He thought about it for a while and Emily was fully expecting him to come up with an excuse not to use them, but he didn't. He actually thought it was a good idea. It would probably mean some re-wiring and plumbing. The ground floor unit would be best as it had more room, and no-one would have to risk climbing the worn stone steps up to his old flat. He had been wondering what to do with the buildings. He hadn't liked the fact that they were standing empty, but didn't know what to do with them. In the meantime they had just been deteriorating. He suggested that the pair of them went and had a look.

* * *

The yard was bigger than Emily remembered. She hadn't paid it much attention previously. When she and Alex first started seeing each other she had been too eager to head up the steps to his flat. Now, looking around, she could see that the area, if cleared of all the accumulated rubbish and swept, would be quite an attractive space. The yard was cobbled and the years' worth of soot, that for generations had coated the granite buildings making them black, was wearing away. Most of the stone was now a light brown to yellow, almost like Cotswold stone. With some flower tubs and hanging baskets the place would look very welcoming.

Alex fetched a bunch of keys from the forge and unlocked the largest of the 5 doors at ground level. Pushing it open, it scraped on a collection of debris that had gathered behind it, and stuck. Stepping through the gap Alex used his boot to clear the ground behind the door, so that he was able to open it fully. He switched on the light which consisted of one bare bulb in the centre of the room. It barely penetrated the depths of the space. Emily wasn't sure whether her eyes adjusted or the bulb was an energy saving one but soon she found she could see. There was one window which was covered in dust and cobwebs: the latter weighed down by collections of deceased bluebottle remains. The floor had at some point been concreted and was flat, which was helpful, if not aesthetically pleasing. Cleaned and scrubbed, with better lighting and some shelving units the room would provide a larger and more useful space for the charity shop. Alex was busy studying the ceiling and explained that he was working out where his flat's kitchen and bathroom were, with a view to feeding pipes down. There was a toilet in the yard which could be used but it would be better if the shop could have its own sink and toilet. He reckoned that it was possible. "So, what do you think?" he asked Emily.

"I think it would be perfect. It needs some work but I think it could be great. With the plumbing, would we be paying for that?"

"Yes, I don't mind doing that. I have also been thinking of letting out the flat but just never got round to it. It needs a bit of an update. So, why not do the two together."

Emily was chuffed. "Can we go talk to the shop, see if they are interested?"

He grinned, her enthusiasm was catching. On the way there they discussed the terms they would propose and Emily suggested that he explained that bit. After all, it was his property, even though technically it now belonged to both of them.

At the shop they both wandered round inspecting the stock until the one customer who was there when they arrived, left.

"Hi, remember me?" said Emily, "I was here the other day."

"Of course I remember you Emily, and this is your husband, Alex. We have never met but I know who you are. I'm Phyllis. What can I do for you?"

"Well, since we talked I, we, have been to see Lady Agnes, who has asked for our help to raise money for St Peter's. After you told me that most of this shop's income goes on rent, I talked to Alex. We were wondering if we could offer you a rent free site, at the forge."

Alex then explained that as well as the property being rent free, he and Emily would pay the utility bills for the first year. The woman looked sceptical until they explained that access would be through the doors that opened onto the high street, about 50yards from the current shop. At this revelation she locked up the shop and insisted on taking a look for herself. The decision wouldn't be hers she explained, but if she saw it she could pass on her opinion.

When they went into the yard Emily was at pains to explain how the area would look, cleaned, tidied and titivated. Alex put forward his plumbing proposals. Phyllis really liked the idea and said she would talk to the shop manager. She wasn't sure but she thought that they would need to give 3 months notice on the current rent, but that would surely give plenty of time to get the forge site ready. Emily hadn't thought of that. It looked like this wasn't going to be the quick fix she had hoped.

* * *

That afternoon, with Alex now at work, she decided to go for a walk, stop off at Bode Well Cottage, and see Lou. As she walked down the high street she stuffed her hands in her pockets. It was bitterly cold and the wind was picking up. Looking up she noticed that the clouds had a bit of a yellow tinge to them. She would be glad when she got to Lou's. Head down, she trudged onwards, her coat held tight against the wind.

"Oy, watch where ya goin'." It was Mr Swire, her ointment 'patient'. "I've bin meanin' a cum warn ya agin, lass. Thiz rumblin's."

Emily looked up, "Sorry, what?"

"I told ye. Summats up. Thiz cats, all o'ert place. It don't bode well. You lot need to do summat. Tek care." With that he doffed his cap and set off walking.

Emily jogged the rest of the way to Lou's. Thankfully, inside the cottage it was lovely and warm. The fire in the kitchen glowed and Emily held her chilled fingers in front of it. Soon Lou handed her a mug of coffee and eagerly listened as Emily told her what had happened since St Peter's meeting, including the strange encounter with Mr Swire. "I was too cold to push him for an explanation: if he had one, which I doubt." She finished by saying how disappointed she was about the 3 months rent, that was probably payable on the shop.

Lou looked thoughtful but offered nothing. Instead she said, "Well, let me know when you have finished the clearing and tidying and count me in for the titivating."

They chatted for a while discussing ideas for making the yard attractive. Every now and again, there would be a thump or a bang from the room above as Nathan entertained himself. At one point there was a particularly loud crash. Lou stopped talking and listened. There was a brief silence, followed by a low scuffling sound. Lou relaxed. There was movement above, but no crying. She continued, telling Emily about her Valentine's meal with Mike and how he had presented her with a pot plant, which was lovely, but it was sitting in a wicker basket shaped like a sleigh. It was obviously left over from Christmas somewhere and being sold off cheaply; the perfect gift!   Emily told her what Alex had done, and what she planned to do this coming evening.

"You lucky sod," said Louise. "Mike would never think to do anything like that. Then neither would I. So, I can't complain."

"Well, thanks for the coffee. I'd better go. I gotta pick up the girls."

* * *

That evening, with the kids in bed, and Alex dressed in the jeans and T-shirt she had laid out on the bed for him, they dined at the kitchen table. Emily splashed the pink fizz into two tumblers, mopped the table, and then served up the Valentine's meal deal. As they finished their chocolate tort and downed the last dregs of the bottle, Emily produced a little cutlass that Alex had used at the triplets' birthday party, and put it between her teeth. Then she winked and said, "Wanna play pirates?" Together they headed for the sitting room, Alex stripping off his T-shirt, as he chased her up the hall.

CHAPTER EIGHTEEN

Just after 9 o'clock, on Saturday morning, the phone rang. Emily crossed the kitchen and picked it up as Alex looked on, curious. It was Phyllis from the Charity Shop. She had spoken to the manager, who had discussed it with the rest of the volunteers and come back to her with a resounding 'Yes' to moving the shop to the forge yard. In fact, the volunteers were keen to help out any way they could to prepare the property, so that they could move as soon as possible. Even though they did have to pay the rent on the current shop for 3 months they felt that, as there was more room in the new place, they would be able to sell more. Also, the new site would be likely to entice more customers, old and new. Emily and Alex were pleased but shocked by the speed events were taking. The theory was fine but now they would actually have to do something about it. The first thing it seemed was to show the rest of the shop volunteers and manager round their new site. So, Alex agreed to go over and open up for 10am.

* * *

Having roped in James and Mike they gathered in the high street outside the double doors of the archway that led to the forge yard. Originally, the buildings to the right had been a coaching inn with stables at the rear. When a by-pass was built in the 1960s, greatly reducing the traffic flow through Much Meddling, the inn had been sold and turned into 2 shops with accommodation above.

When everyone had turned up Alex unlocked the doors and they all filed through. It soon became apparent that one of the volunteers was a retired builder. The others threw suggestions at him and he volleyed them. Some were feasible and some weren't. After about an hour they had formulated a plan. Alex would need to talk to the Council, about 'change of use' of the property, and Building Regulations would need to be consulted. The builder, George, said he would sketch out some plans for everyone's approval, including what Alex wanted for his flat above. When he got home, Emily was amazed. "So, this George, is going to do the work, and for nothing?"

"It appears so," said Alex, "provided, of course, we get the okay from the Council. A group of us have volunteered to provide the labour: even Mike!"

"Really! Amazing what peer pressure can do. I guess he can always make the tea," she sniggered. "So when does all this work start? How long will it take to get approval from the Council etc.?"

"Oh, they aren't interested in waiting that long. They want to start the clearing out this afternoon. I was tempted to just give them the key but I don't know what there is in there. Those buildings have been in need of a good sort out for years," said Alex. "What plans had you got for this afternoon?"

Emily didn't have any plans as such, just catching up on housework and entertaining the girls: not that they tended to need much entertaining, as they entertained each other. Even when they fell out they seemed to manage that amongst themselves, one of them acting as peacemaker. She also had the reassurance that if one of them got hurt, one of the other two would come find her. At times she felt a little superfluous. So, after lunch, with the girls playing happily on the kitchen rug, Alex went off to the forge, and Emily busied herself unpacking that morning's shopping delivery before putting on a load of washing.

* * *

At the forge yard Alex opened up the buildings. They would need somewhere to store all the stuff that they took out of the space which was to be the new charity shop. Looking in some of the other outbuildings he reckoned that there would be room to cram some of the items in there. Then he designated an area of the yard for rubbish and another for recyclables. As the St Peter's volunteers arrived he set them to work bringing everything out so that he could direct where to put it all. As items started to appear he was amazed at the variety of things that were stored there. Out came old gates, a paraffin heater, empty oil cans, random bits of metal, chains, what looked like a log basket made out of horseshoes, spare wheels complete with flat tyres, stacks of old magazines, a wooden stool and a collection of broken brooms. When Alex took a break and went to look inside to see how they were getting on he saw that there were also a number of items hanging from ceiling beams. Covered in cobwebs were horse brasses, chairs, more chains, tankards and an oil lamp.

To give everyone a break he suggested one of them went out to the high street and got milk and some cakes. Handing over a couple of £20 notes he went up into his old flat and put the kettle on.

The volunteers turned out to be a fun bunch. There were 4 women and 3 men, one of the latter being George the retired builder. They were all a lot older than Alex but he found that he was enjoying their company. He was quietly surprised at how hard they had worked. He was feeling a little weary but then that was probably due to all the decisions he had been making over what to keep and what to throw away. They however, all looked eager to carry on and were obviously enthused by what they were doing. They were all also highly interested in the items they were finding; all his old rubbish was like treasure to them.

As they sat and drank their tea he said, "Once I have had time to look through it all I will let you know what you can have for the shop."

"Oh, you'd be better putting some of it on eBay," said one of the women.

"No, I'd auction the bigger items through 'Denbies'," said another.

There was a great discussion amongst them, over various items, until one of them realised that they were busy appropriating all Alex's stuff, with no regards to what Alex might want to keep. At which point there was a stream of acute apologies.

"No, that's alright," said Alex, "I do want to keep some of it but I also should let my wife have a look."

There was agreed understanding at this, and conversation moved on to how they would arrange the new shop to best advantage. George suggested that he build a partition wall at one end. Once the shop was separate it could be opened. Work could then go on behind the partition to give them a storage area, small kitchen and a toilet cubicle.

Once they got to work again it didn't take them long to finish emptying the place. Alex produced a couple of brooms and two of them set to work sweeping the floor. Others used shovels to scrape up bits of rubble and put it into rubble sacks that one of them had thought to bring along. One of the women had found a bucket, which she had filled with water from a tap by the forge door, and was washing the windowpanes with an old towel. This one simple task made a huge difference to the interior. The old uneven glass panes, once cleared of grime, let in the last of the day's sun which scattered its sparkly rays illuminating small eddies of floating dust particles. It was a large space. Even with one end partitioned the room would provide over twice the floor space of the current charity shop premises.

When Alex stepped inside, he found George bent over chalking lines on the floor, marking out the partition wall, small kitchen, toilet, and storage area, whilst the others discussed where to place the counter.

"What are you going to do, if the Council says no?" asked Alex, looking at one of the women who had found an old glass 'fly-catcher' lamp shade and was eyeing up the ceiling light.

"Oh, it shouldn't be a problem, the Building Regulations guy is an old friend of George's." she said, then raised her voice, "George, come here a minute."

"What's up?" said George straightening up and strolling over.

"Alex is concerned that we might not get the go-ahead."

"Hah! There won't be any problems. I'll eat your hat if there is." When Alex looked doubtful, he said, "I have been doing building work in the local area for a long time now, and I know most of the people involved. This is just the sort of site the Council will love being put to use and this is a very simple project for Building Regulations to sign off." Then, pointing at the floor and sweeping his arm in an arc, "What do you think of the layout."

"It looks great. I can't believe that we have got this far already," said Alex. "You lot are amazing."

* * *

Lou was sitting in a chair opposite Gerald, who was leaning on his desk. He was trying to figure out what Lou was really after. He didn't think that she actually wanted to put a conservatory on her cottage and if she was planning on selling she would have said outright.

After Lou and Gerald had exchanged pleasantries and the mention of the conservatory had more or less been dismissed by Lou as something she and Mike were still thinking about, Gerald asked her what he could do for her. So, Lou came right to the point. She had heard from Cheryl, the nurse at St Peter's, who had informed her that the St

Peter's valuation had been done by one Anthony Newton-Smith. Louise wanted Gerald to phone Anthony Newton-Smith and ask him what he had valued St Peter's at. She understood that he probably didn't feel that it would be ethical, as she had no connection with St Peter's. However, as Lady Agnes had asked for help she felt that it *was* her business. She pointed out that the valuation had been done without Lady Agnes's consent, or her knowledge. Gerald's mate might wish to consider that, if at a future date, Lady Agnes *should* decide to sell. After a little more discussion and added persuasion on Lou's part, Gerald rang his mate.

* * *

Lady Agnes sank into her chair and let out a deep sigh. She had just succeeded in walking the length of the room, and it was a large room, with the aid of a walking frame and a nurse. She was exhausted but pleased with her progress. Satisfied, she felt justified in taking a nap, whilst waiting for her afternoon cup of tea to arrive.

A heavy rapping on the door made her sit up straight. The door opened and in walked her son, Simon.

"Hello mother. How are you today?" he asked cheerfully. He crossed the room and bending down, kissed her on the cheek.

Lady Agnes looked at him. She knew full well that he wanted something, and, she was fairly certain that she knew what it was. "No, I...

not …se…ling."

"Well, I have some news."

She looked at him, waiting.

"I thought that maybe, if you knew how much this place was worth, it might change your mind. So, I took the liberty of getting a friend of mine to give us a valuation."

Lady Agnes slid her keyboard on to her lap and started to type.

Simon continued as she did so, "He has valued it at £12.25 million. Anthony is from the best agency in the area, which also has national and international outlets. He could find you a buyer in no time. A care agency if you like. You then wouldn't have to worry about this place anymore and you could move into a nice house with a private nurse.

She looked up from her typing, "Have… very… nice… house… and … ve…ry…good… nur…*sez*." She stabbed at the print button. The printer whirred and Simon went and retrieved the sheet of paper. He read, "Will you be selling it without my knowledge or consent, too?"

"Mother, it is just a valuation: something to think about. I worry about you and all the stress this place puts on you.

"Less…stress…if…you…'elp."

"Look, how about if I get Anthony to come and see you. He can explain what would be involved. He also has some brochures of some lovely retirement villages."

"'Ow…dare…you! This…my…life. My le…ga..see."

"Calm down. You're not well," pleaded Simon, "you must see reason. I'm only thinking of you."

"No, you…think…of…Si…mon. Get…out."

"But mother!"

"Get…out. You…no…son…of…mine."

Alarmed, Simon backed towards the door. He had never seen her so angry. She had never disowned him before. He was at a loss as to how to calm her down. Her hand was shaking and her face was quite red. She was almost screaming, "Get…out. Get…ow. Ge…ow." All he could do was leave. Before he closed the door a cat slipped through it.

In the corridor Simon stopped one of the nurses and told her to go check on Lady Agnes. Then, he trotted down the stairs.

* * *

In the recreation room Sophie was having a game of table tennis with one of the other residents. Suddenly there was a yell and a series of thuds from the hall followed by a string of colourful expletives. Tossing her bat on the table she spun her chair and pushed for the door. Lying in a heap at the bottom of the stairs was a smartly dressed visitor, holding his knee and swearing at Tom, one of the residents.

Tom was attempting to pull the man to

his feet. Sophie rolled over and tugged on Tom's arm. When he looked at her, she shook her head at him and gestured for him to move away. From the floor, the man continued to hurl abuse at Tom.

"He can't hear you," explained Sophie. "He's deaf. He also can't speak. He was just trying to help. Are you hurt?"

"That blasted cat," said the man looking round and letting his glare rest halfway up the stairs, where a large furry ball of mischief sat innocently surveying the scene.

A couple of members of staff appeared and attempted to assess him. They backed off when he got angrily to his feet, unaided, telling them to leave him alone; he could manage, and to get away from him. Endeavouring to ignore his rudeness one of the nurses said, "You will probably have a few bruises and be sore for a few days. If anything gets worse then do take yourself to Accident and Emergency."

As the man picked up his jacket and brushed himself down, Sophie smiled at him and took the opportunity to introduce herself. Then she grinned expectantly at him, her head on one side, quizzically.

With obvious reluctance he said. "I'm Simon." Then as she continued to smile at him he said, "Thank you for coming to my aid. I shouldn't have sworn like that"

"Oh, it's not me you need to apologise to,

it's Tom."

"What, that idiot! You should never try to move someone like that."

"He was only trying to help and he doesn't understand." She looked over to the corner of the hall, where a chastened Tom stood forlornly, half hidden by a tall pot plant. She beckoned for him to come over. After a bit of hesitation, he sidled over looking wary. Simon glowered. Then, before he could stop it, Sophie had him shaking hands with Tom and mouthing 'thank you' to him. Relieved, Tom enthusiastically shook Simon's hand. When he let go, and turned and walked away, he was smiling and humming. Sophie winked at Simon and sped off back to her game of table tennis. Just before she disappeared through the door of the recreation room, she tipped her chair on to its rear wheels, spun 360 degrees, turned back to face him, did a mock bow and wheeled backwards out of sight.

* * *

In her room, Lady Agnes sobbed quietly; frustration, rage and sadness fighting for supremacy. Why could Simon not see how important the home was to her? Why could he not at least give her the time she needed to explain things to him? He must know how difficult it was for her to say anything let alone express herself. It was so easy for him to interrupt her, to talk over her, to shut her down. He had no patience, and deliberately appeared not to notice her distress. So many times, he talked to the nurses, as if she wasn't there. He even made *them* feel uncomfortable. Time and again, bless them, they forced Simon to address her and bring her back into the conversation, deferring to her for answers, of which she knew they were aware. She felt sure that he believed that what he was doing was in her best interests, whilst blindly suppressing his own. He didn't even have the decency to wait until she was dead, and then sell the place. However, for St Peter's to be sold was unthinkable to her. Even if it went to a care agency who continued to provide a home for the residents it would be lost to the Earnshaws. She didn't understand why, but the Earnshaw legacy was also important to her. It made no logical sense: the Earnshaws had treated her abysmally. If Simon didn't want the place then there was still Trevor. He should have the opportunity of inheriting and owning this fabulous ancestral home, even if his father didn't want it.

CHAPTER NINETEEN

On Sunday morning Emily and Alex were noisily awoken by the arrival on their bed of three bouncing excited girls, shouting "Snow, snow, snow." Alex got out of bed and drew back the front window curtains. He looked at Emily and nodded. There was a glaringly white thick covering on everything. Alex squinted and took in the scene. Emily, pulling on her dressing gown joined him and exclaimed, "Wow, just look at that."

There was a good 10 cms of snow on everything they could see. As it was early morning, no-one had trampled any of it yet. It was a beautiful sight. Looking left they could see the church, snow piled high in the angles of its windowsills, each lead pane defined by a thin white line. In the church yard the head stones were topped with snow, their engravings picked out with a sparkly frosting. Yew trees groaned: their branches weighed down. Looking up the high street there wasn't a soul around. To the right the odd duck could be seen swimming in the centre of a much reduced pond: its edges frozen and covered in snow.

"Who wants to go sledging today?" asked Alex. The children looked uncertain but seeing their father's enthusiasm all said, "Me, me, me!" before one of them asked, "What is slejin?" So, Alex explained, and told them that they would go after lunch, but they would need to stop off at Daddy's forge on the way.

* * *

Leaving the children and Emily in the Range Rover, Alex disappeared into the forge and emerged with three small sledges, their shiny runners glinting. After another trip inside he came out with a larger, adult sized one. As he loaded them into the back of the car Emily asked, "When did you make these?"

"About three months ago. I've been hoping we would get to use them this winter. I was beginning to think we wouldn't be able to."

Driving out of the village and up into the hills the car crunched its way up a rough track. At the crest of a hill there was a small car park and Alex drew the car to a halt. In front of them was a magnificent view. The countryside fell away from them in a commanding sweep. Almost featureless, the landscape was a mass of lumpy blue white. To the left a few stone walls could be seen where the sun had melted some of their covering but to the right the only evidence of their existence was the shadows they cast.

Once everyone was out of the vehicle and togged up ready Alex gave each child a sledge. They were beautifully made. The runners were smooth and expertly curved into partial scrolls at the front ends, providing somewhere for little feet to brace themselves. The wooden slats were deeply polished and each of the centre ones had a triplet's name skilfully painted along it. There were even some carriage work markings along the edges of the outer slats. The larger sledge had Emily and Alex written on it.

Emily was delighted, "You are so clever. These are wonderful, Alex!"

* * *

At St Peter's Sophie took up position in the entrance hall, ready to ambush visitors. She had persuaded the staff to provide her with a table, which she had positioned equidistant between the bottom of the stairs and the bank of 3 lifts. She had a white board on a stand to which she had attached a large poster proclaiming 'ST PETER'S NEEDS YOUR HELP! Keep a roof over our heads.' She had a stack of leaflets which explained the need to raise money to repair the roof and also asking for the services of any tradesmen willing to work at cost. She had brochures of St Peter's explaining the work they did, for any relatives who didn't already know, and attached to the wall was a series of colourful speech bubbles containing quotes from the residents saying what St Peter's meant to them and what they had achieved with the help of St Peter's staff. In a prominent position on the table was a collection box, with a sign saying that cheques were acceptable as well as 'bank transfers'.

* * *

Placing a sledge rope in each child's hand, and then doing the same to Emily, with the larger sledge, Alex set off, "This way," and he trudged, explorer-like, towards the edge of the slope. At a suitable point he stopped and surveyed the terrain. Being familiar with the site he knew that there weren't any obstacles for the girls to come to grief over. As a demonstration he suggested that Emily went first. With the children watching he got Emily to sit on the sledge and then instructed her where to put her feet and her hands. Then he gave her a push. With a yell she disappeared down the hillside leaving two parallel lines in the snow. At the bottom of the slope Emily fell over sideways, then got up laughing. Dusting snow off herself she called to the others to join her.

Tansy was already on her sledge, eager to get going. With her feet wedged against the runners and her hands gripping the sides of the sledge she bounced up and down on her seat, "push, Daddy, push."

Alex gave her a gentle nudge to get her going and watched as she glided down towards Emily. About five metres from Emily, she came to a halt. Laughing and giggling she got to her feet and, dragging the sledge behind her, set off up the slope for another go. Next, Violet, and then Lily descended. As Lily set off following Tansy's tracks uphill, Emily noticed that Violet was still sitting on her sledge, motionless. The little girl appeared to be staring into space. Walking in front of her Emily could see that this wasn't the case. Violet's eyes were focussed. Mouth partly open, she was tracking snowflakes as they fell. Emily crouched by her side and held out her hand, catching a large flake. Stretching out her hand for Violet to see she said, "Aren't they pretty? Each one is different. Isn't that amazing?" Together they held out their hands and watched as snowflake after snowflake landed and melted. Their concentration was soon broken as Tansy sped past, shortly followed by Lily.

With all three girls having made it safely down, Emily trudged back up the slope, helping each child as necessary until all four of them got back to the top. She handed the reins of her sledge to Alex. With the children safely out of the way he set off at a run, holding the sledge at chest height. He then launched himself forwards and, landing on the sledge, careered down the hill to end a good twenty five metres beyond the spot Emily had reached. Before Emily could stop her Tansy set off, copying her father. "Tansy, no!" yelled Emily. To Emily's amazement Tansy perfectly executed the flying leap onto her sledge and sped down the hill towards Alex, giggling madly. Alex ran up the slope to meet her. Picking her up and setting her on her feet he asked, "Are you alright? I wasn't expecting you to copy me."

"Yes. Again, again," and she set off up the slope, sledge in tow.

Slowly Alex followed her. Bursting with pride he watched the determined little figure trudge uphill. She slipped and fell a number of times but carried doggedly on. Once or twice she stopped and looked back at him, her little face glowing. Only half of it was visible as her hood stayed static when she turned her head, dark brown curls escaping at the sides. He knew that he would be in trouble with Emily when he got to the top. Thankfully, Violet and Tansy were either more cautious, or Emily had spoken to them. They both made their next descent sitting, with a gentle push from Emily. When he reached Emily he said, "I know, that was stupid of me. I'm sorry. I really need to think about my behaviour in front of the girls."

* * *

Sophie was having a great time. She approached everyone who entered, with a beaming smile and a couple of twirls of her wheelchair. Balancing on the back wheels always gained her a round of applause. Having elicited people's attention she then went on to ask them what St Peter's meant to them, and how they would feel if it closed and their relative had to leave. Most of the people she asked had positive experiences, and were horrified by the thought of it closing. One couple appeared indifferent, which surprised and saddened her. However, they were just two people. Most people put money in the collection. A few wrote cheques and others asked about the bank transfer details.

* * *

It wasn't long before the girls began to tire of dragging their sledges back up the slope and Emily and Alex had to drag them up. Soon they wanted carrying up. So, the family spent some time making a snow man and throwing snowballs at one another. Emily built a barricade to protect her and the triplets from Alex's aim. Then Tansy deserted the girls and went and joined Alex. So Emily got Lily and Violet to make the snowballs whilst she threw them. However, the snow stuck to their mittens and they really struggled to form the snowballs. The production line was very slow and they were no match for Alex and Tansy. When Tansy hit Emily smack in the face with a surprisingly icy snowball, Emily decided that it was time they all went home.

Back at the car they discovered that Violet was missing a boot. Removing a soggy sock to inspect her foot Emily asked, "When did you lose it?" Violet stared back and shrugged. Whilst Alex went off in search of the missing boot Emily leant inside the back of the car and held the tiny foot between her hands. It was surprisingly warm. By the time Emily had strapped the girls in, Alex arrived, "I can't find it. It could be buried anywhere in this lot."

"Let me look," huffed Emily. She trekked back down to the last place they had been and glanced round and surveyed the ground. They she went back to their barricade and moved the snow about with her foot on the spot Violet had been standing. A small area of blue appeared. A little digging revealed Violet's boot. She picked it up, gave it a shake and climbed back up to the car.

* * *

When Sophie finally abandoned her post to go for dinner she handed the collection box and cheques over to St Peter's receptionist, and proudly announced, "Not bad for day one. £263.62p plus promises of more by bank transfer." As Sophie wheeled away the receptionist smiled to herself. She hadn't known Sophie for long, but she knew that the life changing injuries which she had suffered had been devastating for her. She had been a fit and active individual, who spent most of her time outdoors, riding. In one terrifying afternoon her life had been changed forever. As a result of breaking her spine she had spent 6months in a Spinal Injuries Unit. Unable to go back to her flat she had been transferred to St Peters. She had not just lost her mobility but her home, her work, her lifestyle and her social circle. She had a lot to grieve for. Now, today, if Sophie could walk, the receptionist would have said she had 'a bounce in her step'. Being useful and doing something positive had made a distinct difference to her demeanour. St Peter's was again giving at least one of its residents a reason to challenge the difficulties she faced. The receptionist had seen it before; it was the reasons beyond their own needs, which took them out of themselves, that stimulated the greatest success.

CHAPTER TWENTY

O n Tuesday morning as Alex waved goodbye to a customer and started to close the yard gate behind their horse-box, he was surprised to see another vehicle arriving and being waved down by George, the St Peter's charity shop volunteer. It was obvious that George was expecting the arrival of the person in the approaching car. Obeying George's gesticulations Alex re-opened the gate and allowed the mystery visitor to drive in. Almost before the driver had stopped George opened the car door and enthusiastically made introductions, "Alex, this is Tom Atkinson, the Buildings Reg's guy from the Council. Tom, this is Alex the owner of these buildings." Tom stepped out of the car and stood up. He was at least two inches taller than Alex but a lot slimmer. He had a weathered complexion and an easy grin.

"Right," said George, "lets get on wi' it. Have you got the keys?"

"George, I don't have time for this right now," said Alex, "I have another customer arriving any minute."

"Its okay, just give us the keys. We won't bother you."

"I want to be there so that I *know* what is being agreed to," said Alex.

"Don't worry, it will all be written down," said George, unabashed.

Reluctantly Alex went and got the keys. He handed them to George who trotted off towards the out-building leaving a little white cloud behind him as his breath condensed in the cold air. Before following him Tom looked at Alex, and raised his eyebrows. Rubbing his hands together to warm them, and nodding in George's direction he said, "He means well. He's a bit hard work, but he'll do a really good job." Then he turned and ambled slowly after George.

* * *

When Emily got home from dropping the children at nursery James was parked outside, waiting for her. She climbed in the back behind Anna. "Hi. Sorry to keep you both waiting, the nursery teacher wanted to have a word with me. Apparently Lily had called Trevor's dad a 'bad man'." As James set off towards St Peter's Emily continued, "Yesterday, Simon had taken Trevor home early. When he walked into the nursery, Lily scowled and pointed at him and said, 'Bad man'. The nursery staff didn't know what to do. They apologised to him and he just shrugged it off and left. It is so embarrassing. I don't know what to do about it. Did we tell you about the picture she drew? It appears to be a picture of St Peter's with a man in front waving a spade. *Hopefully*, it is meant to be a spade. She drew dark clouds over-head with some very angry looking raindrops."

Lou was waiting by her gate, shoulders hunched against the cold, hands deep in her pockets. She got in quickly and they set off again. "Anna, hello, how's Sasha? Very sneaky of you not to let us see him."

"Sasha is fine. I just wanted to keep him to myself for a bit."

"I reckon there is something wrong with him," said Lou.

"There is absolutely nothing wrong with him. You will meet him, all in good time."

Turning off the slushy main road James pointed the car up St Peter's drive. At the end he found a parking space not too far from the entrance and the four of them walked carefully up to the doors, salt and grit crunching underfoot.

Sophie greeted them and summoned a lift. Together they travelled up to the meeting room. Lady Agnes was already there, as was the nurse manager and a lady that Emily and Lou hadn't met before. Again, drinks and biscuits were offered and accepted. Then the nurse manager, Colette, introduced the newcomer as May Brown, the manager of St Peter's charity shop. May was a petite individual. She sat erect and gave off an air of no-nonsense ability. Having been introduced she launched into a report of the current state of the charity shop's finances and then brought everyone up to date with the latest news concerning a new, rent-free site for the shop. This created a buzz amongst those present and even Lady Agnes let out an 'ooh!' At this point Emily felt obliged to point out that it wasn't confirmed yet, they still had to have approval from the Council and Building Regulations. At which point May Brown shook her head and dismissed the obstacle as non-existent. Emily hoped she was right.

Sophie proudly announced how much money she had raised which, with bank transfers and Monday's donations had reached £510.92. Sophie knew that the donations would dry up, as there wasn't a limitless supply of relatives, but she had other plans that she was working on.

Lou, not knowing whether Lady Agnes knew about Simon's valuation of St Peter's, didn't mention what she had found out from Gerald, but did ask permission to talk to him and the current owner of the old charity shop premises about finding a new tenant. That way they would save some, if not all, of the 3 months rental they were contractually obliged to pay. Everyone was happy for her to do that.

Emily told them that Alex was looking to rent out his old flat over the new charity shop.

After costs, she added shyly, he would give the first two years' income to St Peter's.

"Do you want me to try and find a tenant for that as well?" asked Lou.

"Er, yes, please," said Emily.

Colette then informed them that they had had another valuation for repairs to the roof. They had been quoted £4,500 to repair some of the minor problems to the East Wing section. This would mean that two of the rooms on the top floor could be made usable, after some work. They didn't have quotes for that yet.

James told them that he had a couple of Comedy Caravan Club bookings which would bring in £300, and he may also have a business lunch booking, but that was a little 'up in the air'. He would know by the end of the week.

Anna, who hadn't said anything as yet and had nothing to report, was looking a little uncomfortable as everyone now looked at her. "Could we have a look at the rooms? I would be happy to do some decorating once the roof is fixed."

Colette nodded, "I can show you them now, if you like. Hopefully we will have enough money by the end of the month to get work started on the roof."

"So," said Lady Agnes, "We…are…ge…tin…g, some…where. You…are…all…wun…der…ful. 'Ank…you."

Colette took the little party up to the

rooms on the top floor. As she opened the first door, a fluffy black cat, with white socks and whiskers, rubbed her ankles and entered the room ahead of her. It ran to the windowsill and hopped up, turned, and sat watching as the humans filed in. Sophie made her way over to the window and gave the cat a stroke. Colette pointed out the damp in one corner where the wallpaper was peeling off and speckled with black mould. The room smelt damp. However, it wouldn't take too much to bring the room into use once the roof was fixed. After a brief inspection she led them to the other room which was much worse. Not only would it need drying out but parts of it would need re-plastering. The cornice was starting to crumble and the ceiling rose was turning yellow at the edge. The whole room smelt musty and the carpet was a mess. It was littered with flakes of ceiling plaster. Anna did a walk round the room. Stopping in one corner she bend down and took hold of the carpet, "May I?" she asked. Colette nodded and Anna pulled it back with a ripping, popping sound. Underneath was a layer of brown lino, obviously damp in places. "We could make a start by getting rid of all this. It would give the room a chance to start drying out. The ceiling rose is going to need replacing and the windows stripping and repainting. Ooh, that is a nice window handle. Emily, do you think Alex could make another to match, to replace that missing one over there? AND just look at that view."

The en-suites fortunately were dry, and with a little work would be functional. As Anna got stuck-in to ripping up the carpet and started picking at the lino, Colette excused herself and the others began muttering that they weren't dressed for DIY and perhaps they could come back another day, when they had procured some hazmat suits!

Anna, however, was not to be deterred. "James, you get hold of that end and pull." Together they managed to roll back the carpet to the middle of the room. The lino was stuck in places but came up easily in others. Beneath the lino was a beautiful oak floor. Anna was in raptures. With a clean and a polish it would be terrific.

Sophie suddenly came rolling back into the room, surprising everyone as they hadn't noticed her absence. On her lap was the black cat, smugly enjoying the ride. Sophie had been giving the other room, the less damaged of the two, a closer inspection and she appeared to share Anna's joy. "You know, if we took down that partition in the en-suite to make it wheelchair accessible, I'd be very happy to move in there. It is a fantastic room, much better than mine. Mine could then be used for someone else."

"How is that going to help? It would be just one more empty room," said Emily.

"Yeah, but mine has over-head tracking."

Seeing the blank expressions, Sophie explained, "There is a sling hanging from a track in the ceiling which can carry people from bed to shower to toilet. St Peter's only has a few rooms with that facility, as do most care homes. They can easily fill that room. I don't need over-head tracking. I am independent. The other room, up here, would be brilliant. It is so much quieter; why people don't switch off their TVs when they aren't watching them, I'll never understand. There is so much room and I love that view. I really wouldn't mind the mess."

"But, you can't move into that," said Emily horrified. "It is damp and it smells and, and, you're, you're not... well," she said lamely and blushed.

Sophie spun round in front of Emily and glared at her. "I am not ill. I am as well as you. I am only here because I don't have anywhere to live at the moment. I am not an invalid and I don't need you to decide what is suitable for me. I have looked, and the facilities in that room are perfectly adequate for my needs. It won't take much for it to be usable. I am not going to come to harm because there is a little damp in one corner."

Emily, unable to meet Sophie's eyes looked at the cat. It scowled back, settling protectively against Sophie. Emily stammered her apologies, "I didn't mean..."

"Yes, you did. You think because I am in a

wheelchair that I am not capable of looking after myself or making my own decisions..."

As Emily turned crimson Lou intervened, "What Emily thinks, is that there is no way that she would move in *there*. I know *I* wouldn't!"

Anna, who had disappeared, came back into the room, "You know what, she's right. It wouldn't take much to dry out that corner and make the room habitable, and that partition in the en-suite only needs unscrewing."

"See," said Sophie and set off, complete with passenger, towards the lift, "they can start looking for another resident. That will quickly make up the £4,500 shortfall."

* * *

As soon as he could, Alex went and joined George and Tom. He wasn't too interested in what they did with the space for the Charity Shop but he did care about his old flat. Having made Tom explain to him what George was planning to do, he satisfied himself that what was being proposed was actually what he wanted. He was about to leave them to it again when George handed him some forms. "These are for the Council, for Change of Use. I have filled out what I can to save time but you need to sign it and add the details in the boxes marked."

Alex was about to protest but he quickly scanned the pages and realised that they weren't that lengthy, or complicated. He added what was needed and signed them. Tom said he would take them back with him to the Council Offices and that Alex should hear the result within the next two to three weeks. He added that he had inspected the yard access from the street and that was okay. As Tom and George left, Alex felt annoyed. George had been far too pushy. He had taken control and it irked him. He went back to work and took out his frustrations with his hammer. He tried to tell himself that it didn't matter and that George had actually saved him time and effort. It would have taken him ages to research and find the right forms and he knew that he would have hated doing that. Still!

* * *

Back at home Emily went to see Snokettee and the kittens. It took her a while to find them as Snokettee was increasingly bringing them into the house. She found the little family were grouped around the triplets play box on the rug in the corner of the kitchen. Up until now, she had tried to keep the two sets of youngsters separate but it seemed that Snokettee wasn't as concerned for the kittens' safety as was Emily. Would Snokettee bring them when the children were home? As they stumbled about, Emily watched. When Whoops-a-Daisy fell over and yawned, Emily could see tiny little white teeth starting to show. She couldn't resist, she reached out and gently picked up the tiny ball of fur. Snokettee sat, head on one side, and watched. Emily cradled Whoops-a-Daisy in her cupped hands and grimaced as the kitten commenced chewing her little finger. Though small, the teeth were sharp. Thankfully, the bite wasn't that strong. Emily placed the kitten back on the rug and tentatively stroked it. Spider and Marigold came and joined their sibling and Emily had to stroke all three in turn.

* * *

Apart from the antics of Snokettee and the kittens, Emily hadn't had a good day. That evening, after the children had gone to bed, Emily told Alex about the nursery 'talking to her' about Lily calling Simon a 'bad man'. When she had brought the children home she had spoken to Lily and tried to explain that she mustn't call Mr Earnshaw *that*, but Lily had just scowled at her. When she had tried to get Lily to explain why she thought he was a 'bad man', it was as if she didn't know why, she just knew! At the St Peter's meeting she had managed to upset Sophie, and she felt awful about it but Sophie seemed determined not to accept her apology. She then remembered that the triplets had been invited to another child's birthday party a week on Saturday, which was when her parents were coming for the weekend. It also meant that she would need to buy three gifts, one from each of the girls. It was getting increasingly difficult to find appropriate ones and buying one large gift, had, on the one occasion she had tried this, been met with undisguised surprise. That was the best interpretation she had been able to put on the parent's response.

Alex was also unhappy with his day. His interaction with George had made him grumpy, especially when he recalled the wording on the 'Change of Use' form and realised that it could be interpreted as encompassing all of the buildings in the yard. He hadn't spotted it at the time but now he wondered. Did George have designs on all the out-buildings or was Alex mis-remembering what was written? Emily thought about it and wondered, if that was the case well, was it such a bad idea? It wouldn't do any harm to have the option of converting them to some purpose. Alex reluctantly agreed but still felt that he was being manipulated, and that, he didn't like.

CHAPTER TWENTY ONE

Just after 9am Anna arrived at St Peters and was met by an eager Sophie who had been busy borrowing whatever she could lay her hands on, to assist with cleaning and prepping her new room for decorating. As nurse manager, Colette had taken the pragmatic decision to let Sophie do as she wished, and move rooms. Despite the room not being suitable, in the clinical sense of the word, she was wise enough to realise that any risks were completely mitigated by the boost to Sophie's mental state. She also agreed with Sophie that the facilities available in her old room could be much better utilised by someone else, and to the benefit of St Peter's finances.

After a brief discussion, as to what they were going to do, Anna commenced attacking the heap of carpet that she and James had pulled up the day before. With a Stanley knife, she sliced it into manageable pieces and piled it in a heap by the door. With a long-handled brush Sophie set about knocking all the spiders' webs off the windows and then swept all the accumulated debris off the windowsills and radiators onto the floor. Once that was cleared up they worked at taking up the lino, Sophie pushing it upwards with a garden hoe and Anna peeling it back and snapping bits off. Most of it unstuck easily but the odd patch defied them, requiring a hammer and chisel. As they worked Sophie asked, "What makes you so keen to help with all this?"

"Why not? I love decorating. I haven't been able to do any for a while. My place is only small and it is all 'done'. So, for me, this is great fun. I love making a difference, turning a mess into something pleasing."

"Okay, I understand that but I meant why help with St Peter's?"

"Well, there again, I like making a difference and this place is really worth saving. James has been going on about it for years but I hadn't been here since I was a child, playing in the woods and, of course, to the odd fete."

"Fete, what was that like?" asked Sophie, interest piqued.

"For a child they were great fun. There were stalls of all kinds from the W.I. crafts to fairground type 'try your luck' ones. One year there was even a carousel."

"Really! Did they make much money do you know?"

"I have no idea. They used to have Easter Egg Hunts too."

The two women grew silent for a moment, thinking.

"The Easter Egg Hunt would be quick and easy to resurrect," said Sophie, pulling her phone out of her pocket and starting to tap. "When is Easter?"

"This year it is 21st April. We could really do with something sooner than that."

"How long would it take us to organise a fete?"

As they worked, watched by the black cat, they chatted happily about what they could do and how. Mid-morning, Colette appeared to see how they were getting along. The two mugs of tea she had brought with her were gratefully received. Seeing the heap of rubbish, she went and got them some old laundry bags and a trolley. If they put it all in the service lift and sent it down she would get one of the staff to get rid of it for them. Before Colette left, Sophie pointed at the cat and asked, "What is the cat's name? Do you know?"

"Oh, that is Horace. Not sure what he is doing in here. He rarely comes inside."

Having drunk their very welcome cups of tea, Sophie and Anna went into the en-suite and took a screwdriver to the partition. First, they removed the panel and then unscrewed the brackets that had secured it to the wall and floor. With the partition out of the way the room looked a lot bigger.

After lunch they cleared up all the rubbish and started stripping the wallpaper. Like the lino, some of it came off easily and other bits didn't. Some of it came away clinging to bits of plaster, much to their annoyance.

* * *

Louise, having obtained permission to find new tenants for the charity shop and also to act on behalf of St Peter's, rang the shop owner. After a brief explanation she asked if they would be amenable to forgoing the remaining rent, if a new tenant could be found. Yes, they would. So, having expressed gratitude on behalf of St Peter's she called the charity shop to make herself an appointment for the following day, when Nathan would be safely at nursery, to take a look around the property. She also gave Alex a call to arrange to look round his old flat. Finally, she rang Much Meddling's estate agency and made an appointment with Gerald.

* * *

As the afternoon wore on, Sophie and Anna started to talk about what they needed to do next, to get Sophie's new room habitable. Firstly, they needed to clean the floor. So, a mop and bucket were obtained and they gave the wood floor a clean. It looked great wet, but dull when it dried. It could really do with a sand and polish, but they had no money to hire anyone, or the equipment, to do that.

"Well," said Sophie ruefully, "it isn't as if I will be walking about on it. It will just have to do. Let's see if Colette has some curtains for us and then we can think about wallpaper and paint colours."

* * *

Meanwhile, Lady Agnes was offering James and Emily tea and cake. James had arranged the meeting to ask Lady Agnes some questions regarding her marriage. James explained that, after she had given him permission to check the church records for her Wells' ancestry, he had become curious as to her marriage as he could find no record of that. He felt uncomfortable asking but for him to thoroughly convince Alex that Lady Agnes was related to him and that she meant his children no harm, he needed proof that she had actually married Lord Earnshaw.

Lady Agnes smiled, as best she could following her stroke, and said, "Gre...na...Gree...n." Then she pointed to a folder on the table, indicating that James pick it up and open it. Inside he found some typed sheets and a green wedding certificate dated, November 3rd 1980. Richard Charles Chippendale Earnshaw, bachelor age 27, son of Lord William Earnshaw had married Agnes Clarissa Worsley, spinster age 25, daughter of Clive Robert Worsley.

With it was a photocopy for James to take

with him. The printed sheets had presumably taken Lady Agnes some time to prepare. She had done it with the intention of explaining the circumstances of her elopement and in an attempt to anticipate any of their questions.

Emily was impressed. She had never known anyone who had eloped. It all seemed so romantic, two 'star-crossed lovers', but reading through the pages she realised that it had been anything but. "I am so sorry, that must have been terrible for you."

There was a knock at the door and in walked Simon and Trevor. The atmosphere immediately changed. Lady Agnes was not happy to see her son but unwilling to make an issue of his arrival in front of guests and her grandson, who ran into her arms. Simon smiled briefly at Emily and James and then said to his mother, "I'm not stopping. Suzanne will pick him up, if that is okay?" With that he left. Emily and James thanked Lady Agnes for the information, made their excuses, and followed Simon out.

Outside in the car park Simon turned to James and, with a hint of annoyance, said, "I was going to call you this afternoon. The board have agreed to pay. Yes, please do your act for us. I will send you the details. Bye." With a nod at Emily and a, "Bye Mrs. Wells," he climbed into his car and drove off.

Emily turned to James, "Why wouldn't they pay you? They must know that your act is to raise money for St Peter's."

"Exactly, Simon seemed to think that as the money was coming back here anyway it was daft having to pay! We had quite a disagreement about it."

"Oh, was that why he left the vicarage scattering gravel the other week?" asked Emily, the penny dropping.

"It is the only time he has visited so, I guess so."

* * *

Once Anna had left for the day Sophie went for another look at her new room, trying to decide what she would like, décor-wise. She was torn between something traditional that would suit the room and something more modern that suited her taste better. However, she wasn't certain what that was. She was also conscious that, although she was probably going to pay for the materials, the room would be best served by being appropriate for future occupants too. She liked the proportions of the room and the cornicing and ceiling rose. She particularly liked the casement windows. Part of her liked the idea of living in a stately home and wanted to retain that elegance. She also didn't want to detract from the view, which was superb. Looking at her watch she realised that if she didn't get down to the dining room soon she would miss her dinner. Pulling the door to behind her she headed down the corridor and turned right towards the lifts.

She was surprised to be confronted by a little boy, who was staring at her from further down the corridor. He was outside what she believed to be Lady Agnes's room, the door of which was open. As she waited for the lift he came towards her.

"Hello, I'm Sophie. Who are you?"

The little boy grinned and said, "I'm Trevor. Why has your chair got big wheels?"

Children, they were so direct. "That is because I need them to get about. My legs don't work so I can't walk."

"Gran's chair has small wheels."

"Oh, I see. Can your gran walk at all?"

"Yes,"

"Does someone push her in her wheelchair?"

"Yes."

"Well, I push myself and the big wheels make it easier to do that," and Sophie demonstrated. "Would you like a ride?"

Trevor looked at her with big round eyes and nodded gently. Sophie turned her chair round and instructed him to stand on the two bars at the back and hold onto the back of the seat. She then carefully propelled the two of them up the corridor and back. Trevor laughed his head off. Down the corridor a lady, slightly younger than Sophie stepped out into the corridor, "There you are. Come on we need to go now. Say goodbye to the lady," and to Sophie, "I am sorry if he was bothering you." With that she shepherded Trevor towards the stairs and left Sophie sitting by the lift.

* * *

That evening Emily was keen to show Alex the copy of the wedding certificate and tell him all about Lady Agnes eloping with Lord Earnshaw. "So, she really is a Wells' descendant," said Emily, "and she really doesn't mean the children any harm. She just wanted our help, as relatives."

"Wealthy relatives! Strange she never got in touch before."

"Oh, Alex! Lady Agnes hasn't been well for quite some time, probably since before your great great aunts died. The three of *them* obviously didn't initiate contact, otherwise you would have heard of her. The reason she eloped is probably the same reason that she hasn't been in touch. Have you any idea what it must have been like, being disowned by your own family, simply because you fell in love with the wrong person. Actually, we still don't know why the Wells and the Earnshaws fell out, all those years ago. It must have been something serious for both sets of relatives to be so against the marriage. You would think that there would have been someone, on at least one side, still willing to talk to them. It was only because of the sudden death of his parents, in a car accident, that he and Agnes left Kilmarnock. If there had been a will, Richard probably wouldn't have inherited. Had there been a will, he might have been disowned. Just imagine, what it must have been like for them, suddenly coming back to take ownership of Sycamore Park Hall, with all their relatives unwilling to accept them.

"My heart bleeds," said Alex dryly.

"Well, Lily seems to like Lady Agnes."

"But, not her son, Simon," Alex pointed out.

To distract herself, and calm down, Emily went to see Snokettee. One look at the three little kittens brought a grateful smile to her face. She crouched on the floor and picked up each of the kittens, placing them on her lap. With the three of then nestled in the crook of one arm she gently stroked each one in turn. All her irritations melted into nothing, and she sighed with contentment.

CHAPTER TWENTY TWO

With Nathan at nursery Louise, wearing a skirt and jacket, checked her appearance in the hall mirror and then stepped out of the front door. It was a bit chilly, but she wasn't going far. She would be indoors most of the time and she didn't want to be encumbered with a thick coat. Glancing up at the owner of two amber eyes, sitting in a tree by the gate, she grinned, memories of her cat, Ruby, providing a warm glow. Her first appointment being at St Peter's Charity Shop she crossed the road and headed up the high street. Stopping outside the building she inspected its frontage. The shop window and entrance could definitely do with a lick of paint but otherwise the doors and windows looked to be in reasonable condition. She let herself into the shop and introduced herself to the volunteer behind the counter, who shouted, "May," over her shoulder.

May, the charity shop manager, appeared with a gentleman who she introduced as the owner of the property, and invited Louise through to the back of the shop. As they went round the property Lou made notes and took the odd photo. On each level she drafted out a floor plan. There were three floors and some attic space. Out back there was a small yard, two to three parking spaces and access to the back street. She asked about heating and cooking facilities. Was there gas to the property and when was it last inspected? The owner informed her that as a rental property it had a current gas certificate. She asked several other questions which she remembered as being pertinent, from her purchase of Bode Well Cottage, and then thanked them for showing her around.

Next she let herself through the high street door into the forge yard and sought out Alex, who was busy shaping a horse shoe on his anvil. He gestured at a hook on the wall, and the bunch of keys hanging there. She took it, crossed the yard, climbed the stone steps and let herself in to Alex's old flat. It had been a long time since she had last visited, and her memory of it was vague, but it was noticeably different. All personal items had been removed. Most of the furniture, however, was still there but the place looked a lot bigger. It was light and airy and with a lick of paint it could be completely transformed. Some colour on key walls would make the flat really appealing and cosy. The kitchen would benefit from a new work top and tiles and the bathroom could do with the grout either whitening or a contrasting colour applying, to maximise its letting potential. Again, she sketched a floor plan and took some photographs to go with her notes. Having finished, she let herself out and stood for a moment at the top of the steps to scrutinise the yard. If it was cleared and swept properly, and it was obvious that a lot of the debris was from the work going on in the new charity shop premises below, the area could look really smart. Some planters and a bit of greenery and a bench or two for people to sit on would work wonders. There was also the potential for 4, possibly 5 more shop units, and maybe another flat above them. Enthused, she took the keys back to Alex and set off for her meeting with Gerald.

* * *

Colette had produced 3 sets of matching curtains for Sophie's new room. Sophie didn't like them particularly but they were clean, fit the windows, and were a light peach with a vaguely abstract floral pattern. Ironed, they would do. Colette had also brought a collection of wallpaper rolls left over from decorating other rooms in the home. Again, none of them appealed, but there wouldn't have been enough of them anyway to do the whole room. She would have liked the walls to be plain but, as they had been papered a number of times over the years, the surface wasn't in a fit state to just paint. The rolls of paper did give her an idea though. If the walls were painted and she just used random shapes of wallpaper on the patchy bits of wall she could perhaps buy a roll that she did like and use that. Crisply defined geometric shapes could work quite well and add a bit of fun to the place.

When Anna turned up to take her to a DIY store Sophie was thrilled to tell her that Colette had given them £100, out of petty cash, with which to buy supplies. She was keen to get going. After a bit of a struggle getting into Anna's passenger seat, which wouldn't go back as far as would have been helpful, she instructed Anna on how to dismantle her wheelchair so that she could put it into the boot. Negotiating a couple of cats, sitting in the drive, they set off, Sophie clutching one of the smaller curtains to match paint and paper against. She thanked Anna for agreeing to take her and said she would be really glad when she had her own car. It wouldn't be long. The 'Motability' people were bringing it for a test drive on Monday. If it was okay, she would be keeping it.

* * *

Louise gave Gerald her best smile, explained that she needed tenants for both the charity shop and a flat in the forge yard and presented him with her notes and the tablet which contained the photos she had taken. Gerald offered her coffee, and whilst waiting for the kettle to heat up, studied her paperwork. Placing coffee in front of Louise he sat down opposite her. "You are going to do me out of a job," he said, laughing. "There is barely anything left for me to do. The owners will need to sign contracts of course."

They chatted for a while, Gerald asking her questions, but there wasn't much that she hadn't covered. He would need to visit both properties and retake the measurements, but he had no reason to believe that what she had provided weren't correct. However, based on the details so far, he believed that he had a couple of potential tenants for the flat. The shop would take a little longer but he would phone round and make enquiries. Once he had visited the properties he would put both of them on-line.

After Louise had left, Gerald did some thinking. Again, he scrutinised her notes and looked at the photos that she had transferred to his tablet.

* * *

Back home Lou phoned Emily. She was keen to tell her the ideas she had for Alex's flat and also her thoughts on the other units at the forge.

"It seems such a shame not to turn the other buildings to use. The whole yard could be filled with craft shops. Tourists would love that. Plus a little coffee shop with tables in the courtyard would be a real draw. We would need a name for the arcade of course. Something punchy. Something that sums up what the area is all about."

"Gosh, you're all fired up. I haven't heard you this enthusiastic about anything for a long time," said Emily.

"Well, it feels good to actually do something again. I shall be so glad when Nathan starts school and I can get a job of some sort, something a bit more interesting than just working in a shop, which is all Much Meddling has to offer, otherwise I'd get a part-time job now."

"You don't want to work for me making ointments do you? Growing fruit, vegetables and herbs, and concocting stuff, along with looking after the triplets and Alex, keep me fully occupied. I could do with some spare time."

"No, you can keep your lotions and potions and your weird patients to yourself. I just want to use my brain again. So, what do you think about the yard?"

"Talk to Alex. It is his yard. Just don't be too pushy with it. He has had enough of that lately from the charity shop. Let him think it is his idea if you can."

* * *

At the DIY store Sophie clipped her wheelchair to a trolley and set off towards the wallpaper section, adjusting her angle of attack on the bends, as she got used to the unwieldy lump she was pushing. Anna wanted to help but Sophie insisted that she wanted to do it herself. It was yet another new thing she had to get used to if she wanted to be completely independent. She studied the array of papers on display, glancing down at the curtain on her lap, and grew disheartened. Then Anna produced a roll which was textured, but coloured in a bold cerise. It matched the curtain and, she said that it came in a variety of different colours. She led Sophie round into the next isle. Sophie's mood lifted. She really liked the wallpaper with its choice of strong colours.

"I was thinking," said Anna, "that if we chose three rolls in different colours and did as you suggested with geometric shapes…"

"Sophie's eyes lit up." When Anna showed her the 'End of line bin' she was ecstatic. She found a couple of rolls that she liked, for just 50p each and one from the shelf at full price. Having made up her mind to paint the entire room in white, for speed and simplicity she was thrilled with their purchase. They also bought some wooden beading strips to make borders for the shapes, and sundry other items, and headed for the tills, where it seemed that a couple of plants had also made their way into her trolley.

CHAPTER TWENTY THREE

Having spent nearly all the previous day painting Sophie's room, Anna was really glad that it was the weekend and she could give her aching shoulders a rest. Sasha was coming to stay and she had invited Emily and Louise to join them for lunch at The Three Wells pub. She hoped the meeting would satisfy their curiosity enough for them to leave the pair of them alone for the rest of the weekend.

At just gone 11.30, Sasha's car drew up to the kerb outside and Anna ran out to meet him. After a brief embrace she waited whilst he opened the car's back door and, reaching in, pulled out a large bunch of flowers, which he presented to her. Opening the boot, he lifted out his case and followed Anna into the cottage. Out of public view the flowers were dropped on a table and the case on the floor, where it was quickly joined by Sasha's jacket, as the pair headed for the stairs.

* * *

At 1pm Sasha, with a nervous Anna

sitting beside him, said, "Okay, are you more worried that your friends won't like me, or that I won't like your choice of friends?"

"I really don't know why I am so nervous. You are all really nice people and I don't see why you shouldn't get along, but I feel like a teenager again. Isn't that silly?"

"And there was me, thinking you were," he teased.

The door opened and in poured Louise and Emily who proceeded to gush over Sasha and completely ignore Anna. "I'll get you two drinks, then," said Anna, gratefully removing her red face to the bar, whilst the others introduced themselves.

When Anna returned with a couple of glasses of white wine, Louise turned to her, with a serious expression on her face, and said, "I am very disappointed." With a quick glance at Sasha, she said to Anna, "What is the point… of a French man, with a Yorkshire accent? Does he even speak French?"

"Yes, I do. My family moved here when I was 7. So, I am fluent in both languages. I switch to fit the occasion," he said, looking suggestively at Anna, making her blush and the others laugh.

Once their first course arrived, Anna felt more relaxed. The initial meeting was over and her friends and Sasha were all getting on like they had known each other for years. She had to admit that he was deliberately being more charming than was necessary, to ensure that her friends liked him, but she loved him all the more for that. Yes, she did. She loved him, and it came as a surprise. She realised that she felt comfortable and proud to sit by his side, and when he squeezed her hand under the table, she felt supported and connected: something that she hadn't felt for a long time and something that she hadn't realised was missing. She glanced at him, and he looked at her and smiled.

Sensing a 'moment' Emily said to Louise, "I believe I need the ladies. It must be a good two weeks since I was last here. Do you remember the way?"

Enjoying the 'moment' Louise proceeded to avidly smirk at Sasha and Anna, "No, but do let me know when you find it. I am sure I will need it at some point." Holding out her empty glass she added, "stop by the bar on the way back."

Hauling Louise to her feet Emily marched her away from the table. Heads together, they disappeared into the Ladies, both talking at once and giggling.

Sasha laughed, "Your friends are brilliant. I look forward to meeting their other halves."

When Emily and Louise returned to the table, their main course arrived and they spent the rest of the meal catching up on what they had all been doing, in relation to St Peter's. Sasha asked a number of questions. Whether out of interest as an architect, or just to show interest in what Anna was doing, they couldn't have said. However, he did raise one important question: was St Peter's a listed building and, if so, were there any grants available?

* * *

To entertain the triplets Alex took them for a walk up the crag. Passing up through the wood he made the children stop and look around at the patches of snowdrops that splattered the ground. The odd clump of daffodils stood tall amongst them, intruding. As they continued uphill Tansy startled a deer and sent it crashing away through the undergrowth. She ran hopefully after it, but it was soon lost to view. When they reached the stone steps leading up through the rocks to the top of the crag, Alex stopped and let the girls climb up ahead of him. He found Violet was struggling to get up the last of the steps. Puzzled, he realised that she was attempting to climb one handed, the other clutching a bunch of snowdrops. He explained that it was wrong to pick wild flowers and made all three children repeat, until they could remember the phrase, "In the country, we take only photographs and leave only footprints." If she wanted to pick flowers then they had snowdrops in the garden. Wide eyed, Violet then bemused him by setting off back the way they had come.

"Violet, where are you going?"

"I'm putting them back," and she looked

like she was about to cry.

"Oh, sweetheart, that isn't going to do any good, you can't put them back."   With that she burst into tears. Lily immediately put her arms round her sister whilst Tansy began jumping up and down, intent on landing heavily.

"Tansy, what are you doing?" asked Alex, feeling that he was losing control of the situation.

"Leaving   footprints,"   she   said determinedly, smashing her heels into the ground.

* * *

Sophie had a visitor. She didn't get many. St Peter's was quite a trek from her old home and although her friends had visited her in the beginning, the visits had grown fewer and fewer as time went by. Her riding friend, Lucy, had arrived unexpectedly and Sophie was delighted. The timing couldn't be better. Giving her new room a second coat would be much quicker with two. Although she was capable of reaching the top of the walls with the long-handled roller, she was finding it physically exhausting. She was also getting herself and her wheelchair showered with paint. Having persuaded Lucy to help, together they had finished the ceiling, and were now starting on the walls. If she could get the room finished this weekend, then she could hopefully move in on Monday.

Having caught up on her friend's gossip,

she explained about St Peter's and what she was trying to do to save it, and then she said, "I have just got to tell you this, there's this guy…"

Lucy lowered her roller, and Sophie continued, "He visits someone here. I haven't found out who yet, but we met when one of the cats tripped him up and he fell down the stairs. When I went to help him, and touched his hand… ooh!" and she grinned and closed her eyes dreamily.

"Tell me more, tell me more…" sang Lucy.

"Well, that's it. I have seen him a couple of times since but haven't been able to talk to him. He smiles at me though, which is good, because he was angry when we touched hands. Not with me, but with one of the other residents. Anyway, there is probably nothing going to come of it but I just had to tell someone."

"Ask one of the staff who he is. If you know who he is visiting then you will know where to lurk."

"No, I couldn't do that. I don't want the staff knowing I am interested in him. Besides he…" using her arms, she shifted her seat in her wheelchair. Not saying what was really on her mind she instead said, "He probably has someone, anyway."

CHAPTER TWENTY FOUR

Just after lunch on Monday a couple of St Peter's staff moved furniture, and then Sophie's belongings, into her new room. The corner which was damp had still to be painted, but Sophie didn't mind. Arranging her things, in the room that she had decorated, she felt more at home than she had in the institutional setting of her old room. It was more peaceful, and she felt more in control of her life than she had for a long time. Horace, curled up on the end of her bed, certainly seemed at home.

At 2.55pm she took herself down in the lift and sat by the front door. Spotting a bright red Peugeot approach up the drive she went out to meet it. It was brand new, and if she could get herself in and out of it and manage the hand controls, it would be hers.

With the driver's door open to its full extent, she manoeuvred her chair into the gap and deftly transferred herself into the driver's seat. The next part was more challenging, but with the 'Motability' man's instruction, she succeeded in removing the wheels from her chair and stowing them and the frame inside the car with her. Next, he got her to reverse the process, and get out again. This was irritating as she wanted to get on and drive, but she realised that she needed to be able to do both. It was better to do it for the first time, with help available. Afterwards, she had to admit that he had given her a number of valuable tips which made the process, with practice, slick and not too difficult.

Back in the car again, he got her to drive around St Peter's car park until she mastered the controls. It didn't take her long to adapt to controlling the brake with her hand. Strangely, she found it more difficult to get used to not needing to change gear, the car being automatic.

Going out of St Peter's gate and heading away from Much Meddling was a lovely feeling. When Anna had taken her for paper and paint, it had been the first time that she had been away from the home since she had been deposited there by ambulance. It felt liberating to be leaving under her 'own steam'! She couldn't wait to get rid of her Motability 'minder', nice though he was. So, she was rather surprised and annoyed when he directed her off the route which would take them back to the Motability Centre. Mentally she ran through her memory of where she thought they were going, in case she was wrong. Then when she was about to question him, he told her to head into a petrol station forecourt. Part of her instruction, it seemed, included filling the car with petrol.

He made her park far enough forward so that she could get her chair out, and also have enough room behind to reach the pump and far enough out to be able to access the petrol tank. Whilst she struggled her way through all this, he stood, seemingly oblivious to glares he was getting from other motorists, who obviously thought he should help her. Putting the hose back in its cradle Sophie suddenly realised with horror that she had no money. However, she needn't have worried, the man paid for it, stating that the car came with a full tank of petrol.

Having deposited him back at the Mobility centre and completed the required paperwork she set off, finally free.

After a lengthy drive around the local countryside, she made her way back to St Peter's. As she was getting out of the car, she realised that she was being watched. Simon had just come out of the front door and was making his way back to his car, which was parked not too far from hers.

"Is this yours?" he said, indicating the car.

"Yes, just got it this afternoon. Oh, you have no idea how good it is to be independent again."

"I'll bet."

"So, how are you? Is your hand okay, and

your knee? You took quite a fall the other day."

"Oh, I was a bit sore for a while, but they are okay now. Thank you for asking," he said.

She looked like she was about to say more but a car was coming up the drive. He recognised it as belonging to one of the staff. "Well, glad you are okay," she said. "I won't hold you up," and she pushed off towards the front entrance. It didn't appear as if she wanted to be seen talking to him. "Bye!" he said and got into his own car.

Sophie disappeared inside St Peter's, a wide grin on her face and a flutter in her stomach.

* * *

In the forge yard, work on the charity shop was progressing nicely. Gerald gave it a quick glance as he followed Alex up the steps to the flat. Inside, Alex asked him what he thought would help to maximise its rental value. Having been prepped by Louise, Gerald suggested a bit of colour, new work top and tiles in the kitchen and ideally a new bathroom suite with a power shower, but the flat could be let as it was. The difference would be about £50 a month. However, the update would be likely to reduce problems, so was probably worth it. He took measurements and photos and made notes. Then, as they stepped out onto the top of the steps he surveyed the yard and asked, "Have you thought of doing anything with the rest of these buildings? You've got a right little money earner here: just a thought."

"What do you mean? How much are we talking about?"

* * *

After dinner Sophie headed back to her room. Waiting outside the lift, was Trevor. He had been playing in the corridor and heard it arriving.

"Hi,Trevor. How are you?"

"Hi, Sophie", he said, brightly.

"Is that a ball you are holding? Can I see?" When he gave it to her she asked, "Can you catch?" and she threw the ball in the air a couple of times before tossing it carefully towards his hands. The ball dropped on the floor and he went and retrieved it. After a few attempts he managed to catch it. It took him longer to learn to throw it, so that Sophie could catch it. Then, Trevor was being called again, from Lady Agnes room, and it was time for him to go.

* * *

That evening, Trevor was keen to show his father what he had learnt. His throwing was a bit wild but his catching was successful most of the time. Simon was amused. According to Trevor, the fun lady with the big wheels had taught him.

CHAPTER TWENTY FIVE

O n the Saturday morning Emily was up early. Her parents were coming to stay for the weekend and would be arriving for lunch. It was a while since she had seen them and she was looking forward to it. Alex had agreed to take the girls to their friend's birthday party and whilst he gave them their breakfast Emily walked across the green to the store. She quickly filled her basket with the things she required and headed to the till. Jake scanned and bagged her items for her.

"Jake, I don't know if you have heard of the Well Blessing, or not."

Jake nodded, "Oh, yes. You feed the whole village then, don't you?"

"Yes. I am going to need a large amount of vegetables. How much notice will you need? It will be on Saturday 23rd March and, if you aren't working, you are very welcome to come."

"Thanks, but I get paid more for working Saturdays. If you give me a list, a couple of weeks before, I will have it ready for you to collect on the Thursday of that week, if that is okay."

"Yes, that is perfect. Thanks."

As Jake attended to his next customer Emily headed for the door and held it open to allow Mr Swire to enter. He hobbled into the shop but then, as she left, he followed her out again. Wringing his flat cap in his fists and working his jaw, to get his dentures under control, he looked earnestly and semi-accusingly at Emily.

"Summats not reight love."

"Look, I've told you before; you need to go to the doctor's."

"No. Not me! 'Aven't you seen t' cats? They're all o'er't shop."

"No!"

"Well, maybe not so much at your end o't village, but you need to take note and do summat about it. AND SOON! Any road, 'ave you planted them seed potatoes I giv ya? Ya wanna git on wi it or they'll be o'er chit. Bye."

* * *

At the Charity Shop the volunteers were busily ferrying stock from the back of the shop round to their new premises in the forge yard. May was in her element directing operations. She couldn't wait for Sunday. With the old shop closed they would empty it and shut it up for good. She could then make final arrangements in the new shop where there was much more room to display items, and that was what she loved best. Being situated in a yard meant that they would also be able to put stock outside when the weather permitted. Posters had been made advertising the change and were now plastered all over the high street window. The new shop would open on Monday. Already there was interest. People passing had stopped and read the posters and some had ventured in to enquire, voicing enthusiasm for the new site.

* * *

With the arrival of her parents Emily forgot about her encounter with Mr Swire. Greeting them, feeding them all, and dressing the girls for their friend's party meant that it was 3pm before she felt she had time to breathe. With Alex and the girls out of the house, she made a pot of tea and sat in the living room with her parents, catching up on their news. They were well, and looking forward to a trip to Paris they had planned, later in the month.

* * *

At St Peter's Simon was trying to appease his mother. He had brought Trevor with him again and Lady Agnes understood perfectly well, why.

"You think, I wo... dis...in'erit...you, be... cause...of...Tre...vor. Wrong. I can...leave it...in trust...for...him!"

"What. That's ridiculous. He can't run this place and who would manage it in the meantime – your so-called management committee aren't doing a very good job, or you wouldn't be about to go bankrupt."

"You could...'elp."

"Me. I know nothing about it."

"You... could... learn."

"There is just no talking to you. Where's Trevor?"

"Pro...bab...ly with Sophie. She nice girl. She...'elp, every...one, des...pite...her...prob...lems. Maybe...I ...leave...St... Pee...ters...to... her!"

* * *

When Alex and the girls returned, it was obvious that the children had enjoyed the party. They ran off into the living room to tell their grandparents all about it. Alex, however, raised his eyebrows and gave a deep sigh. There had been a clown at the party. Possibly not the best idea for three-year-olds, as three of the party goers had cried: not the triplets, he was quick to add. They, however, had nearly made the clown cry! Firstly, Tansy didn't understand the slapstick element of his act and physically went to his aid each time, until Alex restrained her. Then, when he performed the odd trick, Lily ruined it by shouting 'it's up your sleeve' and similar. Finally, the clown had a disc with animals on it. When he spun it, the top halves of the animals stayed put and the children had to guess what animals' bottom half it would stop at, making funny mixed animals. Before the wheel finished spinning Violet had told them all the answer, three times! The clown packed up after that and left.

"I love my girls, but sometimes they can be excruciatingly embarrassing," bemoaned Alex, "other parents look daggers at you if you clamp your fist over your child's mouth and pin them to the floor! Plus, I didn't have enough limbs to control all three of them."

That evening, with the girls in bed, Emily and her parents and Alex settled down in front of the living room fire with a glass of wine each, and chatted. When the conversation got round to St Peter's and what was happening with the forge yard, Emily let Alex explain. Having seen the work that George had done he had been impressed and his initial dislike of the retired builder had morphed into grudging respect. Alex surprised Emily by enthusiastically telling her parents of the work and its progress and then he dumbfounded her by saying, "You know, I've been thinking. If we converted the other buildings too, then we could probably bring in around £30,000 a year in rent."

Emily managed to control herself whilst silently sending a prayer of thanks to Lou, for whatever it was she had done, to prompt Alex's change of heart.

CHAPTER TWENTY SIX

On Monday morning, the St Peter's Charity Shop opened in its new home. A steady stream of the curious made their way into the yard, which on its own was a draw: very few people had ever seen what was behind the large wooden high street doors. It was a bright, sunny day and the coloured glass items, that May had deliberately put in the shop window, sparkled and bounced light off the brass ones. She had placed a metal bistro set outside the door and leant an old bicycle against the wall. A collection of wicker baskets and large terracotta plant pots lined the entrance and guided customers through its doors. Inside, there were display shelves for ornaments, crockery, books, toys, and linens etc. A couple of armchairs by the bookshelf meant that people could sit comfortably and read. A series of old paintings depicting Much Meddling dotted the walls and helped legitimise the shop's existence and tie it to its setting. May understood that the shop, in a way, represented Much Meddling. It recycled its history, and she wanted the shop to reflect that, to make the inhabitants proud of their heritage and have pride in their legacy. She beamed with satisfaction, every time the till rang with another sale, and planned all the things she could do to maintain the momentum of the current sales, once the initial curiosity had passed.

* * *

Over the weekend Simon had been thinking. He had bumped into Sophie again on the way out. Having just returned from a trip out in her car, she had been busy shooing one of his mother's cats away from the driver's door, of his car. It had apparently been trying to spray it. When Simon appeared, it had sauntered off, back towards St Peter's: its tail in the air, gesticulating like a raised middle digit. Sophie had seemed pleased and eager to engage him in conversation, until a member of staff appeared in the car park. Had she been flirting with him? He thought back on their different encounters and thought she probably had. He had to admit that he was attracted to her, and it seemed that his little boy liked her too. It seemed she had even bewitched his mother! Sophie was a bit younger than him, but not much, he thought. She appeared somewhat feisty, and he liked that. The more he tried to put her out of his head, the more he thought about her. He tried to tell himself that the idea was ridiculous. Still...

* * *

Louise, keen to find tenants for the flat and the old charity shop, popped into the estate agency to see what Gerald had achieved. He had a couple of viewings booked for the flat, but hadn't yet found anyone interested in the shop. He thought for a moment and then said, "Right now, I need to get these details finalised and online," indicating details of some properties on the desk in front of him. "I was going to make some calls this afternoon to other agencies, but would *you* like to ring them?"

Louise was surprised but delighted. Gerald unpinned a list of agencies from a notice board behind him and she practically snatched it out of his hand.

"You can use that phone over there. Louise, make *sure* you include the third one down."

Puzzled, she looked at the name, which seemed familiar, but she couldn't think why. She was about to ask Gerald but he had picked up his own phone. Louise settled herself by the phone he had indicated, and punched in the number. When it was answered she said, "Hello, my name is Louise Parker, I am calling from Much Meddling estate agency. May I speak to Mr Anthony Newton-Smith please?"

"May I enquire what it is about, please?" said a female voice.

"We have a shop with 3-bed

accommodation for rental in Much Meddling High Street, and we are looking for tenants."

"Oh, Mr Newton-Smith only deals with land sales. He works with the large building firms on development sites, and certainly not rentals. Can I help you? My name is Margaret Walker."

"Oh! really! My apologies! Yes, hopefully you can." So, Lou went on to explain about the charity shop. The lady took the details and said that she had two possible interested parties. She would call back if she had some news. Louise then worked her way through the list until all the agencies had the details.

Before she left, she thanked Gerald. She had more than progress with renting the charity shop to thank him for. Gerald smiled knowingly, and nodded, "You're welcome." He had more than a reduced workload to thank Louise for, hopefully, but first he needed to talk to his business partner.

* * *

Having dropped the kids at nursery, put away her shopping, cleared away the breakfast things and put on the washing machine, Emily went upstairs to make the beds and strip the one her parents had used. As she approached her and Alex's room she thought that she could hear noises, barely audible. She stopped and listened. Yes, quiet squeaks and rustlings could be heard. As she stood still, they stopped. She waited and listened. A couple of squeaks and some scampering began. Cautiously she peered round the bedroom door. There, amongst Alex's heap of shoes, three furry balls with white tipped black tails were attacking his slippers. Snokettee strolled over to Emily and rubbed against her legs. Emily bent down and picked her up. "You gave me quite a scare there," she said stroking the soft white head and peering into two beautiful big eyes. "I think we are going to have to start keeping some doors shut!"

* * *

After work Simon made a detour round by St Peters' and slipped a note beneath one of the wiper blades on Sophie's car. If she didn't want the staff to know about the two of them then that suited him just fine. If he was wrong, and she wasn't interested, then she could just text him and decline his invitation. However, he really hoped that she wouldn't.

* * *

That evening, a delighted Sophie sat in her car and pondered on the note she had just found, along with Simon's phone number.

Dear Sophie, Would you like to go out with me for a drink, or a meal, at The White Horse, Burnlees at 7.30 on Thursday? Simon.

Yes, yes, she would, but she wanted to think before replying. Heading down the drive she set off, as she had been planning, to explore more of the countryside and to be away from St Peter's for a while. As she drove she thought of how she could reply. Would he want to pick her up? That would be nice but then she didn't want the staff to know that she was going out with a resident's relative. She also didn't want them asking her about 'her date'. No, she would drive and if their 'date', she assumed it was a date, didn't go well, then she could escape.

On her way she detoured to Burnlees and drove into the car park of The White Horse. Although most of the car park was covered in chippings they were reasonably compact and she didn't think her wheels would sink. The entrance had a step but one which she would be able to negotiate. Looking at the double doors she realised that she would need help, but at least she could see that they were wide enough.

Back in her room she 'googled' The White Horse. It claimed to be wheelchair accessible; maybe it had another entrance. Helpfully, it had a photo of the toilets, which she had to admit looked okay. Satisfied, she texted Simon and agreed to meet him at The White Horse, at 7.30 on Thursday for a drink.

CHAPTER TWENTY SEVEN

At 9am Louise's phone rang. She could see that it was the estate agency. Hoping that Gerald had found a tenant or two she eagerly answered.

"Hi, Gerald. Is it good news? Have you found any tenants?"

"Not yet, but I do have two viewings booked for the flat. However, that isn't what I am calling you about."

"Oh!" said Lou, warily.

"I have talked to my partner and he agrees – we would like to offer you a job. We could do with an extra person, and you would be ideal. The details you put together for the shop and the flat and your telephone manner calling the other agents were impressive. You would need some training of course, but you appear to have a good grasp of the basics. What do you think?"

Louise had been secretly hoping but never actually believed that she might be offered a job. Having dreams in your head was one thing but she didn't expect them to come to fruition in reality. She had thoroughly enjoyed herself, collecting and collating the information at the shop and the flat, and talking to the other agents from the estate agency office phone but, despite her dreams, being offered a job for real had never entered her head. She must have been silent for some time as Gerald continued, "Never mind, it was just a thought…"

"No, er, yes!" stammered Lou, "but, I mean I'd love to, but I've got Nathan and I'd need to talk to Mike and…"

"Why don't you have a think about it. Talk to your husband and let me know. Part-time is fine. Our only stipulation would be for you to work every third Saturday, but we can negotiate that around any holidays, family commitments, etc."

"Okay, I'll get back to you. Thank you."

As soon as she put the phone down she rang Emily.

"This calls for a celebration," said Emily. "We need a girl's night out."

"I haven't said yes yet. I need to talk to Mike. He might not like the idea of me working every third Saturday."

"Mike will be delighted, if not for you, then with the extra money," said Emily. "What are they offering you – it isn't all commission is it?"

"Oh! I never asked. I was too surprised to ask any questions."

"Well, I suggest that you talk terms, before talking to Mike. He will be all over that aspect like a hot rash."

* * *

At St Peter's, Colette had just put the phone down. A care package had 'fallen through' and long-term accommodation was urgently needed for a young man with a head injury and a number of physical problems which made caring for him challenging. A room with over-head tracking would be beneficial. Colette called a couple of staff and asked them to prepare Sophie's old room, for occupation that afternoon. She then went and told Lady Agnes that they had another resident, funding for which would be made available by the end of the week.

Lady Agnes was relieved. This meant that the home would be able to continue paying the staff for an extra 3-4 months, provided there was no reduction in the current number of residents, of course. There were so many things that needed to happen to save St Peter's, but this was a reprieve, one of many that she prayed for. Mainly she hoped for a change of heart by Simon. She knew that was unlikely. Even as a child he had always wanted to get away. His brother had too. Thomas had taken himself off to Australia at the first opportunity, and stayed there. He was now married with two children, which she saw only rarely. Video chats just weren't enough. Maybe, without St Peter's, it would have been different. Had she driven away, first Thomas and now Simon? Was this obsession with St Peter's really worth it? She had her doubts. Then she thought of all the good that the home had done over the years. The thought of giving it up was an emphatic 'No'! She couldn't do that. Why? She didn't understand. That was just the way it was.

* * *

James was a little apprehensive. He had performed his comedy routine many times on the Comedy Caravan Club Circuit but this was different. This time his audience hadn't chosen to be there, their work had done that for them, and, worst of all, they would be sober. He wasn't sure what the occasion was for, some sort of company presentations, lunch and then entertainment – him! He wasn't certain why he had been chosen, other than the probability that Simon had promised him *gratis* and then, when it was too late to get anyone else, told them they would have to pay. It didn't bode well. However, the majority of his audience would be unaware of that and hopefully gracious in their welcome. He took a deep breath, stepped through the large revolving glass doors into a spacious glass and metal atrium and headed to the reception desk.

* * *

Sophie was in her room desperately looking through her clothes for something to wear. She didn't have much. Since coming to St Peter's there hadn't been an occasion that required her to dress up. Most of her clothes were at home. Perhaps she should have them brought over. This room had loads of cupboard space and her flat would need clearing out soon anyway. She must call her estate agent again, and chase them for news. She realised that there had been no feed-back from the viewings that were supposedly booked, and nothing proposed that would be suitable for her to move into. She had let things slide. Her thoughts had been too much on raising money for St Peter's and not enough on her own situation. Now she had a car she could easily go and view properties. Perhaps she should get another agent. There was a knock at her door. It was Colette. She thought that Sophie might like to know that they had someone for her old room and to thank her for being helpful, by giving it up. Sophie was pleased. In fact she was thrilled. It felt good to have helped.

* * *

James' routine had got off to a bit of a rocky start. Having been introduced as the Irreverent Reverend his audience seemed a little bemused as to why a vicar was trying to make them laugh. Once he had worked his way through his dog-collar jokes and they realised that he was trying to amuse, as opposed to convert them, they got the idea. Simon, it seemed, had been a little uncomfortable when James started his routine, apparently feeling responsible, having booked him. Simon laughed loudly, and at times inappropriately, in an effort to get those around him to join in. James found this distracting and irritating but as his act progressed, and his audience laughed spontaneously, Simon quietened down.

"I wasn't always a vicar. I used to be a fireman, until I injured my back. That was a whole different life. I loved it. I also loved the reaction I got when I told people that I was a fireman. It is an interesting contrast. I am the same physical specimen (he did a graceful twirl, arms outstretched) but when I tell them I am a vicar they look at me with either serene hope (looking angelic with big innocent eyes), or fear (shrinking backwards and biting his fingernails). They think that I am either going to solve all their problems, Huh, or reveal all their secrets (laughing and rubbing his hands with glee). Before, when I said I was a fireman, they would either, 'look me over' (giving his audience a smouldering look and taking-on a super-hero pose) and get flirty (he ran his tongue round his lips suggestively) or, try to out 'kudos' me by claiming pending applications to the SAS or similar. Now, when I tell people I am a vicar but used to be a fireman, the reactions are the same but in quick succession (and he pointed round the room, grinning wickedly at one or two of the women, in whom he had noted the reaction)." Everyone looked round to see who he was pointing at, and the guilty gave themselves away, making everyone laugh.

By the end of his act James found that he had been a resounding success. Members of the audience congratulated him and expressed their enjoyment, and a couple made enquiries about St Peter's. He handed out his card to enquiries about future performances. Best of all, the collecting tin, which he had left by the door, was a good weight when he picked it up to leave.

* * *

At 7.30 Sophie parked in The White Horse car park, pushed her door open wide against the wind, and swore as the rain hit her. Just as she reached over to pick up the frame of her chair a large black umbrella appeared and provided a canopy, over the gap between car and door. Simon was there; bless him, gallantly allowing her to assemble her chair in relative dryness. Conscious that he was getting wet, she tried to be quick. Irritatingly, in her haste she failed to lock one of the wheels in place first time, and was annoyed with herself for her incompetence. Eventually, she was in her chair and heading for the door. She slickly managed the step to the entrance and Simon held open the doors so that she could get inside. Relieved to be in the dry they both started laughing. Simon had booked a table for them.

"What can I get you to drink?" he asked
"An apple juice please."
"Crisps?"

"Okay. Yes. Cheddar and Sour Cream: if they have them."

As Simon stood at the bar she studied him. He looked different somehow: more relaxed, more himself. Although she couldn't know what that was, she thought he seemed more confident, away from St Peters. Visiting a relative there, she understood would be stressful. Perhaps he would tell her in his own time. She wasn't going to pry. As he talked to the barman, he laughed, easy in his manner. When he picked up their drinks and headed her way, he grinned at her and she grinned back. This was going to be okay, she thought.

CHAPTER TWENTY EIGHT

After church the Wells family had a quick lunch and headed over to the forge yard. Having decided to convert the rest of the buildings Alex was keen to sort out all the stuff he had in storage there. The personal belongings from his flat had been moved across the yard, along with some of his Great Great Aunt Myrtle's things, that he hadn't had time to sort through when emptying her home, Fare Well Cottage. With the girls happily tearing round the yard on their tricycles, Alex and Emily made a start on the pile of boxes that contained Myrtle's old things.

* * *

At 1pm Sophie arrived at The White Horse for her second date with Simon. Their first date had gone well and she had really been looking forward to having Sunday lunch with him. Although they had talked for over two hours she had realised, on her way home, that *she* had done all the talking. He had plied her with questions and she had answered. She had asked her own questions but he had quickly followed up with another enquiry about her. She knew next to nothing about him. Still, she could ask him today.

Simon was already there and, she noted, appeared as keen as her. Again he waited whilst she got out of her car and held the pub doors open for her. They settled at their table.

"Would you like to share a small bottle of wine?" he asked.

"Thank you, but I don't drink. An apple juice for me please, and a glass of tap water."

When Simon went to order their food and get their drinks Sophie glanced around the restaurant. At a table, at the other side of the room, she was horrified to spot Anna, having lunch with a man. They were deep in conversation but if Anna went to the ladies she would have to pass Sophie's table and couldn't fail to spot her. Sophie tried to reason with herself that it didn't matter if she was seen with Simon. Anyway, Anna might not recognise him from St Peters. After all, Anna hadn't visited often. Why should she know him?

As Simon headed back from the bar, he noticed the look of concern on Sophie's face and followed her gaze. He spotted Anna. He didn't know her well but having grown up in Much Meddling he had seen her about, and he was fairly certain she would know him. Sophie hadn't seen him look, but when he reached their table he asked her what was wrong. She hesitated but then, when he thought she was going to confess, although he didn't know why she should know Anna, she said that she didn't like sitting so close to the ladies and could they move to the table in the alcove. Also keen to move, as he didn't want his mother finding out that he was seeing Sophie, he agreed. After a discrete conversation with the staff, they relocated.

* * *

Anna and Sasha had just finished their main course of roast beef and Yorkshire pudding and were trying to decide whether to have dessert. They studied the menu and argued with their consciences and decided to compromise by sharing a sticky toffee pudding. She said she would order it, along with coffee, on her way to the Ladies. She had been putting off going, but needs must, and looking up she was relieved to see that Sophie and Simon's table was empty. She had seen them come in. The moving of a chair or two to assist access had made the whole pub aware of their entrance. Seeing Sophie with Simon was puzzling. She didn't see them as a couple and yet they looked very intimate. Why Sophie would want to be with him, when he was so opposed to saving St Peter's she couldn't imagine. Annoyed, she didn't want to talk to Sophie, and certainly not Simon. So, with Sophie and Simon having apparently left, she confidently walked to the bar, placed her order and headed into the Ladies.

With Anna in the Ladies, Sophie raised her head and noticed that Simon appeared to have been keeping his head down too. He looked up from the menu he had been studying. Their food arrived, quickly followed by a dish of horseradish and a jug of gravy. To Sophie's annoyance, Simon asked for some mustard. As the waiter went to pick some up, from a shelf by the bar, he did a little dance with Anna, emerging from the Ladies. Apologising to her, as he went, he led her eyes right over to Sophie and Simon's table. There her eyes locked first on Sophie's, then Simon's. Anna, shocked, walked halfway to their table but then said, "Hi, nice to see you. I won't intrude. Enjoy your meal," and quickly returned to Sasha who had witnessed the exchange and was keen to know what was going on.

So, Anna told him all about Sophie's fund raising to save St Peter's and Simon wanting to sell it and the strangeness of seeing the two of them together. Judging by their faces they hadn't wanted to be seen. Simon was being so horrible to his mother, what on earth did Sophie see in him; she knew full well that Lady Agnes wasn't getting on with her son. It didn't make any sense. Could love be that blind? If that was what this was?

* * *

Alex and Emily had worked their way through two of the nine boxes at the forge. Myrtle had a lot of old documents, letters and photographs. They went back several decades. Alex sorted through them, arranging them in piles, some for saving, some for further scrutiny and some for throwing. The latter pile Emily glanced at, as a final check, before taking the items outside to the bin. With the photographs, they had to make a determined effort to just put them to one side for when they had time to look at them properly. Now, they had too much to do. The girls were getting bored of playing in the yard and would soon need either Alex or Emily to provide some diversion. As Emily ran her eyes over yet another document, she did a double-take. This was a copy of the solicitor's letter she had found amongst the St Peter's papers, of a donation of £72,000 to St Peter's. So, the 'M' in the signature must have been Myrtle, and not Millicent, as she had surmised. She showed it to Alex. Why had Myrtle left money to St Peter's when she died? He couldn't believe it. Yet here it was in black and white: a Wells giving money to the Earnshaws. For a while he held onto the paper, deep in thought. "Why was Lady Agnes never mentioned? Do you think there are going to be any more clues amongst this lot? It is going to take us ages to go through it all.

* * *

Sophie hoisted her legs into the foot well

of the car and Simon waited until she had dismantled and stowed her wheelchair on the back seat. As she was reaching for her seatbelt he tentatively leant in, made eye contact, and then gently pressed his lips to hers. Feeling her hand caress the back of his shoulder and her willing response, he ran a finger down the side of her neck and stopped, just short of her cleavage. As she leaned into him, he pulled away, "If you would like to follow me, I know a beautiful little secluded spot, where we can be alone."

She followed him out of the car park and up into the hills where he drove off the road and up a track and stopped under a tree. She pulled in beside him and waited. Leaving his own car, he got into her passenger seat. Then he reached down, found the catch and slid her seat back as far as it would go. Next, he undid her seat belt and reached over and kissed her. It was awkward, but neither of them minded. For Sophie, being physical with someone again, and having someone want her was dizzying. Having her body respond, deep down, when half of it was numb, was exhilarating and reassuring. For Simon, being intimate after so long on his own was challenging. He didn't want to rush her, or heaven forbid frighten her. He also had many questions.

Feeling that he was struggling to reach from the passenger seat she put her hands at her sides and hitched her bottom so that she was slightly sideways in her seat. He grinned and then reached round her to the seatback control and rapidly turned it so that her seat tilted slowly backwards. To his dismay Sophie started to laugh uncontrollably. When she was able to speak again she apologised, "I'm sorry, but it's just like being at the dentist."

CHAPTER TWENTY NINE

On Tuesday, there was another meeting at St Peter's. This time Anna drove, picking up James, Emily and Louise on the way. Anna was bursting to tell them about seeing Sophie, apparently on a date with Simon. The others were aghast. "What," said, Emily, "do you think his mother knows? Besides, he is married. Do you think Sophie knows?"

Anna shrugged her shoulders as she turned the car into St Peter's driveway. "All I can say is that they both looked guilty, really not wanting me to have seen them." A couple of cats sauntered across the gravel, as she brought the car to a halt.

Louise used the stunned silence to announce, "I have some news. Gerald offered me a job at the estate agency. I start next Monday. It is just part-time, but I can't wait."

"So, Mike was okay about it then?" asked Emily.

"Yes, he thinks it is brilliant, but ...listen to this...that valuation that we think was done of St Peter's by Simon's friend... turns out that the guy only deals in land development. I reckon Simon is looking to sell St Peter's, or at least some of the land, for housing."

"No, he wouldn't. That would be awful."

James, the steadying influence, unhappy about the conclusion, said, "We don't know that, you are just surmising. Please, do not go mentioning it at the meeting. Anyway, well done Louise for getting yourself a job."

As they got out of the car, everyone congratulating Louise, the cats disappeared down into the woods at the edge of the lawn.

With everyone settled, the meeting began. Lady Agnes opened the meeting and then handed over to Colette who asked everyone to report what they had achieved over the past fortnight.

James was able to tell them that he had been paid for his Comedy Caravan bookings and as a result of the last one had two more bookings and a potential third. If it was okay with Emily and Alex he intended using the Well Blessing ceremony to ask for donations.

Louise said that having been given a job at the estate agency she was now personally responsible for the letting of the old charity shop premises and the flat, and would do her utmost to find tenants as soon as possible. She started work officially on Monday but was already busy. Regarding the shop, she planned on doing a survey as to what sort of business the inhabitants of Much Meddling would like, so that she could target her sales pitch at appropriate businesses.

Sophie, not meeting Anna's eye, and giving side glances to the others for clues as to whether they knew about her lunch with Simon, reported that they had received a further £725.25p in donations plus some promises, which she wasn't counting until the money arrived. The growing amount was good but it wasn't going to be enough to save St Peter's. What she would like to do was to hold a fete, along the lines of ones she understood that St Peter's had held in the past. She also proposed it be held soon and suggested Saturday, 6th April. Everyone thought this was an excellent idea and that they should really get together and do that. She would also like to arrange other events such as an Easter Egg Hunt, if she was still here. Now she had her car she was able to house hunt.

"Oh, perhaps I could help you with that," said Louise.

Sophie looked like a rabbit in headlights but quickly saved herself, "I already have an agent, thank you."

Seeing her discomfort Emily began *her* report, "Alex and I have started clearing out the other buildings in the forge yard with a view to converting them into sales units and a couple more flats. Alex has agreed to give 80% of the rental, after costs, to St Peter's for the next two years."

Lady Agnes was thrilled and warmly thanked Emily.

May said that the sales at the Charity Shop were going well and that they had already taken double what they usually made in the old place, and, of course it was all profit, thanks to Emily and Alex's generosity. Emily couldn't help noticing that Sophie looked slightly miffed at this.

The meeting concluded with an agreement to meet at 11am on Friday to plan the fete. Everyone was to come armed with ideas.

As everyone left the room, Emily hung back, seeing that Sophie would be last to leave. With everyone else in the corridor Emily said quietly to Sophie, "I really hope you don't mind me saying, and it really isn't any of my business, but, in case you don't know... I feel... I must tell you... that Simon is married."

Sophie went ashen, "What?" she hissed. "How would you know?"

"His son goes to the same nursery as my girls."

Sophie stared at her, disbelief written all over her face.

"I am sorry. I really wouldn't make-up something like that."

Sophie turned and crashed her way out of

the room, looking daggers at Anna, as the little groups in the corridor stared after her.

* * *

Back in her room Sophie sobbed her heart out. Now it made sense. That was why he was happy to meet at the pub. That was why he got her to do all the talking, so he didn't have to talk about himself, and why he was trying to avoid Anna too. Why was he playing with her? Why would he do that? What about his wife? AND, he has a son: poor kid.

She wanted to call him and scream at him, to let him know what a scumbag he was. She picked up her phone and stabbed in the numbers. It rang and rang and then went to voice mail. No, she wasn't leaving a message. She would challenge him, oh, yes, she would challenge him, but she wasn't going to give him any warning. Having time to stew on the situation she decided that revenge, as they say, is a dish best served cold. Horace nuzzled his way onto her lap, and allowed himself to be cuddled, seemingly oblivious to the cascade of tears, and snot.

* * *

"So, that went well," said James sarcastically, as they drove home.

"I would have thought you would have been in agreement with telling her," said Emily.

"Yes, in principle. However, breaking bad news in the middle of a meeting probably wasn't the best way to go about it."

"When else could I have done it? I tried to do it quietly. How was I to know she would behave so dramatically? Besides, it *wasn't* the middle of the meeting."

"What would you have done," said Anna, "if it had been you? Said, 'Oh, thank you', and carried on politely chatting to everyone."

"I was only trying to help."

As they approached Bode Well Louise told them to keep going and let her out, outside the old St Peter's charity shop. Before getting out of the car she produced a clip board from the large shoulder bag she had been carrying. "So, you lot can be my first pollsters. What business do you think Much Meddling High Street is short of? What would you like to see in the old charity shop?"

"We don't have a shoe shop!" said Emily.

"Or a decent iron mongers. It is a real pain going all the way to Burnlees or beyond, for anything DIY related," said Anna.

"How about a fish and chip shop?" said James.

"Great. I'll put those down. If you come up with anything else, let me know." As she stepped out of the car and prepared to accost her first passer-by, the others watched on in amusement as, limping towards her was Mr Swire. James reached for the window control. The panes quietly slid into their door recesses. It made things a bit chilly but would surely be worth it.

Ten feet away Louise smiled brightly and said a polite and cheerful, "Good morning, I wonder if you would spare the time to answer a few..." She didn't get any further. Mr Swire kept walking and with an extended, bony finger prodded her backwards, until she stumbled into the gutter and sat heavily on the bonnet of James' car. With his face inches from Louise's, Mr Swire glowered at her, and said succinctly, "Bugger off!"

CHAPTER THIRTY

F riday soon arrived and with it a letter from the council informing Alex that Change of Use had been approved, and it did include all the buildings in the yard. The liberty that George had taken still annoyed him, but it did simplify matters and meant that they could proceed, with whatever he chose to do. He needed to talk to George and see if he was willing to do the work. The shop was doing well and Alex was finding that he actually liked having others in the yard and having access to the High Street, via the open gates. The fact that he was putting the unused buildings to use gave him a good feeling.

* * *

Emily was not looking forward to the fete planning meeting. She felt really uncomfortable at the thought of facing Sophie. The fact that the others openly thought that she had been stupid, didn't help. Anna, it seemed, wasn't looking forward to the meeting either, feeling guilty for having blabbed. If anyone had told Sophie, then it should have been her, and in private. James pointed out that probably Sophie wouldn't be happy about it either and would probably feel embarrassed at facing them all, and they should think of her. Louise was the only one keen for the meeting to occur. Rallying from her encounter with Mr Swire she had spent a couple of hours stopping passers-by and getting cold, but hadn't gained much in the way of helpful information. As a result she had turned to the internet and local social media, where it appeared that people were more willing to engage. They also had time to think about their responses. From the suggestions, there was a clear winner. As a result she had been making enquiries and had an interested party keen to set up business in Much Meddling and she would be showing them round the old charity shop that afternoon. If it met their needs then she would have completed her first letting.

When they entered the meeting room, Lady Agnes, the gardener, Colette and Sophie were already there. Sophie smiled tightly and made a point of looking each one of them in the eye. Lady Agnes didn't appear to notice but Colette gave the group an appraising look. Something wasn't right and this group was the cause. After Sophie's dramatic exit from the room on Tuesday, Colette had made a point of talking to Sophie, but could get nothing out of her. It seemed as though Sophie was trying to make the best of it, hopefully the rest of them would behave.

"So, what…are…we…go…ing…to do?" asked Lady Agnes. "Let's…hear…your…ideas. Sophie?"

All eyes on her she took a deep breath and said, "Having asked both Lady Agnes and the staff, I now have a good idea of what happened at previous fetes." At this point she distributed a stack of photographs depicting previous fetes. "Most of the stalls, signs and equipment you see are still here, in storage. So, we can recreate a lot of it. Mr Arkwright here, the gardener, knows where it all is. It might need a bit of a 'touch-up'. I also think it might be a good idea to show-case St Peter's, give people an idea of what work is done here, let people know how much it has helped people over the years, really push the need to keep the place going. With that in mind I have contacted a few relatives and ex-residents who are willing to volunteer their input."

"Have you thought about asking that mobility shop, can't remember their name, to set up a stall? Or the car lot, where you got yours?" said Emily.

"Yes, it had crossed my mind. How about the artificial limb people too? They could help with the three-legged race," said Sophie sarcastically.

"I am sure that the fire service would be willing to turn up. A fire engine is always a big draw," interjected James.

"Yes, yes, as are the firemen," added Louise, with a grin.

"I don't think 'firemen' is the correct term anymore," said Anna.

"Well, I'm not interested in the firewomen," said Louise.

"How about a raffle? That is always popular. Or a tombola?" said Colette.

By the end of the meeting they had plenty of ideas and had distributed jobs amongst themselves, including advertising. As Colette wheeled Lady Agnes out of the room and the others followed, Sophie followed closely behind and made her escape. The meeting was over and Emily was relieved, but it really wasn't going to be easy working with Sophie.

Passing the office, on their way out, they couldn't help overhearing raised voices. A man was arguing with a member of staff. Drawn to look as they passed, they saw it was Simon and the receptionist.

"It had to be here. This was the only place I left it parked yesterday evening and it has been locked in the garage all night."

"Well, if it was done here, I am really sorry, but I can't imagine why anyone here would do such a thing," said the receptionist.

Unable to hear anymore, without stopping, they continued out of the building. Instinctively they all scanned the car park for Simon's Mercedes. Luckily it wasn't far from

Emily's vehicle, so they were all able to walk casually past it, fanning out for a collective view of both sides. Simon's cause for complaint wasn't hard to discern. Someone had written 'SCUM' on each tyre, in white paint.

* * *

Louise was excited. She had dressed herself smartly in a suit, done her hair and make-up, and checked herself in the mirror. Satisfied with her appearance she did a few practice smiles, then picked up her bag and headed out of the door. She was early but wanted to give the old charity shop premises a look around before the prospective tenants arrived, and ensure that she was there to greet them.

Exactly on time, a car pulled up to the kerb and out stepped two men and a woman. Louise greeted them and addressed the older couple, "Hello, Mr. and Mrs. Basak, I am Louise Parker." Then turning to the younger gentleman, "and you are?"

"This is my son, Aslam," said Mr Basak. We are looking to set him up in a business of is own."

Louise shook Aslam's hand, "Pleased to meet you and welcome to Much Meddling. Shall we go inside?"

It didn't take long to show them round. She then waited in the front of the shop whilst they looked around on their own. They were mainly interested in the kitchen area, yard and rear access for deliveries. The shop and large room above would be used for meal service. If they were happy with the place then Much Meddling would have its own Bangladeshi restaurant and take-away. She couldn't wait to tell Mike. First, the Basak's needed to say yes. From what she could overhear, it was all sounding very positive. When they were ready to leave they thanked her and said that they needed to think about it but they would be in touch.

* * *

Sophie was feeling nervous. Half of her wanted to just, not go, but the other half of her was mad. At the end of their last date they had both agreed that they wanted to 'take things further'. The front seat of her car being a limited venue they had agreed that Simon would book them a room. The subsequent awkward conversation they had had about contraception now infuriated her. Yes, she could absolutely have children and she would love to. If he thought that because she was paralysed nothing worked, it did, just the same as any other woman. Now she realised that he hadn't been looking to a future with her, just checking whether the risk of pregnancy was going to be an issue. Seething, she took a deep breath and set off.

Simon was waiting for her in the car park of the hotel he had chosen. She smiled graciously as he waited for her to get out of the car. Then he held the door open as she wheeled inside. It was a lovely place, and expensively decorated. The booths all had large antique style mirrors making the room look larger than it was, and the lighting was subdued and concealed. The waiter led them to a bay with large pot plants, and removed one of the chairs so that Sophie could take her place at the table, which was laid in a cream linen cloth and napkins and what looked like real silver-ware. She was a little unnerved, feeling slightly under-dressed, but quickly remembered that she wasn't here to impress. The waiter poured her some water and then produced a small basket with a selection of breads and a sectioned dish with different herb butters. He then asked what they would like to drink and Simon said they would choose their food first. Looking down the menu she opted for the most expensive starter and main course and then when the waiter enquired about drinks, said sweetly, "Oh, just water for me, please."

Simon gave her a measured look and said, "I'll have the same. Thank you."

They chatted, Simon plying her with questions as usual. Sophie answered, telling him anything that came into her head, and biding her time. She didn't bother asking him any questions as she knew he would avoid answering them anyway. As the meal progressed she became increasingly flippant with her answers and Simon became increasingly uneasy. When their desserts arrived, she said, "So, tell me about you."

"Well, there isn't much to tell. I like playing golf and travelling."   "No, I mean something more personal."

"Well, and you are going to think I am a bit weird, I collect trench art." He was obviously expecting her to ask what that was, but she completely threw him by saying, "Tell me about your wife!"

The venom with which she spoke caused Simon to drop his spoon. Open mouthed he stared at her.

"Yes, your *wife*. Tell me about *her*."

"I thought you knew!"

"What? Do you think I would have gone out with you if I knew you were married? Do you think because I am in a wheelchair that I am so desperate?"

"No, no, of course I don't think that! Sophie, I am divorced." He watched as she processed her confusion and then studied his face for the truth.

With a little bit of hope she said, "Really?"

"Yes, for some time now."

"Oh, I am sorry," said Sophie, baffled as she remembered what Emily had said about Simon's son going to nursery with her girls. Emily, that interfering bitch. This was all her fault. "And, your *son*?"

"Yes, you are a real hit with Trevor. He can't stop talking about you." There was a long pause whilst Sophie's brain went into overdrive, pieces crashing into place.

"You are *Trevor's* father! Then, Lady Agnes must be your mother. *You*, are *the son*! The *monster* of a son. No!" In swift succession she threw her Eton Mess in his lap, pushed back from the table and left him behind with the bill and an audience of shocked diners. In the car park she did what she had planned on doing all along. She fed the contents of the plastic bag, which she had taken for the purpose, through the air vent of his car. During the meal she had surreptitiously bagged part of her fish course. It might take a day or two but Simon's car would need more than a dangly pine-scented tree to smell nice again. Recklessly she drove back to St Peters, barely concentrating on the road. When she slid to a halt in the car park, she sat for a while, not wanting to go inside, not wanting to meet any of the staff. After several minutes just staring into space, she thought she heard a mewing sound. She was about to open the door when a furry face appeared at the window. Horace was standing on his back legs and looking at her, "Meow, prrr…"

Despite herself, she smiled. As she carefully opened the door he dropped down onto all fours and waited patiently whilst she assembled her chair. Once she had transferred, he hopped up onto her lap, and stayed there until they got up to her room.

CHAPTER THIRTY ONE

Sunday was a lovely sunny day, but rather breezy and cold when the odd cloud flitted across the sun. As the Wells family strolled down the gravel path after the service at All Saints Church they found that Mr Swire and a couple of similarly mature Much Meddling ladies were waiting for them by the gates.

"We want a word wi' you two," began Mr Swire. "It's getting worse. Thiz cats every way ya look!"

"Ay, and not a bird in sight," piped up the skinnier of his two companions, whom Emily believed was called Astrid. The lady slid her wire-rimmed glasses down to the tip of her nose and peered over the top. She looked first at Emily and then up at Alex, "Summat's up. Its not bin like this since drought, in summer o' '74, when that fool Earnshaw insisted on doin' switherin' on far side o't village, and wind changed. Damn near burnt entire wood."

"Ay," said Mr Swire, chuckling. "He barely cleared any of 'is stubble but lost two barns. It were just fortunate that midden hadn't got dry and crusty; that would a burnt for weeks. Any road ee cleared all 't wildlife out o't wood into folks gardens...rabbit and venison pie a plenty that 'arvest."

At this point the third of the party, one of Emily's ointment 'patients', who was a pleasantly mild and timid individual who normally said very little, unless prompted, joined in. She had obviously worked herself up and grown impatient with the turn in the conversation. Arms folded and back straight she began crossly, "All that money's gone to yer 'eads. Not takin' care of what's important. It's Well Blessing next weekend. You'd better 'ave it sorted by then." Where upon she turned and headed out of the gate followed by Astrid. Mr Swire, business concluded, politely tipped his hat at Emily, then Alex and set off after the ladies. Then, incongruously, he tucked an arm through one each of the women and the three strolled off companionably down the high street together. Alex and Emily looked at one another, eyebrows raised, obviously with the same thought in their heads.

Guiding the children across the road they headed to the duck pond and Alex pulled some brown paper packets of squashed bread slices out of his pockets and gave a bag to each of the girls. They watched as the mallards motored over expectantly and waited impatiently for the paper-bags to be opened. After a couple of minutes Alex left them to it; it was his turn to make lunch. With Alex gone Emily went and sat on one of the benches. It usually took the triplets a while to finish throwing their bread. Having been instructed to tear it into little pieces and ensure it landed in the water served two purposes, firstly it was better for the ducks' digestion and secondly it prolonged the activity nicely. Emily always enjoyed this time: a little peace and calm and a chance to think, and lunch ready and waiting when she got home. Today, however, she couldn't help wondering what the little posse by the church gates had been on about. Yes, there did seem to be more cats about, but then there were always cats about in Much Meddling. Glancing round she spotted a couple of cats on the vicarage wall, sitting staring in her direction. To the right she caught the movement of a small figure daintily tripping along the church wall. To the left there was one sitting on the windowsill of The Three Wells. Turning round she could see a black tail sailing through the long grass: left to grow as a wildlife refuge, in the middle of the green. The more cats she saw the more disturbed she became. Compelled now, to check *all* her surroundings she looked upwards into the branches of the tree at her back. There, just above her head, was a familiar white figure, with a white tipped black tail. Snokettee ran down the tree's trunk and, jumping up onto the bench, climbed onto Emily's lap.

"What is going on, Snokettee?" Emily and cat looked at each other and bizarrely Emily felt reassured. Stroking the white head and sturdy back, she sighed, "I guess you aren't telling but I do wish you could talk."

"Snokettee," yelled Tansy, who had finished feeding the ducks.

Snokettee jumped off the bench and headed across the grass to the left hand side of the pond. Tansy followed and commenced running round in a circle. Then, to Emily's surprise she spotted three tiny movements: the kittens were there. As she approached, and followed Tansy's motion she couldn't help noticing a brown, dotted ring of toadstools. Then Tansy broke free of the circle and ran an adjoining ring. Changing direction again, Emily spotted a third. There were three separate rings. By now all three girls had joined in. Snokettee sat in the middle and watched.

"Girls, come here. Do you know what these are?" asked Emily. The children gathered round. "They are fairy rings. Don't touch them. You need to leave them alone for the fairies, okay."

"Fairies, fairies."

Job done, Snokettee led the party back across the street to Wishing Wells, the girls skipping and talking of fairies. Emily needed to talk to Alex, but mainly she needed to consult

Angelica's books. Were fairy rings a good or bad thing?

After lunch Emily headed into the front room and pulled a couple of Angelica's books down from a shelf. Finding nothing but a brief description of the natural phenomena splitting the rings into two types, those in wooded areas and those in meadows (both formed when the toadstools cast their spores outwards in a circle) Emily turned to the internet. What she found wasn't reassuring. Generally, it seemed that fairy rings were a bad omen and considered dangerous places for humans. The only good references she found indicated that some people believed it good luck to build a house on a fairy ring and others that sheep which ate grass grown on fairy rings thrived. Ridiculous! Why was she even looking? So, there were toadstools growing on the green.

Heading back to the kitchen she was surprised to hear all three children shouting at Alex and Alex angrily defending himself. Puzzled, she hurried into the kitchen to be met by Lily charging past her, then stampeding upstairs.

"What on earth is going on?" she asked looking first at Alex, then Violet and Tansy. They all started shouting at once.

"He broke them," accused Violet.

"Somehow they have managed to get their necklaces out of the wardrobe," said Alex.

"Put them back," demanded Tansy.

"Put them back Daddy, put them back!"

"No," said Alex, "they are perfectly good as they are!"

"No."

"No."

"Girls, stop it," snapped Emily. Then, looking at Alex, she continued, "What has happened?"

"They want me to put the periapts back on their necklaces."

"Girls," said Emily. "What does it matter? They look just as good, as they are. Daddy and I think they are better without the stones."

As Violet and Tansy started yelling again Lily returned at the run, arm raised, "No, Daddy. PUT THEM BACK." With an ear-splitting crash something slammed onto the stone floor and then skittered under the kitchen table, hit a leg and bounced back to lie at Alex's feet. Alex stared at it and went cold.

The girls were silent now and glowering at Alex. Emily stared at the object, the memory of a broken car seat, evoked. She looked at Alex. Eventually, in a cracked voice, he broke the silence, "Okay. I'll put them back." Silently, Lily bent down, gathered the Cats Eye, dusted it off, and pocketed it.

* * *

There was another text from Simon. Without even looking at it, Sophie deleted it.

She considered going out for a drive but, after her initial burst of freedom, she was now considering the cost of the petrol. Having chased up her estate agent she had a couple of viewings to look forward to and she needed what was left in her petrol tank for those. Picking up her tablet she had another look at the details of the properties. One was a flat, which looked okay but she didn't like the idea of being dependant on a lift. The second was a bungalow with a decent amount of room; it even had an accessible garden, but it didn't appeal. That was probably due to the décor which looked like it hadn't been touched since the 1970's. She tried to picture the rooms with plain walls and empty of the multitude of tiny ornaments and photographs that cluttered them. The bathroom would need completely re-doing. She couldn't bear the thought of using the dated bathing-aids that were already fitted. They were what she needed but they were personal items, and she needed her own.

A knock at the door interrupted her and she called out, "Come in." The door opened and in stepped Simon.

"Get out. I don't want to see you."

"Sophie, please let me explain. There are things you don't know." He hovered by the door, wanting to shut it but afraid it would alarm her if he did, afraid they would be heard if he didn't. "Just give me five minutes and then I'll go. I promise." She said nothing. "I really care about my mother. You have to believe that."

"Strange way of showing it!"

"This place is making her ill. The stress it has caused her over the years has been horrendous. You have no way of knowing. You haven't lived through it like I have. She hasn't had a break in nearly 30 years. She needs to retire and get some enjoyment out of life. Whilst she still can."

"She could if you'd help her, instead of trying to sell St Peter's out from under her *feet*."

"What?" Simon softly closed the door.

"Yes, everyone knows you had the place valued! How stressful do you think she found that: her own son!"

"I was only trying to show her what the place was worth and that she could retire and live comfortably."

"Yes, very comfortably and less bother for you when she dies! Any normal person would be supportive and help her as it is clearly important to her. Any normal person would just wait until she dies and then sell. Instead you are breaking her heart."

Simon sank into a chair. "Have you any idea what it was like growing up here?"

"No, I haven't, and I really don't care."

"I hated it. My brother did too: constantly surrounded by people who moved in funny ways and made strange noises. Half the time I was scared stiff, just getting up to our home on the top floor. I didn't understand that they couldn't help it. All these grounds to play in and none of it felt safe because I didn't know when I was going to meet one of the residents. My friends were scared to visit. At first they thought it was great, visiting the big 'castle'. Then they made excuses not to come, and teased me. My mother, who had sympathy for everyone else, didn't have any for me. She just told me not to be silly, that the residents meant no harm and couldn't help how they were. I should be glad that I was 'normal'. I didn't feel *normal*. The other kids didn't see me as *normal*. So, no, I don't want to keep this place. It only has bad memories for me."

"Simon, I'd like you to leave. You are an adult now. I am sorry that you *feel* you had a lousy childhood, but you are fortunate. As an adult you are *very* fortunate. You have money and you have your health. Go...and be grateful for that." She rolled across the room and held the door open. Horace strolled in and took up sentry by her side.

Slowly Simon got to his feet, "Sophie, I am so sorry."

"Go!" As he stepped into the corridor, he turned. She slammed the door in his face.

CHAPTER THIRTY TWO

With only a week to go to the Well Blessing there was a lot to do. Over the years Emily and Alex, Louise and Mike, James, Anna, and Richard had perfected what they needed to do to make the ceremony a success. Each had their own role. Alex, James and Mike dressed the wells, Louise baked the bread, Emily made the hotpot and Anna helped as needed. During the run-up Emily gathered the herbs and greenery for the well garlands, collected the meat from the butchers and the vegetables from the store. Alex checked the tables and chairs that were stored for the rest of the year in one of their sheds and one of them checked and washed the bucket in the well. Friday afternoon they all gathered in Wishing Well kitchen and made batches of dough for the bread. Water was drawn from the well especially for this. Using the well water for making both the bread and the hotpot was a vital part of the tradition. Making the batches of dough was hard work but it was no longer a stressful event and they all quite enjoyed it.

This year however, for Louise, it was different: she started her new job on the Monday. As she settled herself behind her desk at the estate agency the phone rang. She picked it up. It was Mr Basak. He had a number of questions that he would like her to put to the owner of the old charity shop premises. She wrote them down and said she would find out and call him back. When she did she was able to report that the owner would be happy for them to refurbish the kitchen and enlarge it by knocking through into the outbuilding at the back, and to clear the old wooden structures in the yard to make it more accessible. They also had permission to rewire the shop area and room above. They would meet the owner to discuss it and finalise details. If they could agree, then the Basaks would like to rent the property. In the meantime they would like a second viewing.

In the afternoon she had two viewings, arranged by Gerald, at Alex's flat. Hopefully one of them would want to rent.

* * *

On the Tuesday Emily set about checking and cleaning all the items needed for bread baking and hotpot making. This year she had her new giant teapot from the charity shop which she needed to clean and trial. It had a decent base to it so she was hoping that she could fill it and sit it on the range until it boiled, at which point she could add tea bags. The question was, how many? Choosing a mug which she thought looked about the same size as the ones that would be supplied by the pub, she filled it with cold water and then emptied it into the tea pot. She repeated this 27 times and then put the teapot on the range and waited. When it boiled she plunged 8 teabags in and stirred. A further 4 teabags and it looked a 'decent brew'. She poured herself a cup to test it and was satisfied. What she needed now was a giant tea-cosy. Perhaps she could knit one for next year; a tea-towel would have to do for now.

* * *

On the Wednesday Louise got a phone call requesting a second viewing of Alex flat and the Basaks completed the paperwork to rent the shop, paid a deposit and made their first 2 month's payments. Gerald had been really impressed by Louise's pro-active method of renting out the shop. Following her research she had gone to visit a number of restaurants of the type requested, the most popular being that owned by the Basaks. They were looking to expand and were thrilled to know that Much Meddling had effectively chosen them.

* * *

At Thursday's St Peter's meeting, Louise was delighted when Colette told everyone that the Charity Shop was officially 'off the hook' for any more rent for their old site. This meant that St Peter's was able to go ahead and get the roofers to start work on the area of roof over the side of the building housing Sophie's room and get the adjoining room usable. If the fete went well they would be able to get the boiler and heating updated to make the whole building usable: once the rest of the roof was done.

Louise said that she was hopeful of being able to let the flat in the yard soon. She had shown 2 prospective parties round and one was very keen but had questions. She hoped to have news soon.

At this point Emily chipped in that she and Alex had a number of items from the forge outbuildings that they were giving to the charity shop. This produced a huff from Sophie. Emily continued, "They are planning on sending some of it to auction, as they think they should get more for it that way. There are 2 sets of wrought iron gates and a Victorian Rose Arch which could fetch £800 - £1200. So hopefully, you will be able to get the heating sorted sooner."

"Or, you could just...put your hand in your pocket," sniped Sophie. Everyone stared at her. Unabashed she continued, "The millionaires are giving away their junk and we are supposed to be grateful!"

"Sophie!" warned Colette, "Yes, we are grateful. They are putting a lot of time and effort into this."

"Yes, and it would save us all a lot of time and effort if they just donated a few grand. They wouldn't miss it and it isn't as if they even earned it!"

In the stunned silence Emily pushed her chair back and stood. Mustering as much dignity as she could she picked up her bag and walked out of the room, determined that they wouldn't see her cry. As soon as she closed the door everyone turned on Sophie, all talking at once. Louise got up to chase after Emily, but as she passed Sophie she hissed in her ear, "You nasty little bitch."

"I was just saying what everyone else was thinking," said Sophie indignant and unremorseful.

There was a sudden bang on the end of the table as Lady Agnes thumped it with her fist. "Sophie," she said forcefully, her voice stronger than any time since her stroke. "The Wells family...are ve...ry good to...'elp...at all. I am grate...ful. There...is...a ...lot...you ...don't... know. Wells and Earn...shaws...'ave...long... his...tory. Emily and Alex...are...good...people. You...should...apolo...gise."

Seeing Lady Agnes angry gave Sophie pause. From the looks she was getting it was obvious that the others didn't all think the same as her. She needed to be alone. Deftly she spun her chair and headed out of the room. Leant against a wall in the corridor was Emily. Not having her own transport with her she had no where to go. Louise was trying to console her.

Looking pointedly at Sophie, she said, "Well, have you got something to say to Emily?"

Cornered, she begrudgingly said, "I'm sorry. I shouldn't have said that."

"Yes," said Louise, "What the Wells do with their money is none of your business. Besides it will take way more than they can afford to sort this place out. It needs to be self-sufficient to survive."

"I'm sure they can afford a boiler!"

"Stop it, Sophie. There is a lot that you don't know. Now, how about we all go back inside and plan this fete?"

After that, the meeting was strictly 'business' and they made great progress, everyone making an effort to be polite and helpful.

* * *

After lunch Emily quickly forgot about the incident at the meeting. After removing and cleaning the well's bucket and giving it a test dunk to check the rope she was puzzled and alarmed to find that it came up empty. There was no water in the well. She phoned Alex, who didn't believe her. It didn't take him long to arrive. No, there was no water in the well. He phoned Louise and told her to check *their* well. He would go and check the one at Fare Well.

In the meantime, Emily went to pick up the meat from the butchers and the vegetables from the store. Jake, seeing that Emily appeared agitated asked her what was wrong. So, she told him, but then wished she hadn't. She didn't think Alex would like the news getting round the village when he hadn't had a chance to do anything about it. She made Jake promise not to say anything.

When Alex returned he was able to report that there was water in both the other wells. They were lower than normal but they had water. They would just have to bring water from the other wells.

* * *

On the Friday Alex finished work at lunch time and took and filled a container with water from the well at Bode Well cottage. Emily and Alex started making batches of bread. They were soon joined by Anna and James and a little later Louise, with Nathan. It took them a while but soon the kitchen had batches of dough, in a variety of containers, sitting on most surfaces. Once they had collected the girls from nursery the adults took it in turns to entertain them, out in the garden.

Just after 4pm Anna took a phone call. Sasha had arrived. Excitedly, she ran out to the front of Wishing Well and into the street. Jogging along the pavement towards her cottage she met Sasha and led him back to Wishing Well. There she introduced him to Alex and James who quickly made him welcome by handing him a beer from the fridge. As if on cue, Mike walked through the door, having finished work for the week. Alex handed him a can and the four men pulled their ring pulls more or less in unison and said a collective "Cheers!" Anna watched as the men quickly and effortlessly fell into conversation. Sasha fitted in well and she breathed a silent sign of relief. It really mattered to her that he got on with her friends: another piece in the decision puzzle of their relationship, and a very significant corner piece that slotted in perfectly. Having him at the Well Blessing was going to be fine. She hadn't really had any doubts, but now she was certain. Both he and she would be comfortable. Her friends had seen to that.

When Emily went to feed Snokettee she found that the outhouse was empty. It was at this point that it occurred to her that they really should find somewhere safe for the kittens for the duration of the Well Blessing. However, when she went out in the garden, it appeared that Snokettee had beaten her to it. Drawn by the sound of scampering and little squeaks, she looked up. There, on top of the outhouse, in Kevin's old vantage point, was Snokettee and the three kittens. Kevin had been Angelica's cat that Emily had inherited with the house. He had kept his eye on events from here which gave him both a view of the garden and the village green.

CHAPTER THIRTY THREE

E mily was up early, as she always was on the day of the Well Blessing. The girls weren't awake yet so she was able to get herself a cup of coffee before setting the fire in the hearth under the huge cauldron, used to make the hotpot. This was the vessel that she had first seen when Angelica Wells had invited her in out of the snow and given her a bed for the night. With a village wide power cut the house had been lit only with candles and the odd oil lamp, and the cauldron on the hearth had added to the spooky atmosphere. As she put a match to the kindling Snokettee joined her. She stroked her head and watched as the flames took hold, her mind now wandering to Mr Swire and cats, and the implied legacy. What were the Wells family expected to do?

Her peace didn't last long. Alex came down, shortly followed by the girls. Then Louise appeared and started baking bread. Anna arrived, with Sasha, and helped Emily peel and chop the vegetables and flash-fry the chopped pieces of meat. With the hotpot under-way Emily made everyone drinks. Having brought out the tables from the shed, and set them up, Alex took Sasha over to the pub to help Richard and Mike bring over the glasses and kegs of beer. James put the finishing touches to the three garlands that would decorate the three wells. When he had finished Mike and Alex helped him to dress the Wishing Well well. James and Mike then left, to dress the other two wells at Bode Well and Fare Well cottages.

When everyone went home to change, Alex lowered a huge plastic garden tub to the bottom of their well and filled it with water from the Parker's well. He then carefully filled the well bucket and lowered it part way down. He would only need to serve small amounts of water from their well as, having had water from Bode Well and Fare Well most people were only interested in getting on to the beer by the time they reached Wishing Well. If he gave the water out sparingly he should be able to get away with only three buckets full, and the villagers would be none the wiser.

* * *

At 11.30am James began the service at Fare Well Cottage. He welcomed everyone and thanked them for coming. He then related something of the history of the three wells and the tradition which went back over 450 years. On, or around, the vernal equinox each well would be blessed, and all the villagers would have a drink from each of them. This blessing was intended not only to ensure the village's water supply but also to maintain the safety and prosperity of its inhabitants. Most people had heard it before but still listened intently, enjoying the tradition that was uniquely theirs. As Alex ladled out the water to the file of people he deliberately gave a smaller amount than normal, in the hope that no-one would comment on the tiny amounts he intended giving when they got to Wishing Well.

The first well blessed, James led the string of refreshed residents on to Bode Well where Mike ladled out the water, sparingly, as instructed by Alex. With the Bode Well ceremony complete James set off for Wishing Well, a long flotilla of villagers following in his wake. With everyone crowded into the garden at Wishing Well Cottage James once more addressed his audience. Having gone through the traditional speech for the final well he then surprised Emily and Alex by referring to Angelica, Ruby and Myrtle Wells.

"...three sisters who were loved and honoured for the wonderful work they did for the village. Now, we have a fifth set of triplets to continue the Wells line, Violet, Lily and Tansy." The three girls, who everyone now saw standing behind James, stepped forward. Emily and Alex looked at each other. Neither was aware that this was going to happen. Annoyed, they looked on as the triplets smiled happily at their audience, confident in their new role.

"Right, let's drink from the Wishing Well. Then, I am sure Richard will be happy to refill your glasses with something a little more satisfying...before you get your bread and some very welcome hotpot. Girls, you should start us off. You should have the first drink from this well." The girls lined up, led by Lily, and took their drinks. Then they split up and strolled round the garden, regally greeting people.

As he ladled water into James' glass Alex glowered at him. How dare he present his girls that way. Were they expecting it? It certainly looked like it, the way they had all gathered behind James. As James headed over to Richard at the beer table, Emily approached and Alex remembered that he needed to give out the water sparingly and take care not to spill it. Emily took her water and exchanged a look with Alex; they needed to have a word with James.

Having taken her water Emily headed towards the kitchen, greeting guests as she went. They all seemed to want to talk to her. In the kitchen she filled a tureen with hotpot and took it outside to start serving from it. The tureen was quickly empty and she had to refill it. Inside Anna was busy putting teabags in the huge teapot. She looked up at Emily, "Did you know James was going to do that, with the girls?"

"No, and I am really annoyed about it. Alex looks furious. What on earth possessed him to do that and without even talking to us about it first."

Louise came back in for another batch of bread and had the same question. "What was that about? When did he plan that?"

"Not a clue but it looked like the girls knew," said Emily as she disappeared back out to the garden.

As Louise carried a basket of bread across the kitchen Lily appeared, "Hello, Auntie Louise."

"Hi, Lily. Did Uncle James tell you he was going to talk about the three of you to everybody?"

"No."

"Then why did you all go and stand behind him like that?" asked Louise

"So he would," said Lily in a very matter of fact way.

"You mean, you all wanted him to do that?"

"Yes, it was time."

Louise stared at Lily, not knowing what to say. Anna remained silent.

"We are three years old now. May I have some bread, please?"

"Yes," said Louise abstractedly, "I like your necklace. Is that a fairy?"

"Yes. We all have them. We can wear them on special cajuns."

A series of yells from the garden drew Louise, Lily and Anna back outside. A group of three villagers sitting in deck chairs were all trying to get out of them, expressing alarm and disgust. As others went to help they refused to take the proffered hands. Then further along the garden, there was a scream as a lady stood and started slapping at her dress, in between shaking her hands, in an apparent attempt to rid them of something. Then a man started shouting. Louise then noticed that the eyes of the afflicted were all looking angrily, in one direction. Others were looking on with amused delight and expectation and a small following was building; people were starting to move towards whatever was causing the stir. Through gaps in the crowd she caught a glimpse of a purple jumper and tousled light brown hair. Wading through the people she grabbed Nathan by the shoulder and spun him round. "What are you doing?"

"Mummy, do you want one?"

"One what?"

"Nathan, oozing charm and generosity, put his hand in his pocket. Smiling, he pulled it out again and held out his clenched fist. Her initial reaction was to hold out her hand, palm up. However, from past experience she resisted the temptation, unlike the villagers who had reacted automatically. Instead, she looked carefully at his hand. It looked shiny. Suspiciously, she said, "show me."

Nathan turned his hand over and opened his palm. In a mass of slime was a large slug. Grabbing him by the wrist she steered him through the groups of people, conscious that everyone was looking at them, to the compost heap where she made him drop it. Then she made him empty his pockets. There must have been a dozen to twenty slugs, of different sizes.

"Is that all of them? Are you sure? Right let's go wash your hands."

There was now a long queue for the cloakroom, all waiting their turn to get their hands under a tap. Louise took him through the kitchen and upstairs. The slime wouldn't come off. It seemed that no amount of soap would get rid of the sticky mess completely and she now had it on *her* hands too. Fuming she went back downstairs. "I can't serve bread like this." Grabbing Nathan, she marched him out the front door and took him home to clean him and find him another pair of trousers.

Anna had taken over hotpot duties as well as the bread, as Emily had gone in search of more soap and towels for the cloakroom. She had then discovered that Tansy had taken it upon herself to collect all the slugs from the lawn and move them out of harm's way. She was now covered in slime too. Having cleaned Tansy's hands and changed her dress, Emily returned to the hotpot. Out in the garden people were still yelling, or laughing; the two camps divided into sticky and non-sticky. Soon, the latter were the only ones left, as the sticky had decided to go home, and peace was restored. As they dished out the last of the hotpot the villagers were now starting to make their way out onto the green and, having drunk their free pint, over to The Three Wells pub.

Finally, the hosts were left alone in the garden and Alex launched into James, "What do you think you were doing, parading the girls like that? They are three years old. How dare you?"

"I'm sorry. I don't know. I didn't plan it. They were just there and…"

"And what?" demanded Alex.

"I… I… they are part of the tradition. If you look at any of the history of Much Meddling there have been triplets…"

"You had no right!"

At this point Louise quietly stepped forward, "Alex, I think it was the girls. I asked Lily about it and she said they had stood there deliberately, *because* it was *time*." Then she looked over to the well. They followed her gaze. Lily, Tansy and Violet were all sitting on the grass in front of the well playing with Snokettee and the three kittens.

CHAPTER THIRTY FOUR

Sunday morning was wet and windy, as if the weather had been holding itself in check during the Well Blessing. Fortunately, they had gathered in all the chairs, tables, crockery etc. straight after the event, having perfected their tidying up operation over the years. However, looking out of the kitchen window Emily could see a paper napkin they had missed, being swirled in the wind. As she cleared away the family's breakfast items the doorbell rang. Alex got up and went to answer it.

She heard him coming back down the hall. Whoever had been at the door, had been invited in. She thought that she recognised the man's voice but couldn't place it. Alex led the way into the kitchen. Behind him was Jake, from the store, clutching a bundle of rolled up pieces of paper, wrapped in a sheet of plastic.

"Oh, this is a surprise. What brings you here?" said Emily.

"Hi, I hope you don't mind me turning up like this, but I have something to show you."

Jake took the papers out of the wet plastic, which Alex took from him as Emily quickly made some space on the kitchen table. "Since you told me about the water level dropping in the wells, I have been doing some research." Seeing the alarmed look on Emily's face, he added, "No. You specifically asked me not to tell anyone. So I haven't." Emily and Alex relaxed and he continued, "Something has caused the water level to drop. Something must have happened to the water table." As he spread out the papers, he explained, "My degree is in tectonics, so I know what I am talking about. This is part of my field. This diagram shows a cross section of Much Meddling. As you will see it is built on a slight slope. Your house is at the top end of the village, Bode Well in the middle and Fare Well at the bottom end. As you can see," and Jake pointed to his diagram, "there are two layers of rock with earth on top. At some point, a section of the two rock layers has been pushed upwards, creating a 'v' of the impermeable rock, with permeable rock sitting inside it, and holding the water like a sponge."

"You mean that our house is built on a huge sponge of water-soaked rock, sitting in a basin of hard watertight rock," said Emily.

"Yes and your well goes down through the top layer of earth and into the water-soaked permeable layer. As the whole village is on a slope, your well will run dry first if the water level drops. That is, if the wells are all cut to the same depth." He looked at Alex, who nodded. Then he continued, "As the amount of rainfall has increased in recent years I don't believe it is drought that has caused the water level to drop. Something must have happened to the impermeable layer of rock, letting the water escape. It could be something underground, of course, but looking at the geological surveys of this area it is more likely that something has happened to the edge of the impermeable layer. I suggest you monitor the water levels in the wells. It won't affect the mains supply to Much Meddling as that comes from a reservoir, these days, but it would be good to know what has happened."

Spreading out a second roll of paper, which was a map of Much Meddling and the surrounding area, he pointed out a number of streams emanating from springs in the hill side. All on the same contour line, they surrounded the crag. These he explained were where the water overflowed from the water-table.

* * *

Sophie was miserable. She couldn't stop thinking about Simon. She had been so happy. She had really enjoyed his company. She couldn't wait for their dates. But now! She really didn't like what he was. She couldn't love someone who behaved the way he did. Love: had she been in love with him? She had certainly started to think that they had a future. How could she not have seen the real him? What he was doing was so wrong. He was uncaring and selfish: not just to his mother but also to the residents of St Peter's. Some of the terms he had used to describe them were awful, admittedly he was expressing his childhood views, but he hadn't made any attempt to show they had changed. Still, despite that, he had gone out with *her*. Or, was that simply because Trevor liked her and Simon thought that she would make a good mother without the complications of any further children. Well he was wrong about that, she would love to, and could have children. She wasn't going to let him sell St Peter's. She was determined to make the fete a success so that they could afford to provide accommodation for more residents. She just didn't have the energy anymore. Simon had taken it all.

* * *

After lunch the wind had died and, although the sky was overcast, it was dry. Alex suggested that the family went for a walk. He led them all out of the back gate of the cottage and through the kissing gate to the road. They crossed over, climbed the stile and headed across the fields towards the stream. It was a lovely spot. Expanses of limestone projected from the hillside in ledges. Over the years the water running over it had carved smooth sided channels through it. The main channel was deep and wide enough to sit in and slide down on the occasions when the water was high, and the weather warm enough. Just below the waterfall was a large flat area which made a terrific picnic spot. The whole area was surrounded by trees and shrubs, making it nice and private. It was a while since the family had visited. The place was so near, but they rarely thought to come here.

As they approached, Alex looked at Emily. She too was listening intently. Normally, at this point so close to the stream, the rush of water could be heard. Now, all they could hear was birdsong and the gentle rustle of the wind through the leaves. As they stepped onto the slab of limestone, Alex almost ran to the edge of the waterfall. It was dry. In the rock pools there was water, but it was no longer flowing. He climbed up the rocks tracing the usual line of the stream and kept going until he reached the spring, where the water usually emerged from the hillside. There was nothing. It looked like it had been dry for days.

* * *

There was a knock at Sophie's door. "Come in," she shouted. There was a pause before the door opened tentatively. Sophie had been expecting one of the staff.

"Hello, I hope you don't mind me calling. I am Trevor's nanny," said the lady.

"Oh, yes. Suzanne isn't it?" said Sophie, not knowing what to think.

"Yes, I wanted to talk to you. Simon doesn't know I am here, and I don't plan on telling him." Without being invited further she quietly closed the door and sat herself down in one of the two window seats. Sophie pushed over, not knowing whether to object to this intrusion.

"It is probably out of order for me to say this but I am right, that you and Simon have been seeing each other, aren't I? It is just that, piecing things together from what Trevor has said and how Simon reacted to him, I have come to believe that you *were*, but not any more." As Sophie made no denial, Suzanne continued, "Simon was so happy, a completely different person. He hadn't been happy for a long time. The fact that *Trevor* liked/likes you delighted him. Honestly, he hasn't talked to me about any of this. I just can't stand seeing him so unhappy and, I have to say, that *you* don't look happy either."

Sophie didn't know what to say. She didn't want to talk to this woman but she couldn't find any words.

Suzanne studied Sophie, took a deep sigh and said softly, "Simon is a kind, caring man who adores his son. I don't know what went wrong between the two of you but...one of you needs to make the first move."

"No, you're wrong," said Sophie, quietly and forcefully. "Please leave. Go on. Just go. Get out." Suzanne got to her feet. It seemed an age to Sophie before she left the room and closed the door behind her. Alone, Sophie burst into tears.

* * *

Emily ended her phone-call. "That was mum. She wants me to go over next Saturday to show her how to download photos from her camera and attach them to e-mails. I'd go during the week but she wants dad to be there. Do you mind?"

Alex shrugged his shoulders. "Yeah, I can look after the girls, but don't your parents want to see them?"

"No, I don't plan on staying all day and I'd like to do some shopping afterwards. I could do with something to wear for the fete."

"So, do we know what we are doing yet … for the fete?"

"Probably manning a stall. I'll find out on Tuesday," said Emily. "I think we will need to go and help set up some of them on the Friday. Sophie and the staff are planning it all but there is bound to be plenty of 'humping and dumping' to do."

"That, I can manage," grinned Alex. "And, I am sure I can find a few items from the forge and the yard to donate for the raffle and tombola. Also, I was wondering whether the donkey sanctuary might be interested in setting up a stall. I can ask them, if the 'fete committee' thinks it is a good idea."

"Ooh, if they could bring some donkeys…"

"I'm not sure about that but let me know what St Peter's say."

"Donkey rides would be a great attraction."

"No. Those donkeys have been through enough. Actually, now you have brought them up. I have been wondering about buying the field at the back of the forge. It is just across the road and the sanctuary could do with some spare capacity. Also, I thought it would be nice for Tansy."

Emily grinned. "As long as I don't have to look after them then yes, go ahead. Just don't ever expect me to do any mucking out."

Alex stepped forward and wrapped her in his arms. As she looked up at him he gave her a great slobbering kiss. She squealed and, laughing, pushed him away. "Tansy will love that, but what about the others? "

"Well, I will think of something. Or, they can learn that life isn't always fair. Instead of expecting equality, they can learn to expect the unexpected."

"They may be wiser than their years but they are just 3 years old!"

"Then, I will get them a donkey each." He took her in his arms again, "You can have one too, if you like," and this time kissed her gently on the lips. She grinned at him. Encouraged he said, "Fancy playing pirates this evening?"

"Mmm, there must be a bottle of

something we can put in the fridge."

"Daddy, Daddy." Lily had arrived and was tugging at Alex' sleeve. In her other hand was a sheet of paper. "For you Daddy."

Alex took it and thanked her and she ran off, presumably to join the others, who were playing upstairs. On the paper was a crayon drawing of what again looked like St Peter's with the bad man and spade and dark clouds. What was different about his picture though, was that it had what looked like a dragon, lying on its back in a large brown pool.

"Is that meant to be blood?" asked Alex, as Emily took hold of the other edge of the sheet so that she could see it too.

"No, she knows blood is red."

Alex looked sideways at Emily, "Maybe it's congealed!"

CHAPTER THIRTY FIVE

The Tuesday meeting at St Peter's soon rolled round again. It was now less than 2 weeks to the fete and there was a lot to get through. They needed to work out where all the stalls would go. To assist with this Collette had projected a plan of the home's grounds onto the white board on the wall. There would be 12 stalls for attractions, raffle, tombola and crafts. The fire brigade were bringing an engine and the local search and rescue team would be putting on a display. St Peter's would have its own stand showing what they offered residents and displaying some of the crafts they had produced.

Emily asked if she should get Alex to talk to the donkey sanctuary about a stand. As everyone liked the idea, she said she would. She also asked if she could help with some of the painting that was needed to smarten up the stalls, which Anna was also keen to do.

Sophie was able to report that she had got them some advertising space in the local newspaper and had posters and leaflets that she would like help with distributing to various businesses in the surrounding towns and villages. She would put messages out on social media and repeat them, as a countdown, leading up to the event. She had a list of volunteers, from the residents and their relatives, both for the day and for odd jobs next week. As her report came to an end she looked visibly tired. Lady Agnes noticed and said, "Sophie, 'ank you. I won't for... get...what you are do...ing. I am ve...ree grate... ful."

Collette took up the thanks and started a round of applause. Sophie smiled, but it was a weak one. However, the recognition had been welcome and as the applause died her smile became genuine.

Collette picked up a marker pen and proceeded, with everyone's help, to label the stalls. There was the odd alteration to ensure that the layout was appropriate and logical, such as putting the cakes stall next to the drinks stall, and at the far end so that everyone had to pass all the other stalls to get there. And, once there, people didn't have too far to go to the toilets.

* * *

Louise was delighted. She had just had verbal agreement on the rental of Alex's flat. A 32 year old man, who illustrated children's books for a living, was keen to move in as soon as possible. Louise was particularly thrilled as the man was just the sort of person she thought would fit in well with the plans she had for the arcade. Not that it was really any of her business but she kind of liked the idea of having a collection of arts and crafts shops and a little café in the forge yard. She phoned Alex to let him know that his flat had been let and to arrange with him to sign the paperwork and remind him that he needed to get spare keys cut. Whilst on the phone she asked him if he had any ideas of what to call the yard, as it needed an address. She pointed out that if he was going to do-up and let the other units it would be good to have something snappy that would attract attention and make people want to visit: something that gave a clue to what the yard had to offer. Once the other units were in use the place would be a sort of charitable arcade. Alex said he'd think about it and ask Emily for her thoughts.

* * *

After lunch, with a bit of time to herself, Emily decided to go over to the forge yard and sort through some more of Myrtle's paperwork in the hope of making further discoveries. As she collected the key from the forge office Alex told her what Louise had said.

"I want the name to be something lasting and multi-purpose. I don't want the name to limit the yard's usage," said Alex.

"Why don't we use the fete? People can give us their suggestions. We could charge 50p per entry and give a prize for the winner."

"What sort of prize?"

"I don't know: something from the forge. Maybe one of those big metal flower-shaped bird baths you made, the coated ones that don't rust," suggested Emily. "I like those."

"Er, yeah okay. I think I still have one."

So Emily went off and busied herself sorting through Myrtle's boxes. It wasn't long before she found herself engrossed in a pile of photographs. Seeing the younger versions of the Wells sisters was strange, but fascinating. Crazily she found that she could tell which sister was which. She wasn't certain how she knew but when there were names on the back of the photos she found herself to be correct, more often than not. Sometimes their activities gave them away and others their attitudes. Perhaps being the mother of triplets had made her more attuned to the subtleties of their different personalities. Part way through the afternoon she went over to the forge to get herself a brew. She found Alex dusting off a metal birdbath.

"Hmmm, that is *really* nice. I wouldn't mind that for *our* garden."

"Would you like one for your birthday? I'm considering fitting a glass bowl to one. It'll be an experiment but I'm going to see if I can make something attractive by melting these old glass milk bottles. It should work; the melting point of glass is a bit less than that of the metal I use."

"Can I stay," said Emily. "I love watching

you work."

"I'm not planning on doing it now but you can come over when I do, if you want."

So Emily went back to sorting through Myrtle's things. In one box she found a large musty brown packet. She took it over to a packing case where she sat, and carefully eased out the packet contents which were equally friable. Delicately she unfolded the top one. It was a faded map. Taking out her phone she switched on its light for a better look. It appeared to be a map of Much Meddling. The church was there and the three Well's cottages. The three-storied terraced row which had the Three Wells Pub at one end and the coaching inn in the middle, with its archway through to the forge was there, but the inn and forge businesses were distinctly separate. The duck pond was marked and Anna's row of cottages, but everywhere else was marked as fields or woodland. The second sheet she unfolded was also a map but covered a larger area and included the crag and the land at the far end of the village where St Peter's stood: except it wasn't on the map. There was no building there, just farmland and a scattering of farm buildings. She looked at the legend to see if she could see a date. There was something there, but it was so small and she marvelled at the skill of the printers who had set the tiny type. She switched her phone to camera mode and took a photograph. She was then able to enlarge the image and read 'Well's land 1782'. 'Well's land: there had been Well's land!' If so, then which was it? The legend seemed to be indicating that a red line denoted it. Looking back at the map she could now see some faint red boundary lines enclosing different parts of the map. The three Wells' cottages were marked including a significant area of woodland beneath the crag adjoining Wishing Well Cottage. The Three Wells pub was there, but most curiously, there was a red line enclosing the large area of farmland on the edge of the village where Sycamore Park Hall (St Peter's) had been built. Really! Had the Wells owned the land? If so, what had happened? She didn't think that Alex knew as she was fairly certain he would have said at some point. She was about to go and ask him when a quick glance at her phone showed her it was time to go and pick up the triplets from nursery. Carefully she put the maps back in their packet and took them with her. She more or less threw the keys at Alex and headed home for her car.

That evening, with the children in bed, she took out the maps and showed Alex. No, he hadn't known. However, it started him thinking. There had always been something unsaid, something that his family avoided talking about. As a child, he realised that there were certain subjects that he learned not to raise. At the time, it was just one of those things he didn't question, one of those things that just were. Now, he realised how odd that was. Maybe that was why he hadn't heard of Lady Agnes, who he now realised, was actually his late father's cousin. Did Agnes know, and if she did, would she say?

Together, she and Alex checked the other two items in the packet that Emily hadn't had time to look at earlier. The first one was a detailed map of the land on which St Peter's now stood and which included an area of crag and woodland behind it and also fields and woodland to the front and sides. The second document was a change of ownership from Cyril Montague Wells to Archibald Noblet Earnshaw dated 1821.

"There is no money mentioned!" said Alex. "No transaction. Normally with documents like this there would be a stated amount, but there isn't. What was the land worth? Were there any other documents?"

"There is nothing else in the packet. There might be more documents over at the forge. I didn't manage to get through everything. Perhaps we should bring it all over here. There is plenty of room in the cellar and we need to get that place cleared out anyway. It will be easier to go through it there."

"Okay, I'll try and remember to bring some home with me every day. You never know, we might find we own more land than we know about."

* * *

Sophie was busy looking through

property details. Having chased her estate agent, she had been sent details of some new properties. There was a very nice bungalow with a superb garden that she particularly liked the look of. It was in the outskirts of Barnlees and was near to local shops and not too far from her friends. It would need a lot of updating but, practically, the building was just right for her. It was a good size with decent 'turning circles' in both kitchen and bathroom; she would have little difficulty manoeuvring. The drive was also a decent width as it was designed for two cars. She had a viewing booked for the following Monday. If all went well she could leave St Peter's and hopefully forget all about Simon Earnshaw. He was still phoning her and leaving messages. At times she was tempted to answer but resisted the urge. Her heart missed him but her head just couldn't rationalise her feelings for the person she knew him to be. She needed someone kind and caring, not selfish and self-serving. Could he not see what he was doing to his mother? Did he not care? Was money more important to him? So, the poor little rich boy had had a miserable childhood. Lots of *poor* kids had miserable childhoods too. Half of her wanted to hate him but the other half wouldn't. Why was he such a bastard?

Shaking her head to rid it of images of Simon she forced her attention back to the sheets of To Do Lists that she had in front of her, but her mind instantly went to the question of why she was doing all this to save St Peter's, when she knew that Simon would just sell it at the first opportunity.

* * *

Louise phoned Emily to ask if she would take over the painting of St Peter's stalls, which she had promised to do this Saturday. If she wanted to attend the fete the following Saturday, she would need to work this one. Emily said that she could do some painting in the morning but she had promised to sort out her mum's laptop in the afternoon. Emily was bemoaning the fact that her mother was pretty useless when it came to technology and often needed help.

"You're lucky," said Lou. "The last time *my* mother needed my help it was to carve her toenails and sandpaper her heels!"

"Aren't there Chiropodists for that?"

"Apparently it is much nicer when I do it; she doesn't need to leave the house."

"Ah, now I know what to buy you for your birthday, an electric sander. Would you like one that also buffs?"

"You are such a wit Emily Wells. No, thank you. I'll let Anna know that you will be painting with her instead of me, but just the morning. What you don't finish I can do on Sunday. I am quite looking forward to this fete. It should be good fun. Nathan can't wait. I have been telling him about all the different stalls. He is especially keen to have a go at 'Splat The Rat' and 'Dunk The Ducks'."

"Yes, they will be right up his street," said Emily. "Okay, see you Sunday."

CHAPTER THIRTY SIX

Emily left early on Saturday morning leaving Alex to entertain the girls. She was aware that he had vague plans for them all to spend the day with Mike and Nathan. Louise was working. Emily arrived at St Peters for 9am keen to get as much painting done on the stalls as possible. Inside one of the outhouses there was a selection of brightly coloured paints and some multicoloured brushes which had obviously been used before and not cleaned too carefully. Just as Emily and the other volunteers were hunting for suitable items with which to remove the paint tin lids, Sophie appeared with a collection of new brushes and a big bottle of white spirit.

"If you take a paint can each, you can go from stall to stall touching up *your* colour wherever it is needed. If you need steps there are some propped against the wall, over there. If you need anything else, just let me know. Thank you everyone."

Emily got a can of buttercup yellow paint.

She was delighted until she realised that most of the lettering on the stalls was yellow and therefore not the easiest of the paint jobs on offer. Also, as most of it was along the top of the stalls it meant balancing at the top of steps with nothing much to lean against to steady her hand. At around 11.30am Sophie came along and, despite their history, generously gave Emily some praise for her artwork. Emily took the opportunity to make her excuses and leave and made it to her parents just after 12 noon.

It didn't take Emily long to show her parents what they needed to know to transfer photos from her mother's phone to their computer, and a couple of test 'sends' to Emily's phone proved that they had grasped what she had taught them. Emily knew that over the next few days she would be inundated with pictures overloading her inbox. Still, she had plenty of material, in triplicate, with which to retaliate and double that if you counted the kittens.

She had lunch with her parents and then went shopping. By the time she got back home it was late afternoon and she was pleased with her buys. Not having the girls with her meant that she could have a leisurely time trying on both clothes and shoes and her haul consisted of two tops, a pair of jeans, a dress, a pair of shoes and some sandals.

Entering the house she could hear male voices and laughter coming from the kitchen.

She abandoned her bags in the hall and pushed open the kitchen door. Nathan was turning circles in the middle of the floor, whipping round a piece of string. Tied to the end by its neck was one of the girls' toy rabbits. Lily and Tansy were crouched on the rug collectively holding Marigold, Whoops-a-Daisy and Spider. As the rabbit swung past them, the girls released the kittens which tore after it, racing round in ever decreasing circles and skidding madly on the flagged floor, tiny claws failing to find a purchase.

"What are you lot doing?" asked Emily, amused.

"You don't have any dogs," said Nathan, pointedly, "So we have to play *cat* track instead." Distracted, he wrapped the string round a chair leg. The kittens caught up with their prey and commenced disembowelling it. Tansy started sobbing and Lily put her arm around her.

Staring thoughtfully at the mess Nathan said, "We are going to need another rabbit."

"Nathan, I think that is enough 'Cat Track' for now," said Emily. She rescued the remains from the kittens, and then inspected several tiny needle marks in her skin before heading to the sink to give them a rinse. Tansy continued to cry, and Nathan started to sulk.

In a bid to cheer everyone up Lily said, "The dog track was great."

Now, Emily looked over at Alex and Mike

who were standing by the kitchen table, and said levelly, "You took our children to the dog track!"

"Yes," said Alex, cautiously. "We all had a great time." Silently he patted the pile of notes he and Mike had been counting.

"Violet won loads of money," said Lily excitedly.

"What?" said Emily, "You had them gambling!" Now she looked over at the sofa where James and Violet were sitting looking at a comic together apparently doing a puzzle; Violet was pointing and James was making circles round her choices between differently patterned tops and caps. On the back of the sofa, looking over Violet's shoulder, was Snokettee.

"James, were you there too?" asked Emily. James nodded and Emily shook her head, "I *don't* believe it. Don't *you* think it is wrong to take children gambling?"

"Well, technically it is only gambling if you don't know which one is going to win," he said tentatively. Then seeing that this didn't pacify Emily, in fact by the look on her face it made it several times worse, he added, "It is all for St Peters. It is in a good cause..."

"I don't believe this. Does no-one else see anything wrong in this?" The men all shrugged but looked suitably cowed. Looking back at James, who had now laid the comic flat on his lap, her attention was drawn by Violet's moving finger which now pointed to another top and cap. Emily stared, her brain slowly whirring. That wasn't a comic. She snatched it up, turned it cover up and confirmed her suspicion; it was a copy of The Racing Post and Violet was helping James to pick winners.

Mike, feeling the need to diffuse the situation, or rather set light to it said, "Yes, if she can win 750 quid on the dogs, just *think* what she can do on the horses!"

"Does Louise know you took Nathan gambling?" said Emily, menacingly.

"Er, no", said Mike.

"Well, she soon will. Out. Everybody out!"

Mike shepherded a dejected Nathan towards the door. He was still holding the remains of the string and viciously whipping anything that came to hand. James approached Emily and, after bizarrely putting his hands together in an unconscious silent prayer, reached out and tentatively slid The Racing Post from her grasp. Tucking it under his arm he then sidled over to the kitchen table, raised his eyebrows at Alex, and silently scooped up their winnings. As the front door clicked shut, Emily felt a tug on her elbow. It was Tansy, no longer crying, but bright as a button, "Mummy, can we have a whippet?"

* * *

At St Peters Sophie busily ticked off items from her to do lists. The different topics included catering, parking, volunteers, additional helpers, stalls, safety, priority, weather etc. The sheets of paper were all fighting for space with a pile of bunting that she had been making on a sewing machine, that the home's Occupational Therapist had leant her. She really needed a bigger table, or ideally another one. There was still so much to do and only a week to go to the fete. Most of the painting was now done but there were a number of small maintenance and repair jobs that needed doing that she would have to delegate. From the likely volunteers there was only one that she could trust to actually do what she wanted and not 'use their initiative'. She had only discovered by chance that the substitute 'rat' for the 'Splat the Rat' had had a bladder of blood inserted, 'for authenticity'!

Checking the time, she reckoned that she would be able to finish sewing another row of bunting before dinner. So, she stacked her sheets of paper and moved in front of the sewing machine. She found handling the pretty floral print cotton relaxing, and she rapidly joined together another 10 triangles on two sides, ready for turning the right way out and then ironing. By the time she had finished it was just gone 5.30 so she switched off the machine and headed down for dinner.

As the lift doors opened she saw Trevor, standing transfixed in the middle of the hall, staring at something in the day room off to her side. A woman was calling out for a nurse. His little face was pale and he looked as if he was about to cry.

"Trevor," called Sophie and pushed towards him. As she approached he turned and flew into her arms. She half dragged, half lifted him onto her lap where he buried his face into her shoulder. As she soothed him she looked into the day room. Suzanne was knelt on the floor struggling with a resident Sophie recognised as Peter. The man was thrashing about and Suzanne was desperately trying to keep him from banging his head on the floor. With Simon on her lap Sophie wheeled round towards the office but a nurse was already on the way. Sophie took Trevor over to a corner of the hall and held him until Suzanne turned up.

"Oh, Sophie, thank you so much for looking after him. I didn't know what to do. There was no-one about and I couldn't just leave the man. As a nanny, First Aid is part of my training." She crouched down and turned Trevor towards her and held his face in her hands. She wiped his cheeks with her thumbs and smoothed his hair. "Trevor, that man is alright now. Unfortunately, what you saw can happen to some people. We are lucky. You, me, your daddy and Sophie, that doesn't happen to us. To those it does happen to, well, we need to help and look after them, until they are better." She helped him off Sophie's lap. "Now, we need to be going and Sophie needs her dinner. Are you okay Trevor?"

He nodded and took her hand. "Say thank you to Sophie for looking after you."

"Thank you Sophie," said Trevor.

"And a big thank you from me," said Suzanne. "I am so glad you turned up. You are brilliant with him by the way. I was so relieved when I saw you there. Will you be at the fete next Saturday? Of course you will, you are organising it aren't you! Stupid of me! Well, hopefully we will see you then. Come on Trevor."

Sophie watched as Suzanne led Trevor to the stairs and waited until they disappeared down to the entrance and out of sight. Seeing Trevor's reaction to a resident having an epileptic seizure was very sobering. How often had Simon been subject to such sights as a child? As an adult it had alarmed her the first time she had witnessed one at the home. She had never been exposed to anything like it before. She had been very naïve. Some people had horrendous and embarrassing difficulties to cope with. Living at St Peter's had really opened her eyes. She was finding that she was much more tolerant than she used to be.

As she took her place in the dining room she looked round at the other residents and mentally worked her way through their conditions. She had no idea what most of them were, but she had seen their effects. The variety of neurological conditions that despite heavy medication caused uncontrollable antisocial behaviour had alarmed and even frightened her until she got to know the individuals afflicted. Some she had grown to like and now called friends. Some made her laugh, treating their afflictions as unruly friends. However, even here there were intolerances and division. There was a distinct social separation between the long and short term residents. It both disappointed and amused Sophie.

CHAPTER THIRTY SEVEN

Emily and Alex were awoken on Sunday morning by a mysterious, intermittent tapping on their bedroom window. Alex got up and drew back the curtains. A long-tailed tit was flying at the window collecting bits of cobweb in its beak. Alex' presence interrupted it briefly but as soon as he got back into bed the bird made a couple more passes and then flew off. It wasn't long however before it was back again. Realising that she wasn't going to get any further sleep, Emily got up. As the bird was currently absent, she wandered to the window and looked out. It was a lovely day. The sun, not yet fully arisen, was shining on the tops of the trees at the back of the cottage. She watched as a pigeon completed a couple of dips of its roller-coaster flight and then turned her attention to the garden. A squirrel was sitting on top of the well, munching something, apparently oblivious to Snokettee settled stone-like on the nearby rockery. Instead, its attention was focussed on the three little kittens playing on the lawn; a lawn which she now saw had three interlocking brown rings. The girls would be delighted; they had their own fairy rings. Alex, however, would not be.

After breakfast she suggested to the children that they went out into the garden to see what they could find. They all trooped outside. Lily went straight to the ring of toadstools and, as the others gathered at her side, she nodded and clapped her hands. There was an exchange between her and Tansy, as if they had been waiting for something. Emily joined them and said, "So, what do you think of *that*?" pointing at the rings.

Again, Lily and Tansy looked at one another and appeared to come to a silent agreement. They looked at Emily and, as one, said, "It's good."

"All will be well," chirped Violet.

"Not yet," said Lily and scowled at her sister.

Emily was about to ask what she meant but Alex called her from the kitchen: a slight edge to his voice. She went inside.

"I have just had Mike on the phone; their well is dry too."

"Really? What can we do?"

"I don't know. Mike and I are going to check Fare Well and I am going to phone Jake."

* * *

Sophie was busy organising. Three more tables had been moved into her room and she was gleefully sorting and grouping lists and items. One table had a collection of money boxes, volunteer badges and packets of raffle tickets, marker pens and labels. The sewing machine table had a stack of bunting (still to be completed) and a striped awning that needed its remaining ties attaching. Another had itemised lists pertaining to each individual stall and the names of the volunteers who would staff them. She was glad she was busy as it distracted her from thinking about Simon and wondering if Trevor was okay. She had had a further two texts pleading for a meeting, one purportedly from Trevor saying he missed her. She had no intention of torturing the boy by prolonging their friendship, much as it hurt her.

There was a knock at the door. It was one of the nurses come to let her know that the St Peter's display board was finished. Would she like to come and inspect it? She followed the nurse down to the corner of the entrance hall. A four-panel display stand, with a large St Peter's logo top centre and a series of coloured photos with explanations of the homes aims and the activities on offer to residents, stood proudly on display. There was also a brief history of the building, with photographs of its time before it became a care home. Sophie was pleased. They really had done a very good job.

"Wow. Who did this?" she asked, and a couple of residents stepped forward. "This is a really professional job. I don't suppose you would help me with some of the other display work that needs doing, would you?"

The two, positively beamed. Yes, they would be delighted to help. So, Sophie led them up to her room and started delegating.

* * *

"Did you tell Alex about the photo?" asked Louise.

"No! Just the well. Can't you tell her?" said Mike as he headed out the door to meet Alex at Fare Well, to test the water level there.

"I can, but you were already speaking to them."

Ever since the Well Blessing, Louise had been haunted by a memory that she couldn't place. Yesterday, when she got home from work and the house was empty, she had gone up to the attic. Sitting on a rolled up old rug on the floor boards she had rifled through an old packing case of Ruby's belongings. She had been through them all before, and had been tempted to throw them out but couldn't; they were part of the history of the house and its former occupants. Besides, if anything, she should give them to Alex as Ruby was his relative. At least ask him before disposing of them. However, the longer that she lived in Much Meddling the more interested she was becoming in its history. The documents, and in particular the black and white photos, had become precious to her and she felt possessive of them. Knowing that if Alex or Emily asked, she would hand them over, she was a little reluctant to reveal their existence. This one photo though, she couldn't keep to herself.

* * *

Back at Wishing Well Cottage, Emily gathered the triplets round her and asked them to tell her what was going on, what was good, what would be well but not yet? The children stared at her and then looked at each other. Eventually, Lily spoke, "Something."

"What do you mean?"

"Something is bad."

"Okay, but what?" pressed Emily trying to hide her exasperation. "Is it to do with the 'bad man'?"

All three children nodded gravely. Then Lily ran off and came back clutching her dead dragon picture and handed it to Emily. "Daddy has to help," she said.

"Then, all will be well," said Violet.

"But how? What has Daddy got to do?" said Emily.

"Help."

"But how?" pleaded Emily and the girls all shrugged. The phone rang and the girls went to play on the kitchen rug. Emily picked up the phone and saw it was Lou. "Hi, I am so glad you called. I could really do with a chat," said Emily.

"Why, has something happened?"

"Yes, no, I don't know."

"Empty wells getting you down? As long as our mains supply doesn't dry up I don't see why it matters," said Lou.

"It is partly that, but the girls are still on about the 'bad man' and saying that Alex has to '*help*', but they don't appear to know how, or why, or even what is wrong! However, the fact that we have three interlocking fairy rings on the back lawn seems to be a good thing. They are all behaving like it is some sort of good omen."

"You do live in a crazy little fantasy world, don't you. Have you considered therapy?"

"I've considered alcohol. Fancy a girl's night out? We can catch up on what is happening with Anna and Sasha. I know they have been seeing quite a lot of each other lately but haven't provided any feedback."

"Good idea. How about tomorrow night?" said Lou.

"Sounds good to me."

"Right, I'll get in touch with Anna and let you know. Anyway, the reason I called you is because I have something to show you; something I found in a box in the attic."

"Ooh, I love boxes in the attic," said Emily.

"Well, I don't remember if I said, but I thought that the necklace Lily was wearing at the Well Blessing looked familiar. It has been driving me nuts but, well, wait 'til you see the photo…"

"Is that all you are going to tell me?" asked

Emily.

"Yep, see you 7pm, tomorrow. Gotta go."

* * *

When Alex got back he was quite agitated. There was still water in Fare Well but, as expected, the level was a lot lower. He had managed to contact Jake, who had joined them. It was a significant drop and a significant loss of water. Jake was going to contact his university and see if he could get a team to survey the area to try to ascertain what had happened, or rather what was happening, as it didn't appear to be stopping. He would also get in touch with a team of speleologists as he was aware that there was at least one cave system under the crag; they may be able to tell what the water level had been and what it was now, plus see if there had been any cave-ins or new openings which could account for the escape of water. In the meantime he wanted Alex to take daily readings of the depth of the well at Fare Well. It would help them to calculate the rate at which the water level was dropping.

Feeling the need to do 'something' Alex suggested that after lunch, the Wells family went for a walk on the northern side of the crag to inspect the accessible land there. Not much of it was public right of way but they might as well look at what was. As it was a bit far for the children to walk, they took the Range Rover.

As they climbed down from the vehicle

the children, as usual, were keen to get going and Emily's attempts to apply sunscreen to their faces didn't go down well, especially when Alex insisted that it was only March and the sun wasn't that strong yet; a bit of sun would do them good. Tansy was the first to reach and negotiate the high wooden stile that gave access to the crag. Alex climbed over ready so that when Emily helped Lily and Violet up, he could help them down the other side. He then helped Emily down, just 'cos she enjoyed him helping her. The pair of them followed their children up the limestone path that wound its way between last year's mounds of broken brown bracken: fresh green shoots starting to poke through and unfurl. Ahead, Tansy's curly brown head could be seen now and then as she worked her way up the hillside: two further dark curly heads in pursuit. Gradually the children slowed, and Alex and Emily were on the verge of catching up with them when Alex said, "Where are they going? There's no path over there," and he started to run, "Tansy! Come back."

Emily broke into a jog, confident that Alex would deal with the situation. As she drew closer, she heard noises. A frantic bleating could be heard and the girls all talking at once, urging Alex to help. Caught fast in a barbed wire fence, was a ewe, its newly born lamb struggling to get to its feet: unable to reach its mother. Alex got hold of the ewe and tried to free it, but its struggles had ensured that its fleece was tightly bound to the fence.

"We need to cut it free. If only I had a knife or something," said Alex racking his brain for a solution.

"I've got some scissors," said Emily, "They are only small, but..." and she ferreted in her shoulder bag producing a first aid kit from which she took a pair of scissors and held them out to Alex.

"You're going to have to do it, I can't let go," said Alex.

"Oh," said Emily alarmed. Tentatively she stepped nearer. The sheep jolted and kicked Alex in the shin.

"Get on with it," he said.

Emily leaned over his shoulder and felt along the barbed wire and started snipping. As she freed more and more wool the animal was able to fight more and more. When it was almost free Alex told her to step back and get the girls out of the way. She dragged Tansy away from the lamb, where she had been crouched looking at it with deep concern. With the girls at a safe distance Alex let go and ran over to join them. A couple of bucks and kicks and the ewe became free, and able to join its child.

From a distance the family watched as the ewe licked its infant and, much to Alex relief, the lamb started to suckle. Content that all was well he found a rock to sit on where he rolled up his trouser leg and inspected his shin. The skin was scuffed and a large bruise was forming. Emily produced some antiseptic cream and a large plaster with a teddy bear printed on it, which amused the girls. Wounded soldier patched up they headed back to the path.

When they reached the point, that was the purpose of their trip, it was just as Alex had expected, the hillside was dry. Where, in Alex life, there had always been a stream, there was just a jumble of dry rocks. Leaving Emily and the girls he walked along the contour looking for evidence of a disturbance to the ground, but there was nothing apparent. He kept going for a couple of minutes more and was about to turn back when he heard machinery. It wasn't the sound of any farm machinery that he recognised and curiosity kept him going. In the distance he could just make out the top of something yellow. As he approached he could see three men and a machine which appeared to be drilling. Just beyond this was a set of farm buildings. Not caring whether he was trespassing Alex went and asked them just what they thought they were doing? After an initially angry exchange which amounted to 'Get off my land it's none of your business' Alex managed to calm down the farmer and explain why he wanted to know. Now, the farmer was very keen to talk as he too would like to know why the water level had dropped. Having no mains water to his farm he was drilling a new, deeper well in the hope of accessing water. After explaining what Jake was intending, the farmer was eager for Alex to give Jake his details and give him access to his land.

When Alex rejoined Emily, she was angry that he had been gone so long but interested to hear about the farm. Fortunately, the farmer was able to pump water up from the river in the valley bottom for the animals, as there was plenty of water in that.

* * *

At Suzanne's insistence she and Simon had brought Trevor to St Peter's again. Simon had been livid when she had told him what Trevor had witnessed and was adamant that it should never happen again. He had persistently counselled her about ensuring that Trevor went directly to his mother's room and at times of the day when he was least likely to encounter anything 'unsavoury' as he had put it, to Suzanne's dismay. Unfortunately, on this occasion, when they walked into reception there were others waiting for the lift so she had chosen the stairs, arriving in the upper lobby just as Peter had fallen to the floor. Even though Simon accepted this explanation, it was yet another incident. He had initially been annoyed when he had discovered that Trevor had met Sophie. To his knowledge, his mother had been the only person occupying a room on that floor. However, he had relented when he understood how much

Trevor liked her and had become curious enough to get to know her.

Suzanne wanted Trevor to meet the gentleman whose seizure he had witnessed, to show him that the man was alright. With the staff's permission and Peter's agreement they knocked on his door. Peter greeted them and invited them in. He thanked Suzanne and Trevor for helping him and made a fuss over Trevor's part in 'being there'. He told Simon what a marvellous little boy he had and that he should be proud of him. By the time they left Trevor was completely comfortable in the man's company and, unexpectedly, Simon found that he was too.

CHAPTER THIRTY EIGHT

The children climbed onto their seats at the breakfast table and Emily fastened a bib round each of them. This was getting less necessary but was still a good idea for boiled egg and soldiers. During the preceding week she had deliberately made sure that each child knew how to crack open the tops of their eggs. This they had achieved with varying degrees of success. As each picked up their spoon she watched closely. Tansy, as expected, was the first to attack her egg. It caved in easily and Tansy stared, and then poked, then did some further smashing, before looking at her mother. The others, eggs now crushed, did the same.

"April fool," said Emily laughing.

Alex entered the kitchen and approached his egg. The girls all watched, gleefully waiting.

As he sat, a disgusting, splattering, 'farty' noise, erupted from his chair.

"April fool," laughed Emily.

The girls were delighted but puzzled. As Alex did a few test 'sits', amusing the girls, and, it seemed, himself, Emily explained about April Fool's Day.

Alex took up his spoon and commenced knocking the top off his egg. The girls watched in anticipation and then laughed uproariously when Alex found it was hollow: Alex playing to his audience.

* * *

Simon drove thoughtfully to work. He had been such a fool, such a huge fool. It was April Fools' Day and he was the biggest fool of all. His stupidity had lost him Sophie and he couldn't see any way that he could win her back. Fresh actions couldn't change his past deeds. He missed her desperately and even worse, Trevor did too. His little boy was being deprived of someone he had grown to love, and it was all Simon's fault. He mentally went back over all their encounters to see if there was anything he could have done differently. Maybe, if he had been honest from the start, but that would only have meant Sophie questioning him more deeply about his ex-wife, and that subject was completely off-limits. As he pulled into his parking space at work, the car slid slightly on the gravel.

* * *

Sophie met the estate agent in the driveway of the bungalow she was to view. It was all very '1930s' with bow-windows and a stained-glass panel over the front door. The estate agent, Julie, led the way up the ramp to the front door which she unlocked. Inside, the hallway was plain white but the anaglyptic paper on which the paint sat was starting to peel. The front room was a good size but felt oppressively small due to its busily-patterned wall paper. The fireplace however, was a modern gas one with a remote control. As Julie pointed out, plain walls would make a huge difference to the room. The kitchen, again, was a decent size and the units were only a couple of years old, with appliances to match. The two bedrooms were different sizes. The larger of the two would be hers and the other would make a good guest room. When she pushed into the bathroom she was amazed; it hadn't been apparent from the property details but the bathroom was completely new. There was a bath with hoist, a roll-in shower and a transfer bar by the toilet. Practically, it was perfect, and it looked brand new. Julie explained that it hadn't been used; complications had meant that the intended occupant had needed to go to a care home instead. At the back of the property there was a large patio and some raised beds with a small pond. It couldn't be better. Sophie did another circuit of the property and told the estate agent that she would like to think about it but would be in touch.

* * *

Louise had been mentally populating the forge yard. Her little fantasy now had four craft shops, a clothes boutique, the St Peter's Charity shop of course, and a coffee shop. The latter had pretty little tables arranged on the sunny side of the yard, with an orange and yellow striped awning for really hot days, or rain. Its windows would be filled with cakes and pastries, displayed on delicate tiered stands. Coffee would be served in huge mugs with the yard logo, and tea in dainty floral cups. As the rental from these businesses would go to St Peter's she was excited about the name she had chosen for the yard. She just needed to convince Alex. On her lunch break she took the opportunity to nip across to the yard and tell him her idea.

When she arrived in the yard she was surprised to find Cheryl, the nurse from St Peter's, in uniform, clutching pieces of metal. She had come to see if Alex would fix some items needed for the fete. The bracket that held the bell at the top of the 'test your strength' machine was badly rusted and looked like it would break at any moment and the lever that catapulted the block up to the bell had become bent over the years. The other item was a pole and its cup from the coconut shy, which should have been all one but was now in two pieces. Alex didn't need the extra work but took them and said he would get them done by Friday if she would like to collect them.

With Cheryl gone, Alex turned his attention to Louise. Sensing that Alex now wasn't in the best of moods she excused herself, saying 'it didn't matter, another time would do'. Alex didn't argue, so she left him to get on with his work.

* * *

"So, Anna, how is it going with you and Sasha?" asked Louise as she raised a glass of house red to her lips. "When is he moving in?"

"We are taking things slowly. Everything is just fine."

"Is he coming to the fete?" asked Emily.

"Yes, he'll be here for that. We are quite looking forward to it and it is an excuse for him to see St Peter's. Architecturally, it is *quite something*, apparently. He has been looking it up online. My fault I guess, as I have been talking about it quite a lot."

"Okay, that's enough small talk," said Lou. "I have a photo to show you both. She rifled through her bag and pulled out an envelope. From it she withdrew an old black and white photo: a bit 'dog-eared' round its cardboard edges. She placed it on the table in front of Emily who picked it up and scrutinised it.

Looking over her shoulder Anna exclaimed, "Oh, it is the Wells sisters as children. They must have been about nine or ten years old when that was taken."

"Yes," said Lou. "Look closer. See anything familiar."

Emily gave a gasp and, a little slower on

the uptake, Anna let out an 'oh!'

"When I saw Lily's necklace I knew I had seen that fairy somewhere before. It has been driving me crazy. It took me ages to find that photo again. Are those the others?"

"Yes, the fairies on those rings are identical to the ones on the children's necklaces. I am sure of it," said Emily. "So, how did Lady Agnes get them?"

"Well," said Anna, "there could have been several made at the time. Gifts like that for children could have been 'ten-a-penny' back then."

"I doubt it. Alex said that they weren't cheap. They are very well made and solid gold. Also, he said that when he took the periapts off there were strange lumps on the backs of the fairies. If they were originally rings that would explain it."

"So," said Lou, "if they are one and the same, how did three rings become three necklaces and get into the hands of Lady Agnes?"

"Anyone want any crisps?" asked Anna as she headed to the bar for another round.

Whilst she was gone Louise took the opportunity to ask Emily what she thought of her name for the forge yard. As it would be a charitable venue and an arcade, she liked the idea of calling it the Arcade, but spelling it A.R.K, A.I.D. What did Emily think? Emily thought it was great but wasn't sure Alex would like it as he didn't want to limit the use of the yard. They may not want it to be a charity for ever. Also, she was planning on using the fete to generate ideas. However, she said she would see what Alex had to say. When Anna got back Louise was a little crestfallen.

"So, how's work?" asked Anna. "Seen any interesting houses yet?"

"One or two, but none I am prepared to discuss until they are on the market, and then only in a purely professional way, of course," snipped Lou, nose in the air.

"Hah! You're such a gossip, Louise Parker. You'll never keep anything interesting to yourself," laughed Anna.

"I can be professional. Emily, did I tell you that Sasha had put Anna on his car insurance, or, that she had given him a key to her cottage?"

"No, I can attest to the fact that you did not," said Emily.

"Well, there you go then: case proven."

* * *

With the children in bed Alex turned his attention to the falling water level in the wells. Jake had contacted him late afternoon to say that a team of speleologists would inspect the larger of the cave systems at the weekend. His university was interested and to his delight wanted his assistance, for which he would be paid a small amount. He had also been in touch with the local council but, as it didn't affect the water supply to the surrounding villages, they weren't interested. It seemed to Alex that only he and Jake were concerned. To those who were actually investigating, it was just an interesting puzzle. To Alex though, it went deeper. It was unthinkable to lose the wells. Legends aside, he felt deeply responsible. The wells were his inheritance and his legacy. He needed to be able to maintain that legacy for his children. Logically it didn't matter but, to his heart and to his soul, it meant everything.

* * *

Sophie had come to a decision. She wanted the bungalow. With the sale of her flat and her accident insurance money she could afford it. Once the fete was over, there would be no reason to stay at St Peter's. She needed to get on with her life. Horace jumped onto her lap and pushed his furry face into her neck. She wrapped her arms around him and kissed the top of his head. In the morning she would put in an offer. If she didn't get it she didn't know what she would do. That prospect didn't bear thinking about. She also ought to start thinking about a job. It was over a year since she had worked. Over a year since her life had been 'normal'. One tiny incident and her whole life had been changed for ever. One minute she had been happily riding along a country lane, preoccupied with where she was going to spend Easter, and the next minute she was being air-lifted to hospital.

The first day or so was a blur, faces, questions, pain, panic: mostly panic as the reality of her paralysis began to dawn. After that, endless days and nights followed of anger and despair interspersed with rage, lashing out, physically and verbally at those who cared about her and who tried to care for her; the rage that was always there, just under the surface: the learning to physically cope: the learning to behave as if everything was okay now, when it wasn't and never would be, ever again. A squeal from Horace let her know that she was cuddling him too hard.

* * *

When Emily disappeared to the 'ladies', Lou brought up the subject of the dog track 'winnings'. She hadn't been happy that Mike had taken Nathan but was amused that apparently Violet had successfully chosen the winners and that now the men were convinced that she could do the same on the horses. Anna had mixed feelings about the moral aspects of it but was delighted that St Peter's was receiving the money. They were still deep in discussion and having fun thinking about the possibilities when Emily returned and asked what was amusing them. Emily, however, wasn't amused.

"Oh, come off it," said Lou, "You don't seriously believe that Violet has the ability to manipulate the outcome of a race or 'know' which one is going to win, do you?"

"No. Look, I don't know. It just isn't right,

taking children gambling, and it is morally wrong if you know the result."

"You didn't seem to have a problem with Ruby giving you a winning lottery ticket," said Louise.

Emily opened her mouth to respond but then closed it.

"AND, once again, case proven m'lud."

"That was completely different. Ruby wasn't under age and we have no way of knowing that her win wasn't pure luck!"

Louise and Anna started to laugh and then, following Lou's lead, they cackled and rubbed their hands together like old crones.

CHAPTER THIRTY NINE

It was the last meeting before the fete and it was spent going over and checking what everyone needed to do to make it happen successfully. There were jobs still to do and Sophie divided them between those present. She had sheets of instructions for everyone and impressed upon them the need to be there promptly at 9am on Saturday. The gates would open to the public at 1pm and there was a lot that could only be done on the day. When she had finished Collette told everyone that there would be a wrap up meeting the following Tuesday for anyone who would like to attend. By then they would be able to announce how much money they had raised. This met with approval as everyone was keen to know the results of all their hard work, and whether it was enough to give St Peter's the reprieve it needed to continue.

As everyone was leaving Emily asked to have a private word with Lady Agnes. When they were alone, Emily produced the photo that Louise had found in her attic of the Wells sisters wearing fairy rings. Lady Agnes smiled knowingly. "Yes, they are... the same... fairies. When I was...thur...teen, the sisters...gave me them on...a...neck...lace, for my birth...day. They said, it would protect...me, and always... bring...me safely...home." This was the phrase that Angelica had used when she had given Emily her periapt.

"Were the periapts on the back then?"

"Yes."

"But why, if your families weren't speaking, did they do that?" asked Emily.

"I wasn't an Earn...shaw...then. I was their brother's grand...child."

"So, all this happened before you got married and then, when you did, neither family would speak to you."

"Yes."

"And, you had the necklace made into three new ones for the girls."

"Sorry! what?"

"The necklace, you had your necklace made into three new ones for my girls."

"Yes, sorry, I am tired. It has been...long... meet...ing..."

"Of course, I will let you get back to your room."

Lady Agnes pressed the buzzer attached to her chair and a nurse, who had obviously been waiting in the corridor, came in. Emily had other questions she wished to ask but, frustratingly, they would have to wait.

* * *

Back in her room Sophie waited anxiously for the return call from her estate agent. She had been expecting it all through the meeting, but it hadn't come, and the agency had been engaged when she had just called them. She made a couple more 'bunting' flags and tried phoning again. This time the line was free and was soon answered by Julie who was adamant that she had been 'just about to call'. It was good news. The owners had accepted her offer and, as there was no chain, she could expect to move in around six weeks. Suddenly, six weeks seemed an awfully long time. She pushed over to the bed eager to look at the property details again. Tossing a sheet and flinging a pillow she found them. What had been three stapled sheets, slightly curled at the edges, was now a punctured and shredded bundle of wastepaper. Papers in hand she pushed over to the window seat where Horace was sitting, minding his own business. Ignoring the evidence, he jumped on her lap and started purring: no admission of guilt or contrition forthcoming. She took his head in her hands and stared into his eyes. The connection she felt startled her and the suspicion that Horace had known exactly what he was doing, was hard to ignore; she had heard the rumours about the Much Meddling cat population. Ridiculous!

* * *

Back home Emily unloaded the items that she had been given and took them inside. She had a box full of wooden ducks that needed their eyes re-painting and the numbers redoing on their bases. Some also needed new hooks screwing into their backs. There was a stack of bunting flags that needed sewing onto strips of ribbon and nine coconuts that needed faces painting on them. In an idiotic attempt to please Sophie she had also volunteered to make two cakes for the cake stall. She was tempted to go to the bakery and order a couple but didn't think 'splashing her cash' would go down well.

She made a list of cake ingredients, had lunch, and then set off to the store. As she stepped through Wishing Well gates she spotted Mr Swire, sitting on a bench on the green. Aware that he had seen her she strolled over; there not being much choice of an alternative route that wouldn't look like she was deliberately avoiding him.

"Hello, how are you?"

"It's not getting any better. And before you start, it's not me leg." As if to prove it he struggled to his feet and waved his stick in her face. "You know full well what I'm talking about. Tell that Alex, 'ee needs to pull 'is bloody finger out." With that he set off, hobbled across the road and into the church yard. A couple of cats hopped down from the church wall and fell into step behind him. To her surprise, one of them appeared to be Snokettee. Puzzled, Emily decided to follow. She wound her way through the yew trees, trying to stick to the grass so as not to make a noise on the chippings. She soon lost sight of Mr Swire but was able to keep at least one of the cats in view. At the back of the church the party veered right, away from the graves of Angelica, Ruby and Myrtle. When they reached the older part of the graveyard, the cats disappeared too. A huge square yew tree stood between her and her quarries' last known position. She crept round the tree and was confronted with Snokettee, a black tortoiseshell cat and Mr Swire.

"I may be a bit mutton these days but I just bin waxed." To illustrate the point he stuck a finger in each ear and gave them a good 'squelchy' rattle. He removed his fingers, glanced at them and then held them up for Emily's inspection. "You'd a bin no good in my unit. Yu'd a bin 'eard in Berlin." He was obviously much older than she thought. "Come 'ere," and he pointed at a row of graves a few feet away, with their backs to the church yard boundary wall. "Go on, take a look."

Emily wandered over, carefully avoiding treading on any of the graves in her path. The first stone she looked at startled her. It was a Wells' grave. On inspection of the others she realised what she was looking at. These weren't just graves of Alex' ancestors but specific ones:

ones with matching birthdays and they came in threes. She strolled along the row. There were gaps where other graves had been placed over the years, but then she would come across another three. In all there were three lots of Wells triplets, four if you counted Angelica, Ruby and Myrtle. Emily wondered why she hadn't discovered these before and why she hadn't even considered how many other Wells may be buried here. It was logical that they would be, and now she remembered that James had mentioned them at the Well Blessing. She was the mother of a fifth generation of Wells' triplets. It suddenly felt like an enormous responsibility. She turned to Mr Swire, but he and the cats were gone. Emily, lost in thought, headed to the store.

Jake was eager to know how the well depth measurements were going. As far as Emily knew the water was dropping at a rate of about half a centimetre a day. There was only about a metre to go and that well would be dry too. Jake looked grim. It would take more than a heavy rain shower to replace the lost water, even if they knew how to stop it draining away; it took a long time for surface water to seep through.

* * *

Alex downed a pint of water and went back to work. The items from St Peter's that he had been asked to repair didn't represent big jobs in themselves, but they were fiddly and he was getting quite frustrated. He really didn't need the extra work. He had to make templates of all the pieces before starting work on them as the finished items needed to fit into their original fastenings: which he didn't have. As all the pieces were broken or out of shape, making the templates was largely guesswork. If he could get them finished today then if any adjustments were necessary, there would be time to make them. With a deep sigh he plunged another piece of metal into the furnace.

* * *

With one cake out of the oven and cooling Emily set off to collect the children from nursery. Driving down the High Street past the forge reminded her that she had neither told Alex of Lou's suggestion for naming the forge yard nor asked St Peter's about holding a naming competition at the fete. Perhaps if she asked Alex this evening and he liked the name she wouldn't need to bother asking St Peter's. Besides, there would be enough to do at the fete without complicating things with a competition of their own, albeit one linked to St Peter's Charity Shop, via the yard.

She collected the girls and headed home. As they passed the entrance to St Peters the girls all started talking and pointing. From her position in the driving seat she was unable to see what they were pointing at, but looked about anyway. It seemed that there were cats, on the walls, in the trees and strolling down the side of the road. As she drove into Much Meddling there were felines in gardens, in shop doorways and under the benches on the green. Mr Swire had not been exaggerating; there were cats 'all o'ert shop'.

"What's going on girls?" said Emily as they rounded the green.

"Bad man!" said Lily.

* * *

That evening, as Alex got the children into bed, Emily scraped icing out of a mixing bowl and placed a dollop of it onto each of two large buns, made from the extra cake mix she had deliberately made. Then, as she heard him coming downstairs, she served up their dinner. After Alex had had a good grumble about the extra work St Peter's had foisted on him, he pushed his empty dinner plate to one side. Emily handed him an iced bun and took the opportunity to bring up the naming of the yard, knowing that this would remind him that he also had a bird bath to complete, without her having to mention it. However, if he liked Lou's suggestion the bird bath would be off his work list. To her surprise he thought that 'The Ark Aid' was a great idea and not, it seemed, just because it reduced his workload. That might have been an element of it but she didn't think he would accept the name if he didn't actually like it. Enthused, he grabbed a piece of paper and a pencil and started sketching out letters that he could fashion out of metal. From Emily's vantage point it looked like the letters were to incorporate lights. When a boat and a series of animals appeared on his piece of paper she raised her eyebrows and started clearing the table. Standing by the sink, she texted Lou, 'Score – The Ark Aid is a success! BUT, Let Alex confirm.'

CHAPTER FORTY

As Emily pulled back into the drive, having dropped off the children at nursery, she was hailed by James who was coming out of the church. He was hoping to catch her. He had an envelope for Alex from Lady Agnes. He would have pushed it through the letter box but he had been instructed to ensure that he and Emily were present when Alex opened it.

"Well, do you want to bring it round this evening, after the girls have gone to bed?" asked Emily.

James looked hesitant so she suggested that perhaps she could get Alex to come home for lunch.

"Yes, that would be better: when the girls aren't around."

"Okay. Come around 1pm. I'll let you know if Alex can't make it."

After James had gone Emily set to work to make her second cake. Once that was in the oven she went to the outhouse and began painting eyes on the little wooden ducks. This was fiddly but fun. She could vary their expressions by the way she positioned their eyes: high and wide – surprised: low and close together – suspicious.

At just after 12:30 Alex arrived with a couple of pasties from the bakery, curious to know what the envelope contained and why it was important that James was there, and the girls weren't!

When James arrived they had finished their lunch and cleared the kitchen table, ready for whatever the mysterious envelope contained.

"Sorry for all the drama but Lady Agnes wasn't sure how you would react to what you are about to learn," said James. With that he opened the envelope and pulled out two stacks of printed sheets. He handed one to Alex and the other to Emily so that they could both read at the same time.

I know that you both have many questions about my history, of the Earnshaws and Sycamore Park Hall and how it all fits into the Wells' history. It has been very frustrating for me not to be able to explain everything, but talking is difficult and exhausting since I had my 'strokes'. I have composed the following to hopefully answer your questions and included some relevant documents. It has taken me a long time to complete this. I would have liked to tell you earlier.

Since long before I was born there was a rift between the Wells and the Earnshaws.

As you may have discovered the Wells owned much of the land on the Much Meddling side of the crag and farmland to the east. (The text now included copies of the Much Meddling maps Emily had found amongst Myrtle's belongings, but the outlines of the Wells land were clearly defined. It also showed land beyond that of the map which Emily had found.) **There was always a certain amount of friction between the two families going back to the Wars of The Roses: Much Meddling being on the Lancashire/ Yorkshire border. To most members of both families this was ancient history. However, for our ancestor Cyril Wells and for one Archibold Noblet Earnshaw, it was very much alive. The two men hated each other. As teenagers they had physically fought on a number of occasions, Cyril usually getting the better of Archibald. As adults they learnt to avoid one another. Unfortunately, both choosing careers in politics meant that they frequently clashed verbally and publicly at Council meetings. Moving in the same circles they were forced to socialise.**

Cyril liked to gamble and was apparently quite good at most card games. Over several weeks he took a moderate amount of money off Archibald. Then, Archibald taunted Cyril into gambling his land, putting up a couple of his winning racehorses as his stake. Cyril laughed at the absurdity of Archibald being so bold as

to challenge him so recklessly and accepted the bet. It was claimed afterwards that Archibald cheated but it was never proved. There were claims and testimony from both sides by those who had been present. However, as Archibold now had the greater amount of influence, most villagers being employed on the land, opposition quickly died. Archibold took the Wells land, leaving them with just the cottages to live in and The Three Wells pub for income. In subsequent years, in an effort to recoup what he had lost, Cyril built up significant debt and they had to sell The Three Wells pub. When he died the family was more or less penniless. They all moved into Wishing Well Cottage so that they could rent out Bode Well and Fare Well Cottages. They earned a living any way they could: herbalism being one of them.

In 1823 work started on Sycamore Park Hall and Mr Earnshaw took the title Lord. With income from the land and his political connections Lord Earnshaw became a very successful businessman and the family lived exceedingly well. Over the years concerted attempts were made by the Wells' family to prove that the land had been taken illegally but the Earnshaw money and connections ensured that all attempts were quashed.

So, when I met and fell in love with Richard Earnshaw, he and I were ostracised by both families. We ran away and married at Gretna Green. When Richard's parents died unexpectedly, not having left a will, he inherited Sycamore Park Hall and we came back down here from Scotland, where we had been living. We discovered that no-one knew who we were. Both families had done such an effective job of wiping us from their lives that, to the villagers, we were just 'relatives from Scotland' when we inherited Sycamore Park Hall. Those that did know who we were, never talked to us, or about us.

So, I am sorry Alex that you didn't know about us until now. Sadly, your great, great, aunts didn't make contact with me and they must have known who I was. Maybe they regretted giving me the periapt necklace. After all, I did come back home. However, I don't believe that the three of them ever did anything without purpose and they were good people.

If you have any further questions I will gladly do my best to answer them.

With love from your cousin Agnes

Alex quietly put down the papers, his face impassive. To James relief there had been no outburst as Lady Agnes had feared. Alex appeared to accept the information as old history.

"Wow," said Emily. "What happened to Cyril?" If the Wells family refused to speak to the Earnshaws how did they treat *him*, the idiot who took the bet and lost all their land? So, I guess that explains why there was no value on the land transaction. How awful. Then to see that huge hall built on the land…"

"Yes, I wouldn't have liked to have been in his shoes," said James. "Right, best get going. I guess I'll see you on Saturday, unless, of course, you are planning on resurrecting the Wells/Earnshaw feud. Jousting; that would be a fun event."

Alex stayed stony faced and Emily said, "Hmm, still a little too soon!"

* * *

Lady Agnes was working hard. Intensive physiotherapy and speech therapy were having their effect. She could now walk from one end of her room to the other and back, with just a stick. More times than not, she could stand unaided. She still tired easily but was determined to improve and having a goal was giving her the incentive. To a certain extent, Sophie had inspired her. Seeing the young woman take on the fund raising for St Peter's and organise the fete which, she had to admit, was on a grander scale than anything St Peter's had achieved before, was galvanising. Part of her felt in competition with Sophie and part of her sought the young woman's approval. If she wasn't currently physically or mentally capable of 'pulling her weight' in organising the fete, then she would do what she could to be a living advert, and advocate, of the work that St Peter's did. She was determined to stand at the St Peter's stall and talk to people.

* * *

Simon was in 'two minds'. He knew that Trevor wanted to go to the fete. He also knew that Suzanne was determined to take him. He realised that, as her employer, he only needed to say 'No' but he also knew that that would create difficulties. Should he just let the pair of them go?

He took a couple of phone calls and started typing an e-mail but couldn't concentrate. He looked out of his office window. It was bright and clear outside. Inside, the air-conditioning was making him cold and he reached for his jacket. The forecast for the weekend was good. His mind went back to the fete and he just knew that he couldn't stay away. He had to see Sophie.

CHAPTER FORTY ONE

It was the day of the fete. Sophie had been up since 5am checking and re-checking her lists. Now she was anxiously awaiting the arrival of her volunteers. At 8:45am a car worked its way up the drive, shortly followed by another. She directed them round to the back of the house leaving the main car park clear for the paying public. By 9am, all her volunteers had arrived.

Emily asked Sophie if there was somewhere cool she could put her cakes until the fete opened. She was directed to a ground floor room which appeared to be a storage room for the kitchen. There were other cakes already there and she placed hers alongside. Returning to her car she collected her box of ducks and bunting and took them to the relevant stalls. She helped put up the bunting and then went to take a look at her stall. It didn't take long to set up as the equipment was already there and just needed some cash for the money tin, which she would be given later. When she had first been told that she was getting the 'Splat the Rat' stall she had been disappointed. However, she quite liked the selection of soft toys that she had been presented with for prizes and arranged them at the back of the stall, and placed her seat at an angle so that she could keep an eye on everything. Lou had got the Hoop-La stall and Anna was going to be on the gate. James would be taking his turn answering questions on the St Peter's stand.

Late morning they were all called in to St Peter's entrance hall. Lady Agnes was there, and to everyone's amazement, standing.

"I want to 'ank you all for all the a... mazing work you have done, and for what... you are going to do today. St Peter's must...go on. The staff here are wonder...ful. Just see... what they can do." She then walked across the foyer, steadied herself and turned sideways. She was now side-on to her audience who started clapping. "Not just for me but..." and she pulled at a large, draped satin sheet, which slid to the ground revealing the St Peter's display stand. "Please, en...courage every...one to read it. 'ank you, and good luck."

As everyone commenced clapping again Sophie shepherded them into an ante room where there was a selection of sandwiches, cakes and drinks.

"Right," said Sophie, "We haven't got long. Would you all please be at your positions by 12:50. Gates open at 1pm. Does anyone have any last questions?"

"What do we do if we need to leave our stall?"

This had been covered but Sophie patiently replied, "Just stick your red flag on the front of your stall and someone will come and relieve you." The woman didn't look convinced but a woman who would be on the adjacent stall said she would keep a look out for her, which seemed to appease the woman.

Emily walked back to her stall, counted her collection of small change and then sat, stroking her rat, waiting.

* * *

Alex bundled the girls into the Range Rover and drove down the road to St Peter's. It wasn't long before he joined a line of cars and crawled the rest of the way at about 5mph. At St Peter's entrance a villager he recognised was in the road, directing traffic, alternately letting a vehicle from either direction into St Peter's drive. Alex was surprised. He hadn't expected so much interest. Eventually, he was into the grounds and handing cash over to Anna, who told him to follow the directions of the man in the yellow jacket. He did as he was directed and got one of the last spaces on hard standing. Behind him cars were being directed onto the grass.

As he was getting the girls out of the car his attention was drawn to raised voices. At the head of the line of cars was Simon, holding everyone up and arguing with the man in the yellow jacket. Guessing what the issue was Alex strolled over. "I don't mind moving if you want my space. I am happy to put my Range Rover on the grass."

Suzanne said she would get out and mind the girls whilst the men re-arranged their vehicles. The man in the yellow jacket muttered to himself and Lily stood and glowered. Cars parked, Alex made his excuses and steered the girls away from Simon.

* * *

Emily's stall was doing well. She had plenty of people wanting to 'Splat the Rat'. Everyone was convinced they could hit it and nobody managed to. She took their money, held the 'rat' at the top of the drainpipe. The customer stood, bat poised, and waited. As she let go of the rat they would swing wildly and the rat would drop out the bottom of the pipe to land, untouched, in the bucket below. As another customer took up their position Emily became aware that Mike and Nathan had joined the audience, Nathan patently keen to have a go. When his turn came, he gave his bat a couple of test swings. Amusingly it looked like he had been paying attention to the techniques of those who had gone before him. He placed his feet apart and stood sideways and nodded his head to acknowledge that he was ready. Emily dropped the rat. Somehow he had anticipated her timing and the rat smacked against the back of the stall.

Amongst the audience's amused approval there was a loud shriek. A little brown curly-headed figure rushed from the crowd, and as Nathan did a victory dance, arms in the air, Tansy hit him mid chest and drove him several feet backwards, into the side of the next stall. As Nathan lay gasping for breath she stood over him, angrily waiting for him to get back to his feet. Mike, quick to rescue his son, flung her out of the way. With a cat-like lack of intimidation she instantly regained her balance and resumed her position. By the time Nathan had got his breath back and everyone was happy that he was okay, there was no sign of the rat. No amount of 'blackmail' could make Tansy reveal what she had done with it and explaining that it wasn't a real rat, did no good. A very apologetic Emily let Nathan choose a prize from the collection of soft toys. Having chosen a multi-coloured Dinosaur Mike took him off to see the fire engine. Alex led the girls in the opposite direction to see the donkey stall which would hopefully take Tansy's mind off the rat trauma. He felt slightly guilty at this, as it might be seen as praising her, but secretly he was amused and proud. He was no rugby fan, but he could appreciate a good tackle when he saw one.

So that the stall could continue to operate Emily used her initiative and chose a replacement rat. Her choice was limited as not all the soft toys would fit down the drainpipe. For a while she continued to take money, but not much. It seemed that Much Meddling's appetite for 'Splat the Kitten', was limited.

* * *

Simon wandered round the stalls. Suzanne had taken Trevor to the little boys' room and so he was on his own for a while. Sophie wasn't on any of the stalls so he headed to the entrance hall. Inside he was astonished to see his mother standing and talking to guests. He couldn't believe it. Haltingly she was answering questions and pointing to a display board. He watched for a while and then wandered outside again. Eventually he spotted Sophie. She was going along the row of stalls, speaking to each of the volunteers in turn. She collected money from some, and gave change to others. She caught a passing helper and sent them off to the house for more raffle tickets. Then she collected a rubbish bag from one stall and sent a stall holder off for a break as another turned up to relieve them. She was fascinating to watch, so animated and in control, so alive and, and... stunningly beautiful. As she turned towards him he stumbled back into the anonymity of the crowd and she passed within feet of him. He didn't know why he was hiding. He had done it instinctively, not wanting to spoil the flow of her, not wanting to take away the magic of her. As she disappeared from view a humbled Simon found one of the residents smiling at him. It took a moment for Simon to remember. The man was grinning at him and holding out his hand, the hand that Simon had shaken once before, at Sophie's insistence. Simon remembered that the man was deaf and made a conscious effort to look him in the eye and enunciate clearly. At first nervous, but increasingly confident the man took it upon himself to introduce Simon to other residents. Using gestures he encouraged them to explain how St Peter's had helped them.

* * *

The afternoon was coming to an end and people were starting to drift off home. Emily, having consulted Sophie, was packing up her stall. She was just putting her remaining soft toys into a bag and retrieving one that had fallen down the back of the stall, when she spotted a donkey walking along the bottom of the field. Registering the sight but not thinking much of it she turned round to find Alex approaching.

"Aren't the children with you?"

"No," said Emily.

Alex was running his hands through his hair and looking around frantically. She was just about to mention the donkey when his face relaxed and she felt a tug at her elbow. It was Violet, "Can we have the car keys?"

Looking round for the other two Emily asked, "What? Why do you want the car keys?"

Nathan stepped up beside her from behind the stall and plonked a conspiratorial hand on Violet's shoulder, "We need somewhere to put this lot," and he yanked into view an orange sledge piled with random items, all with pink numbered tombola stickers attached. "Then we are going to need more money. We still have the 'Hook-a-Duck' stall to do."

As Emily pondered how to respond, Violet and Nathan stood side by side in innocent expectation. Alex continued to scan the crowd, out of which stepped a man in a high-viz. jacket with 'Search and Rescue' printed along its back and front pocket. The man stopped, placed his hands on his hips and addressed Nathan.

"That's a fine haul you've got there young man, but I am going to need my stretcher back."

"No," said Nathan, "When she picks the ducks we'll need it again." Violet beamed at the man. "She's very good," added Nathan.

Ignoring the exchange Alex asked Violet if she knew where her sisters had gone. She pointed down the field at the back of the stall, "Fairy rings." Now Alex could see a donkey at the bottom of the lawn and he set off at the run.

Mike, who had just appeared in search of Nathan set off too, leaving Nathan and Violet with Emily, who tried to explain to the Search and Rescue man that the two missing girls looked exactly like the one in front of him. He held down the talk button on his radio and let his colleagues know that they had some children missing.

As Alex got nearer and the lawn levelled

out he could see Tansy happily skipping round in circles followed by a donkey, but only Tansy. There was no sign of Lily. "Where's Lily?"

Unconcerned Tansy pointed to a gap in the trees. Mike arrived at Alex side.

"Lily went in the wood?"

"Yes," said Tansy.

"Why?"

"Bad man," said Tansy.

Alex ran into the wood and after only a few paces came to an abrupt halt, unable to see. The light contrast between the sunny grounds and the dense trees was too much. Removing his sunglasses he paused for his eyes to adjust and shouted his daughter's name. "Lily, Lily." Just visible ahead was a fork in the path.

Mike said, "You take that one, I'll take this."

"That way daddy," said Tansy, pointing up the right-hand path which the men could now see clearly marked out by a string of cats' eyes, a row of furry heads all turned their way, checking what the noise was.

"No," exclaimed Alex, "Not that way, please not that way." As a teenager he used to play in these woods and he knew that path well; it terminated in a 20foot drop into a rock pool. He used to dive off that ledge but there was only one spot that was safe and the path to it was loose and slippery. Again he ran, cats scattering.

Ahead he could see the gap in the trees

where the top of the ledge was, but there was no sign of Lily. He halted at the top of the ledge and looked down. It was much different to how he remembered it. Strangely the drop looked greater, the opposite to how the reality of memories usually presented themselves in later years. The rocks at the top were how he remembered them, but there were far more rocks below, the pool seemed much smaller, and the perimeter of it was somehow more open and less secluded.

"Daddy, help, help."

Alex couldn't see her, but he headed recklessly down the side of the slope, cannoning into tree trunks and grasping at branches to slow his descent.

"Daddy, help me."

"I'm coming love. Daddy's coming."

Scrambling through the undergrowth he emerged by her side.

"Help, help!"

He took a moment to assess the situation. There was no immediate danger to her that he could see, and physically she looked okay. As his heart continued to pound he gathered her in his arms but she fought him.

"No Daddy. Help," alarmed, he let her go. She bent down and put her little arms round a thick grey hose and started tugging at it. Now Alex looked, his eyes following the hose. It rose from the water and went over the edge of the rocky ground that surrounded the pool and disappeared into the undergrowth. Now, he became aware of water, rushing away down the hillside. The hose was siphoning water from the pool, and at a terrific rate. Alex grabbed it and heaved. Nothing happened. Then he noticed that there were cable ties holding it in place.

Alex now found that he and Lily weren't alone. Mike had made his way down and joined them, as had the Search and Rescue man. Alex turned on him, "You must have a knife, or something."

"Well, I've got this," and, after a bit of fumbling, he produced some wire cutters, "but I'm not sure that we should be interfering. This is private property, isn't it?"

Alex snatched it off him and deftly cut the ties. He then grabbed the hose and threw it angrily down the hillside. From the top of the ledge there was a shout, "There are another two, over there." Alex looked up to see Sasha. He was pointing at two spots, just along from where Alex was standing. Quickly the hoses were found and unceremoniously removed.

Alex handed back the wire cutters and offered his apologies. The man shrugged and pushed his radio button, "The girls have been found, safe and well." He looked at Alex, "That is all of them, isn't it?" Alex nodded and the man set off back up the slope, passing Sasha, who was on his way down. At the top were Emily, Tansy and a couple of firemen. The latter seemed to have been informed that all was now well as they waved and set off back up the path.

Alex escorted Lily back to the top of the ledge and handed her over to Emily. "You take the girls back. I want to have a look around, check that this is the extent of it."

"So, this is what was causing the water level to drop in the wells?" asked Emily.

"Looks like it," said Alex, shaking his head and mouthing a few expletives over the top of the children.

When he got back down to the pool and looked around, he was shocked by the amount of devastation to both the vegetation and the ground. Someone had been trying to lower the side of the pool, but when solid rock prevented them they had resorted to siphoning the water. The three huge hoses would have been emptying gallons every minute. He wished he had been able to show the firemen; they would probably have been able to estimate the quantities.

Alex went back to the pool. Sasha was pacing back and forth and questioning Mike. Now, he asked Alex, "What is up there, beyond these trees?"

"Well, you've got the road along the bottom and the trees thin out and end and you've got fields going round the base of the crag."

"And the rock pools?"

"If I recall there are several of them all

along here. This is the biggest and deepest. They are quite shallow up that way, just dried mud at times," and he pointed beyond where Sasha was standing.

"Well, speaking as an architect, and going on what Anna has said over the past few weeks about St Peters and its land being valued etc., I suspect that someone is trying to drain these pools to allow the building of an access road. Are there any newts or Natterjack toads along there?"

"Oh, there have always been newts," said Alex.

"Are they Great Crested ones?"

Alex shrugged. So Sasha knelt down and put his finger in the waters edge to wet it, and sketched out a Great Crested newt on a slab of rock.

"That's Lily's dragon!" Furious, Alex set off for St Peter's. The others followed, doing their best to keep up.

* * *

Simon had come to a decision. His mother was no longer in the foyer so he headed up to her apartment. He found her there, looking out of her living room window, watching the dregs of the home's guests trickle down the drive, and a couple of people running about trying to catch a donkey. Her door was open so he had walked straight in. She was a little surprised to see him. Without any expectations she said, "Hello,

Simon."

He picked up a chair and carried it over so that he could sit next to her. Slowly and thoughtfully he sat, choosing his words. "I hope it isn't too late, but I want to help." Seeing her look of disgust, he continued, "No, not with the fete, I know it is too late for that, but with the home. I want to help you run it."

Lady Agnes looked at her son and studied him. She was tired and she didn't want a fight. She wanted to believe that he genuinely wanted to help her, but she just didn't. She realised that she had a pain in her chest, a pain born out of disappointment, a little knot of despair. He was her son, and this new duplicity was tightening it. "So, I guess... you are afraid...that St Pee... ter's might survive. Afraid that I will...give...it ... Sophie."

Simon went pale, "I never believed you were serious... You wouldn't?"

"I know you have...been see...ing her. I know she wo't...'ave...you. So...now you think... only way...is ...get...in...my...good...books!"

"No, mum, that isn't true. It is the fete that has done it: this wonderful fete that Sophie organised. I have been wandering round talking to people and I think I now understand. St Peter's really is doing a wonderful job. So many people have been telling me so, residents, ex-residents and relatives, even people with no connection to the place have been impressed by the work here.

I had no idea." Seeing a softening in his mother's eyes and struggling to surmount the lump in his throat he continued, "Up until now I have only seen St Peter's through a child's eyes. Today, for the first time I am looking at it as an adult. You have achieved something incredible here and yes, it is really important that that continues."

"Simon!" Sophie crashed into the room, her entrance betraying the fact that she had been listening at the door and that she didn't care if they knew it. "Oh, Simon, I am so pleased to hear you say that. Do you really mean that?"

"Yes. Tom took me round and introduced me to people. Then we met Peter and he joined in and Andrea told me all about her car accident and how St Peter's helped her get back to her feet and taught her how to wash and dress herself with muscles that would no longer do her bidding. Tim told me all about the tricks, sorry, techniques that he has been taught to cope with his speech impediment and ways to manage his memory loss... "

Lady Agnes listened and watched as her son became animated, and was heartened by his genuine enthusiasm. Slowly, the knot in her chest relaxed, and she reached out for Simon's hand, daring to believe him.

With a rush, Trevor ran into the room. Suzanne walked in, at a dignified pace and came to a halt whilst she assessed the significance of Sophie's presence. All seemed well. This, however, didn't last long. There was a thundering of feet and Alex burst in, closely followed by a breathless Mike and Sasha. Alex was about to let rip when he checked himself, Trevor at least shouldn't be exposed to what was to come. Suzanne, good nanny that she was, escorted Trevor from the room with a promise of 'let's see what we can find in the kitchen'.

When Alex was certain that they were out of earshot he commenced a barrage of expletives that left Simon in no doubt that he had made some kind of error, but he didn't know what. Lady Agnes and Sophie just stared. When Alex paused for breath, Sasha tried to explain.

Looking directly at Simon he said, "Someone has been siphoning gallons of water, emptying the ponds in the wood." Simon went beetroot. "It has reduced the water table in Much Meddling, drying up the wells. It is even affecting farms at the other side of the crag." Everyone looked at Simon. No denial was forthcoming. "Knowing that you had the land valued," continued Sasha, "we suspect that you are trying to drive the Great Crested Newts out of their habitats so that there will be no opposition to an access road, allowing you to build on the land to the side of St Peters."

Lady Agnes gasped and started to sob. Simon now lost all colour.

From the doorway a solemn little voice said, "Bad man."

Ignoring Lily and continuing to stare at Sasha, Simon started to rally. Not very effectively though, as the first thing out of his mouth was, "Who are you?" looking at Sasha.

"*He* is an architect, and *my* fiancé," said Anna, her revelation adding to the disarray, briefly stealing the attention from at least half of those present.

"And *you*, what's it got to do with *you*?" retorted Simon.

"I have lived in this village *all my life*." Having started she couldn't stop; an articulate and vitriolic diatribe of rebuke on behalf of the inhabitants of Much Meddling followed, amazing those present. Normally quiet and easy going she laid into Simon with the skill of a Roman orator. When she came to a halt Alex and Emily took up the reins, joined by Lou and Mike and even James, who had also now appeared.

Simon seemed frozen to the spot: Lady Agnes, too. Then, and Sophie had no idea what caused it, whether it was the condemned look on Simon's face, or the fact that Horace chose that moment to rub round Simon's ankles, she never knew, but she suddenly had the over whelming need to defend him. It wasn't rational but her heart leapt to his defence. She was furious with him but that, she felt, was her prerogative. No-one was going to abuse her Simon. She pushed in front of him and turned to face the others.

"Stop it. Stop it," she screamed. "He plainly

didn't understand the consequences. At least give him a chance to explain." As everyone fell silent she backed up and positioned herself beside Simon and took his hand. Horace jumped on her lap and pushed his head against their joined hands. Simon used his other hand and stroked Horace's head, giving himself some time to gather his thoughts.

"I just wanted to lower the ponds enough so that the newts would move down the valley. I didn't want to harm them. I had no idea it would affect the wells. Of course, we must stop it immediately."

"We already did that," seethed Alex. "It will take years for that water table to fill again."

"I'm sorry. What can I do?"

"Do! There is nothing that you can do. As I said it will take years to undo what you have done!"

"Alex," said Emily. "I think that it is time that we were going. We need to get the girls home and get them their tea."

"Yes," said Lou, "We should be going too."

With that they all filed out of the room leaving Lady Agnes, Sophie and Simon alone.

CHAPTER FORTY TWO

As the Wells family headed up the church path Emily spotted Mr Swire and his two lady friends, waiting just inside the porch. She took a deep breath, put a bright smile on her face and continued putting one foot in front of the other.

"Ye did it then. I can tell. Cats are leavin'. A knew ye wud. 'Ere, I got summat for ye," and he held out a string-bag full of onions. "I just pulled 'em. This some garlic in ther too, a bit exotic, I know, but I wan'ed to give ye summat special." Alex took the bag. "And, I got summat for you three kids an all." He reached in his pockets and pulled out three small brown paper bags and handed one to each child, "Careful. Keep 'em that way up."

The girls slowly and carefully unwrapped the bags and looked inside. Each bag contained an egg cup with a face on it and each was filled with soil. "This cress seed in ther. Keep 'em lightly watered," he chuckled, "and thill all grow green 'air. Reight, best get inside."

At the front of the church and to one side, obscured by a column, and a plinth with some candles and foliage, Emily thought she could see the back of Lady Agnes' head. It was a surprise, and she could have been wrong, but the thought occupied her all through the service. Emily knew that there weren't any seats in that area which added to the possibility that she was right, as it would be a good spot for a wheelchair. When she went up to the altar for Communion she took the opportunity, on the way back, to have a proper look. She was right, it was Lady Agnes, but she wasn't alone. Sat by her was Simon and, next to him, was Sophie. Surprised, Emily failed to notice the two steps down and went full length, landing heavily on the thinly carpeted stone floor. With her communion wafer stuck to the roof of her mouth, it was a while before she could reassure everyone that she was okay. She wasn't, lots of bits hurt, but removing herself from the 'spotlight' was worth further damage to any possible broken bones. Alex helped her back to her seat and she gradually faded back into the crowd, where she could quietly assess her injuries. She had a bruise on her left knee and a bruised and grazed wrist. Her hip she would look at when they got back home.

At the end of the service Emily took her time as she wasn't sure how her hip and knee would work when she stood. She checked the girls had all their belongings, including their

Sunday School artwork, and hobbled painfully to the door. Outside, a lot of the congregation were gathered round the Earnshaws all talking about the fete and hoping that it would be an annual event. When the Wells family emerged attention shifted. Mr Swire it seemed had been singing their praises and lauding the triplets as the new village guardians. "Thiz onli yung, so it took 'em a while but they did it. All is well now." Most of the crowd had no idea what he was talking about and Mr Swire himself didn't know the details, but three delightful and happy triplets, cockily cute, took their attention.

Waving regally, and thanking everyone, Alex led the 'village saviours' back to the sanctuary of the cottage. Emily hobbled along alone. She looked, but the Earnshaws and Sophie were nowhere to be seen.

* * *

At the end of the fete, when everyone else had gone, Sophie had set about healing the rift between Simon and his mother. Suzanne had taken Trevor home, as Sophie had said that she would give Simon a lift, later. So, the three of them were alone and Sophie prompted Simon to describe to his mother, how he had experienced his childhood. Lady Agnes had had no idea how unhappy he had been and finally came to understand why he had hated St Peter's so much. She also understood why he hadn't wanted Trevor to grow up there. She was heartbroken but she understood. He was able to convince her that he had had no plans to bully her into selling any of the land, just to show her what was possible as a way to save St Peter's. Yes, he had to admit that he would have sold it once she died, but simply because he didn't want to live there and had no idea how to run St Peter's, even if it were a successful business. The fete, though, had been a revelation. The people he had spoken to were so grateful and enthusiastic and had made him realise how special the place was and what an incredible thing his mother had achieved. There was a lot more to be said but the events of the day had exhausted Lady Agnes and Sophie and Simon had left her to rest.

In Sophie's room, they had talked and talked, and Simon had finally phoned Suzanne to say he would be out over night.

* * *

Emily inspected her hip. There was bruising, but that was the extent of it. She could feel her muscles were stiffening up and she knew she was going to ache. However, everything worked. She was supposed to be going to St Peter's, to help take down the stalls, but she didn't feel capable. Alex would have to go instead. She knew he wouldn't like that, but if neither of them went it would look like they were avoiding going, because of what had happened.

* * *

After lunch Sophie took her tablet and

notebooks to Lady Agnes' room: the pair being eager to count up their funds. Sophie felt a little uncomfortable having spent the night, only a few doors away, with Lady Agnes' son. It was unlikely that she knew, but one of the staff may have told her of their early morning departure, to drop Simon back home. However, there was no indication that Lady Agnes knew or, if she did, disapproved.

First they emptied all the cash tins onto Lady Agnes' dining table and added the notes Sophie had brought up to Lady Agnes room for safe keeping, during the fete. They arranged it in piles according to denomination and then counted each pile, making a note of the amounts as they went. Then, on-line, Sophie brought up the account, set up specifically for the recent charity events, and added the amount in that. Next, she consulted her notebook for the promissory amounts, and added that to the total. The final amount was significant, even without the promised amounts.

"Sophie, I can't thank you enough. I am so grate...ful. We can now start... planning. This is enough for the heating, and we can start... the...roof. Next, we should do the Easter ...Egg... Hunt."

Sophie looked at her, "I don't think I will be here for that. I am buying a bungalow which should complete soon and I am looking for a job." Seeing Lady Agnes disappointment she added,

"I need to concentrate my efforts towards that. Besides, it only needs a load of eggs buying and scattering and a bit of advertising. Anyone can do that. Simon said he wanted to help..."

"Well, yes, I suppose. What did you do before your accident?"

Sophie explained that she had worked for a travel company. She was a resort rep. for a while but then became an inspector and trainer, which she enjoyed. She travelled a lot. Her firm had kept her position open and had suggested that she tested resorts for accessibility, but she didn't fancy that. She didn't want to be defined by her wheels. They had also offered her a job in the office but she didn't fancy being sat behind a desk all day, plus it was a bit far from her new bungalow.

* * *

Alex hadn't been thrilled at going back to St Peters but went anyway. The amount of physical labour involved, dismantling and stowing the stalls, gave him a reasonable work-out and he had to admit that Emily was in no fit state to have done it.

* * *

Sophie and Lady Agnes had a long chat about St Peter's, with Sophie making suggestions both for the home and for the outbuildings and how to make money out of them. Sophie was just leaving when Simon turned up with Trevor. Wanting to give Simon some time with his mother, Sophie sat Trevor on her knee and wheeled him back to her room. There she kept him entertained with a ball, paper and pens, and Horace, until Simon came to collect him. Trevor was a happy little boy. His daddy and Sophie were getting on well.

CHAPTER FORTY THREE

At the Tuesday meeting everyone turned up early, eager to know how much they had raised and what it meant for St Peter's. Colette put a copy of the account on the screen on the wall so that everyone could see the amounts. All the money had now been paid in. The total was a staggering £47,789.23p. Sophie went down the list explaining the source of each one. There were the initial collections made by Sophie from her 'accosting people in the foyer campaign' as she called it, James' Comedy Caravan monies, random donations, amounts that would previously have gone on rent at the Charity shop, the fete gate takings and the money from the fete stalls. Lastly there was a mysterious £22,678 which had been paid in, in cash, the day before, but not by Sophie. She was at a loss to know where it had come from. There were mutterings but no-one admitted any knowledge. James, Emily noted, as Saturday's Grand National popped unbidden into her head, stayed strangely silent.

Lady Agnes thanked everyone for their hard work in saving St Peter's, but there was one person in particular that she wanted to thank, and that was Sophie. When the applause had died down she told them that she had an announcement.

"I am ve...ry pleased to tell you that St... Pee...ter's has a new Event's Manager. Sophie has...agreed to work for us."

There was much congratulating and genuine joy that she was staying. With her enthusiasm and input, everyone agreed, St. Peters had a bright future.

Back in her room she texted Simon to let him know that she was tired and instead of going out as they had planned could they just eat in her room. There was a brief exchange but her being tired won out.

* * *

Simon arrived around 7pm, hungry and keen to eat. When Sophie let him in, he was disappointed that there were no signs of food, not even place settings on her table by the window. Sophie, however, was wearing an elegant calf length dress with fitted low-cut bodice, necklace and earrings. Her make-up, more than he had seen her wear before, was flawless. She looked stunning. Seeing him looking at her, she did a twirl and then rolled over to him. He made to push the door to, but she shook her head and told him to put his jacket on the bed and follow her. Puzzled, he did as he was told. She led the way down the corridor and pushed open the next door. This room, to Simon's knowledge hadn't been used for years. Intrigued he stepped inside.

The curtains were drawn and the room was weakly illuminated by one candle in its centre. Sophie rolled in and clicked a switch, lighting the room with a thousand tiny fairy lights. In the centre of the room, where the candle sat, was a beautifully laid table for two. Silverware gleamed and a cut glass decanter, its burgundy contents glowing, matched the two sparkling glasses it accompanied. Simon looked at Sophie with raised eyebrows and a grin, "Tired, huh?"

"Please, take a seat," said Sophie. He sat and she joined him at the opposite side of the table. A discreetly sent text message produced their first course, not Simon noted, the home's usual fare. They had a wonderful meal, talking animatedly about all sorts of subjects. When Sophie texted for their coffee Simon spotted the signal and was thankful that he had brought along the ring with which he had planned to propose, at the meal out that Sophie had scuppered. He had been mortified when she had ruined his plans, but this setting was perfect. When the coffee arrived, and they were alone, he would get down on one knee.

Suddenly, Sophie backed away from the

table. He thought that she was heading for the door. Instead she turned and positioned her chair alongside his, facing him. She reached out and took his hand. He stared at it for a while, his mind racing. Then he looked her in the eye. She was smiling at him but her hand was shaking. She opened her mouth and swallowed a couple of times, her mouth apparently dry. "Simon Earnshaw, when we first met I certainly didn't see this coming, but I love you. I really do. AND, I love your son. I know that we haven't known each other long but I have learnt that life can be short and unpredictable and when you know something is right, it is stupid to wait. Will you fulfil my dreams and marry me?"

Simon was dumbfounded, *she'd* proposed to *him*.

Sophie was terrified, he was hesitating. He didn't know what to say. Had she got things so wrong?

Then Simon laughed, and without saying a word he reached into his pocket and pulled out a small blue box, which he opened. Inside was a gold ring, a disgustingly large diamond at its centre. "Yes," he said, and took her left hand, pushing the ring onto her third finger.

When the coffee arrived, it was accompanied by a large, chilled bottle of champagne.

14 Months Later

As the radiographer slid the probe over Sophie's large belly and confirmed that their baby girl was healthy and progressing nicely, Simon couldn't believe how happy he was. Sophie had proved to be the perfect mother for Trevor. Suzanne had been brilliant with him but with Sophie around as well, he had positively sparkled. With Sophie working full time at St Peter's it was decided that Suzanne should stay on. By the time Trevor started school, the baby would be born.

Their wedding had been a large affair. At Lady Agnes insistence The Wells family had been invited, as had most of the village. She was adamant that the Wells-Earnshaw feud would end, and it had. Alex had forgiven Simon. Even Lily could be trusted to be polite now her 'dragons' were safe. There was evidence that the wells were starting to fill again. The speleologists had found nothing else to explain the drop in the water level and Jake was satisfied that no permanent damage had been done to the water table and that it would return to its former level over time.

Simon sold his house and converted one of St Peter's large outbuildings into a home for the family and Horace, who seemed to approve of the arrangement; he moved himself in. Simon continued to work for his old company for a while but gradually he was learning how to run St Peter's and he found that he actually enjoyed the challenges posed by managing a large estate. When Lady Agnes gladly handed over the reins to him and retired, she also moved into Simon and Sophie's house. She grew stronger and was eventually able to walk unaided, for short distances, and her speech improved. She and Sophie became close and she eagerly awaited the birth of her granddaughter. Further revelations to Emily explained the £72,000 donation that Myrtle had made to St Peter's. In her will Myrtle had paid the last of the debt owed to the Earnshaws by the Wells family. It was a large amount of money and would have been a phenomenal amount at the time the debt was accrued. When Emily tentatively expressed her surprise to Lady Agnes that the Wells sisters hadn't used their 'abilities' to pay off the debts she was told sternly that none of the Wells sisters, of any generation, would ever do that. They only ever helped other people.

Alex converted the rest of the out-buildings in The Ark Aid and Lou found tenants, largely of the variety that fulfilled her little fantasy. The St Peter's charity shop flourished and the Basak's opened their restaurant-cum-takeaway, to the joy of Much Meddling in general.

Alex went ahead and bought the land at the back of the forge. He had apologised to the

Donkey Sanctuary for the trouble they had had retrieving the donkey that had escaped at the fete, strongly suspecting that it had had help. He had offered the land as an extra facility for them. In exchange they let him provide a home to the donkey whose hooves he had clipped. Tansy had been delighted.

Anna and Sasha had been married by James and were looking for a property in the area, a little larger than Anna's, and somewhere they could park two cars. Lou was on the look out for them. Fascinated by the architecture of the building which had been Sycamore Park Hall Sasha had offered his services as an architect to help sympathetically restore those parts of the building that needed work and had applied for, and made appropriate use of, available grants. With the Earnshaws' permission and support, he show-cased some of his more radical designs when turning the stables, at Sophie's suggestion, into extra income as holiday accommodation.

Emily was content. Her family was happy and healthy. The girls were older now and behaving like other children their age. She was starting to think about what she would do when the children started school. She didn't actually need to 'do' anything. They didn't need the money. In one way it wouldn't be much different to now as the girls were at nursery each day, but as a bus took the village children to school, she would have much more time. She wouldn't constantly be checking her watch and driving to and fro. She was thrilled that Alex was enjoying his little empire. He got on well with his Ark Aid tenants and was merrily making small items that he sold through one of the craft shops, eliminating his need to advertise, which he hated.

Snokettee's kittens continued to thrive, their individual personalities becoming more pronounced over time. There were no more reprimands from Mr Swire and the number of cats spotted around the village grew less. Things were back to normal, it seemed. All was well, once again, in Much Meddling.

THANK YOU FOR READING MY BOOK

If you have enjoyed Fairy Rings of Much Meddling then do tell your friends, and please consider leaving a review on Amazon.

Coming soon:

Cats' Eyes of Much Meddling

Happy reading,

Pauline

ABOUT THE AUTHOR

Pauline Potterill

The author grew up in the northwest of England, on the edge of The Lake District, but has since lived in many parts of this beautiful country.

"I love local history, tradition and folk lore, and believe that everyone should have a sense of their roots and be part of a community. I try to put a sense of this in my novels, hopefully in an amusing and affectionate way.

I aim to keep readers guessing and like to surprise them. Although Wishing Wells is a romantic comedy, subsequent novels centre more on family life, but do include love stories. Inspiration comes from a fun-filled childhood, which I set against the back-drop of a romanticised version of village life."

BOOKS BY THIS AUTHOR

Wishing Wells Of Much Meddling

Wishing Wells, the first of the Much Meddling novels, is a feel-good, comedy romance with a touch of mystery and a fast-paced plot.

When Emily Hope is caught in a snowstorm she has no idea how radically her life is about to change. The inhabitants of Much Meddling are plotting, individually, each with their own little scheme. Emily, it seems, features in every one. Co-incidence? No! As Emily comes to learn, nothing in this beautiful little village happens by chance. Events have been managed for a long, long time. Just ask the cats.

As Emily becomes embroiled in village life and attempts to come to terms with her fate, whatever that might be, she struggles to understand her own needs: assuming of course that the mysterious periapt is just a harmless pendant, and she actually has a choice.

Cats' Eyes Of Much Meddling

Coming Soon...

In this, the third of the Much Meddling novels, Emily is wondering what she can do to entertain her children during the long summer holiday. However, before it has even begun, the mysterious Catolith appears. Unnervingly, it seems the girls were expecting it.

More mystery and romance, as the inhabitants of Much Meddling go about their lives. What are the children up to in the woods, with an axe? Why are the older villagers so disapproving of the vicar's new house keeper? Who is the secretive stranger and what does he want?

As the children cope with what the Catolith has brought, Emily discovers what the cats' eyes have to reveal.